TAPED

Trevor Barnes

NEW ENGLISH LIBRARY

British Library Cataloguing-in-Publication Data

Barnes, Trevor
  Taped.
  I. Title
  823.914 [F]

  ISBN 0-450-55676 X

Copyright © Trevor Barnes 1992

First published in Great Britain 1992

Published by New English Library,
a hardcover imprint of Hodder and Stoughton,
a division of Hodder and Stoughton Ltd,
Mill Road, Dunton Green, Sevenoaks, Kent TN13 2YA.
Editorial Office: 47 Bedford Square, London WC1B 3DP.

Photoset by E.P.L. BookSet, Norwood, London.

Printed in Great Britain by Biddles Ltd,
Guildford and King's Lynn.

To Sally

ACKNOWLEDGMENTS

Although a long series of acknowledgments at the beginning of a novel can appear tedious, I wish to thank three police officers who have been kind enough to help me: Detective Chief Inspector Jackie Malton of the Metropolitan Police, in particular, saved me from some crass errors by reading through an early draft in great detail; Acting Chief Inspector Tom Millest of the Met assisted through various stimulating conversations about the police; and Assistant Chief Constable Alison Halford of Merseyside Police, despite difficult personal circumstances in 1991, found time to offer me some valuable insights into the problems faced by women police officers. A special word of thanks also to my wife, Sally, who has borne with great fortitude the difficulties created by a husband exiled for a year to his word-processor while this book was written.

'Television? No good will come of this device.
The word is half Greek and half Latin.'

Attributed to C. P. Scott

AUTHOR'S NOTE

TV London – its building, its franchise and its staff – is a creation of fiction. No resemblance whatsoever is intended by the author between any characters in this novel and any person living or dead.

PROLOGUE

There was no pain at first. She had time only to see something glint in the light before it thumped into her stomach. And then came another blow, and another, and another.

It was too late to voice her terror. The woman had been winded by the first lunge and, although she tried to scream, the only sound that emerged was a pitiful gurgle. Her tongue drowned in warm liquid. Her lips quivered impotently, unwilling to do her bidding.

Another blow sliced into her body, and another, and another.

She thrust out well-manicured hands to ward off the flashing blade. The steel simply ripped through her, slicing skin and crunching bone. The woman turned to the door to escape. Her body refused to obey. It merely slumped back against the wall, and for a second the stabbing ceased. The woman's eyes snared those of her attacker, glittering with the fear and anger of violence. Their breathing was loud and hoarse in the small room.

She had not expected this. None of it. She was badly hurt, she knew that, but this could not be the end. Her life could not finish like this, in a cubby-hole where people escaped from the office to whisper gossip or view tapes in peace, the room where she had snatched one or two secret kisses from David.

She wanted to scream out her fear, plead for mercy, but she was so crippled by terror she could not even do that. For the first time in her life she sensed the pain of true hopelessness.

It was then that the other pain began – a deep, searing agony as though someone was playing a blowtorch over her heart and lungs. She did not care any more. All she wanted was for the pain to end.

Another blow thudded into her chest. Another into her throat. With the voiceless pain strangling her heart, she lost all desire to resist. Out of the corner of her eye she caught her white blouse oozing the shocking red of blood, her hands scarred with wounds, flaps of skin hanging loose. She felt herself dragged down into a dark tunnel, the moss on the brick walls chill but soft against her skin. In the flint black she could breathe no longer. Her lungs burned. She coughed for air. She was choking. Still the eyes showed no mercy. Still the blade thumped into her body.

Suddenly she felt released, the agony distant, as though it was not her body that was being savaged but that of another woman. The afternoon, when she had sat in the shadow of the editing suite watching her film about homelessness, was only a few hours away. But already it seemed as golden as childhood. She had looked at herself with pride. The piece to camera at the hostel was particularly good – as Simon said, in his Oxbridge way, 'striking the right note of pathos without being mawkish'. Television after all was only theatre. She was on the verge of success, a breakthrough in her career. She knew the job, the job she had always wanted, was hers. She had been promised it. She had fought so hard for it, taken so many risks. Her lucky break had come at last. Her face would be known across the country, staring out from the tabloids, whispered about furtively when she shopped in the local supermarket. She would be rich. Everything was going so well. She had made David see reason. And his job was safe. She had even felt confident enough to make those jokes in the video. If only she had been more suspicious. After all she had been playing a dangerous game. She had been too trusting. She closed her eyes on the face of her murderer, a face which had not promised harm.

The agony returned, burst open in her chest and suddenly ended. And as she slipped into the endless sleep of the dead, she saw herself again, as she had appeared that afternoon frozen on the screen: an icon on videotape. Lips fluttering, eyes brimming with concern, she would live for ever. She had been taped for eternity.

CHAPTER
ONE

As the first evening of April fell, bringing with it a spring chill, Dexter Bazalgette finished brushing up the dead leaves and spilt compost on his roof terrace. The detective sergeant stood back and looked at the day's work with pride. The climbing rose that was being trained around the door had been pruned, and he had cut back his hardy fuchsias so that the brown stems showed just above soil level. He had always been fond of fuchsias. A line of earthenware pots stood near the edge of the terrace furthest from the house, brimming with summer bulbs and corms of gladioli. Through the window a couple of propagators peeped at him, sown with the seed of various annuals the sergeant would prick out once the frosts were over. He liked colour – bright reds, yellows and purples – all jostling for his favour, not pastel shades, so subtly understated that they were no sooner seen than forgotten. That was not Dexter's style. He liked things big and bold and brassy.

The terraced roof-tops of Shepherd's Bush rolled away in front of him, the tiles and dead chimney-pots rising and falling in waves, their clear rhythm broken only by attic extensions and the tangle of television aerials. Away in the distance rose the delicate towers of arc-lights that burned away the night when Queen's Park Rangers played at Loftus Road. It was a landscape that made Dexter happy, one in which he felt at home.

He glanced down at his hands – the fingers long and delicate, the palms a shocking pink against the deep chocolate of the skin on their backs. He asked himself once again what the hell made the son of Jamaican parents, a child of urban London, a detective sergeant in the Metropolitan Police, take up gardening. His boss had asked him the same question once. Detective Superintendent Blanche Hampton had no time for gardening, of course. She said she found it boring, preferring to unwind over a good book and a bottle of wine. Her passion was her work. Dexter smiled. She would never understand.

Dexter supposed his love affair with plants had started with that one fuchsia – the sad, dessicated stump he had found on the window-sill of his first rented flat. He had simply watered it at first, as much out of curiosity as pity, like searching for the pulse of an accident victim. The plant repaid his kindness by pushing forth green sprouts. So Dexter repotted it and the fuchsia grew and blossomed. The sergeant bought another and another, and within months his flat was bursting with pot plants and flowers. And he had loved gardening ever since. It renewed his faith in nature. So much of his work was clearing up the mess left by human destruction – lives ruined by rape, assault, robbery, even murder – that he needed a means of escape, a means of preventing himself becoming jaded and cynical.

The idea of love made him think of Georgie – the sparkling eyes, the smile, the cute buttocks glimpsed under the jeans. The memory of Georgie mingled with that of the gardening to put Dexter in a good mood. He began to whistle as he cleared the table of his dirty dinner plate, smeared with ketchup from fish and chips, and turned on the taps for a hot bath. He felt excited at the prospect of the night ahead. The previous Friday, he had met Georgie at a pub – a pert little number who worked as a nurse, with just a touch of mascara around the eyes, and who wore the most heavenly scent. Georgie had proved charmingly timid and they had agreed to meet the following Monday evening in a pub on Shepherd's Bush Green. Now that Monday had come.

Dexter towelled himself down while whistling a passable

impression of Bob Marley's 'Is This Love?'. He then flexed his muscles and admired the resultant pose in the mirror. Six feet two inches of shimmering ebony, he thought, irresistible except for the rather spongy nose some bastard had given him while playing rugby at the local comprehensive. Still, as he knew from eyeing up some of the fitness fanatics down at the gym, perfect beauty is all the more perfect when highlighted by a small defect.

Dexter glanced down at his watch, a counterfeit Rolex, and saw it was one minute to nine o'clock. He had almost forgotten: Blanche would never forgive him if he missed her. He snatched up his dressing-gown, vaulted over the sofa and flicked on the television with the remote control.

The Crime Show was the usual rubbish pumped out, in Dexter's view, for voyeurs of human misery. The only moment of light relief was provided by a camp presenter who trotted round an Aladdin's cave of stolen antiques, asking the audience whether they recognised anything. Dexter thought of phoning in and claiming the Charles II solid silver candelabra. After all, it would have looked great on the dining table next to his signed photograph of George Benson. But he resisted the temptation and the next second the camera cut to another presenter who recited the facts of the rape cases that Dexter and Blanche had been investigating. A map of central London followed, marked with four red crosses to show where the assaults had taken place. The presenter swung to her right to reveal the reason why Dexter was watching the programme: his boss, Detective Superintendent Blanche Hampton. Dexter knew she was excited and nervous because Blanche stumbled over her first few words. He felt sympathetic: he knew she had never appeared live on television before. It was strange seeing her on television, the woman he worked with almost every day. She looked more glamorous, her brown hair glistening under the studio lights. But all her spark and humour had gone, extinguished – he supposed – by nerves and the desire to be taken seriously. Always a danger that, he pondered chin in hand, the urge to be taken seriously, as Blanche

15

rattled off the description of a man they wished to interview who had been seen near one victim's flat. An artist's impression of the rapist flashed up and then the programme swept on to an armed robbery. Crime as entertainment, the sergeant thought with a smile, designer titillation.

Dexter finished dressing at a leisurely pace, changing his mind three times about what shirt to wear to impress Georgie. He dreamt about how he might have looked on television instead of Blanche and wondered whether Blanche's plea would have jogged any memories. He was at the door when the phone rang. With the image of Georgie's body in mind, the sergeant toyed for a second with pressing the button of the answerphone, but decided against it.

'Dexter, we've got a murder.'

The sergeant did not need to be told whose voice it was. He had recognised Blanche immediately, breathless and preoccupied. 'Sure, but . . . '

'But what?'

He could not say he had arranged to meet someone for a drink in a pub. It was too pathetic for words. 'Nothing.'

'Just get over to TV London. They'll tell you where to find me.' The tone was polite but curt. The phone was slapped back into its cradle.

For a moment a vision of Georgie nursing his cold pint of lager, a day's growth of designer stubble blurring his chin, drifted in front of Dexter. But as the sergeant snatched up his car keys and sprinted down the stairs, the bad mood faded as quickly as it had begun. Dexter told himself he did not want to get involved with yet another young boy. And, besides, he was fearful of disappointment. Georgie might have stood him up.

16

CHAPTER
TWO

The detective sergeant leant back against the polished rail in the lift and stared at the floor. Although relatively new, it was already worn and stained by the passing of thousands of feet. Dexter wondered how many of them belonged to the familiar faces he had seen on TV London in the last couple of years, and whether any had been left by the person whose murder he was about to investigate. As yet he did not even know the identity of the victim. A detective constable in reception had simply led him to the lift and then pressed the button for the fourth floor. Their eyes met and Dexter smiled in lieu of conversation: he was a good-looking boy, even though every feature of his face – nose, ears and lips – seemed one size too big. 'You from Chester Row?'

'Yeah. That's right, sir.'

'I expect that's where we'll stick the incident room then.'

'Hope so.'

'Why, you keen to be on the squad?'

'If there's a chance, sir.'

The lift jolted to a stop and a disembodied voice issued from a speaker on the wall: 'Fourth floor, going up.'

The sergeant smiled. 'I'll have a word with the guv'nor.'

The constable led Dexter along a corridor that stretched away into the distance. It was lined by doors on both sides with white name-plates and, every few paces, sections of frosted glass in the upper half of the walls. The offices could have belonged to an insurance company as easily as to one that made television programmes and Dexter detected a nagging sense of disappointment. He was an avid consumer of television and he somehow expected the offices to reflect the glamour of the medium. He was not sure how – perhaps a wider corridor, a plush carpet beneath his feet, a few abstract paintings on the walls, beautiful people with harried expressions on their faces scurrying past. Instead it was very ordinary. Just like life itself – or death come to that. The only people he could see were fifty yards ahead. They had harried expressions all right, but no one could have called them beautiful – a knot of uniformed constables. As Dexter loped closer he heard the familiar crackle of police radios.

Blanche was framed by the open door of Room 495, talking in her usual animated way to a constable. The cut of her business suit was stylish, with a narrow skirt and a collarless jacket that was pumped up with shoulder-pads. She had dressed for her television appearance to resemble one of those groomed, efficient women in business magazine adverts except, Dexter thought, Blanche rarely quite looked the part. There was often something rumpled and preoccupied about her appearance, although few noticed it because of the energy of her face and shining eyes. Especially when she smiled. And she smiled then as Dexter strode into the room.

The smile only lasted a second, a look of recognition and comradeship. Dexter knew Blanche was not one for grand gestures. She was not, like her sergeant, a natural extrovert. Over the years she had hardened herself to lead from the front, drink pints with her men down at the pub, even laugh heartily when at office parties she had been given a vibrator as a present. But somehow, against all the odds, she had managed to keep her femininity, her individuality, that ability to care that Dexter had seen squeezed out of so many officers. She demanded the best from her men, and from herself. But she still cared, she still had compassion.

It was a large, open-plan office with windows opposite the door – great sheets of glass through which the sergeant could see the dim, glittering lights of Belgravia. The desks were scattered in little knots of three about the office, their backs forming the shape of a T, each bristling with a computer terminal. Most were strewn with books, yellowing newspapers, photocopies and videotapes. All around the office were television sets, gazing down like watchful eyes from pedestals high on the wall. Most were silent, just a jumble of flickering images, but the one nearest them whispered out an American comedy show which Dexter enjoyed watching. Blanche prodded at the off button when she saw her sergeant's distraction and the screen went dead. Unlike him, Dexter knew, she did not like television very much.

'The body's in there,' she began, nodding towards a large cubicle without windows in the far corner of the room. 'It's what they call a viewing room apparently, where they go to look at videotapes.'

'Well, it couldn't have been more convenient, could it, ma'am? What with you downstairs in the studio.'

Blanche trained her deep brown eyes on Dexter with a smile. 'I don't somehow think convenience entered into it.' Her gaze clouded and swung away to the viewing room. She said the dead girl was Nicola Sharpe, a reporter on a programme called *Inside Out* and it was their offices the police were standing in. Blanche added that as yet she knew little more about Nicola except that she was twenty-eight years old and married. The voice of the female detective was clear and well articulated, without a trace of regional accent – a legacy of her mother's snobbery and education at a girls' private school. She had not tried to change it since she had joined the police and Dexter respected her desire to remain herself.

'Do we know how she was done in?'

'Stabbed. We haven't found the weapon yet. The pathologist might be able to tell us a bit more. When he bothers to turn up.' The superintendent flicked a glance at her watch, squeezing her lips into a tight line. 'We've got some new boy called Attwater.'

Dexter noticed Blanche was still wearing thick, television make-up. She obviously had not found time to clean it off.

19

The sergeant thought it made her look blowsy and made a mental note to mention it in a quiet moment. He glanced across towards the viewing room, noticing the harsh, bright light framing the half-open door. The police photographer was already at work. The laboratory liaison officer, a detective sergeant in his mid-thirties with whom Dexter had worked before, stood to one side chatting to a constable, his personal radio crackling out incomprehensible messages. He acknowledged Dexter's wave with a friendly nod. Lab liaison was waiting to begin a minute search of the room once the pathologist had completed his examination of the corpse.

'Anything turned up so far?' Dexter asked.

Blanche puffed out her cheeks and shook her head. Sometimes, at the start of an investigation, she reminded her sergeant of a dog tugging at the leash, eager to be let loose. Dexter reached into the pocket of his leather jacket for a packet of cigarettes but put it back when he caught Blanche's frosty look of disapproval. He realised he would have to wait in agony for at least half an hour before he could smoke. Blanche had weaknesses but unfortunately, from his point of view, they did not include addiction to nicotine. The only person, she told him once, whom smoking tobacco helped to solve difficult cases was Sherlock Holmes — and he had never existed.

'The body was found by a man called O'Mara. Ken O'Mara. Apparently he edits *Inside Out* — or at least he did until a few days ago. He's down the corridor at the moment having a cup of tea.' Blanche pressed her hands together as if about to pray and raised them to her lips, her eyes narrowing with concentration. She murmured that O'Mara had been at a party on the sixth floor, a party to mark his departure from TV London. He had popped down to the office at around ten to pick up a tape of one of his old programmes and found Nicola Sharpe dead in the viewing room. O'Mara said he had phoned the police immediately and then run upstairs in a panic to tell everyone at the party. Blanche had arrived a few minutes later and found him sitting in a silent stupor.

A thin, tall man tiptoed in through the door of the office, blinking through a pair of thick spectacles. 'Dr Attwater?' Blanche enquired.

'Yes, that's right,' the man replied, although he did not sound at all sure. His young but withered face was raw with acne, his shoulders narrow and hunched. He swayed nervously from one suede shoe to the other, his colourless eyes devoid of all expression. Attwater struck Dexter as so timid the detective sergeant feared he might faint at the sight of an uncooked hamburger, let alone a dead body.

The viewing room was about twelve feet long and ten feet wide. It was lit by two strip-lights on the ceiling and had no windows. On the left were two stands on wheels which held videotape machines and TV screens above: the corpse lay half hidden behind the one furthest from the door. On the right was a metal rubbish bin crammed with soiled paper plates and polystyrene cups, and a tall cupboard stuffed full of videotapes. An office chair lay on its back by the door. A square segment of the prefabricated ceiling was missing and a tangle of cables hung down into the room. The impression of chaos was heightened by various notices stuck to the walls with Sellotape: one about 'Self-Drive Vehicle Hire', another about how to operate the video machines, yet another about the procedures for borrowing VHS recordings of *Inside Out*.

As Blanche had said, no specialist was needed to reveal to the world how Nicola Sharpe had been murdered. The dead woman sat slumped on the carpet, propped up against the wall. She wore a smart suit, cut from a dark grey wool with a faint pinstripe, but the jacket, and white blouse she wore beneath, were stained purple with blood. She had been repeatedly stabbed in the chest and neck.

'I've seen her before,' murmured Blanche to no one in particular. 'Didn't she read the local news sometimes, as well as do *Inside Out*?'

Attwater shrugged vacantly as he opened up his pathologist's briefcase. The sergeant studied the dead girl's face for a few seconds and nodded. He knew Blanche had a remarkable memory for faces and, much faster than he, had recognised the woman behind the blank mask of death. With a jolt, he remembered seeing Nicola Sharpe on his TV screen at home only a few nights before. She had been just another face on the box — blonde hair shining under the lights, wide grey eyes highlighted by make-up, her lips shaping words in which she pretended to be interested.

'I only saw her once or twice,' Blanche added. 'I have to say I didn't like the way she read the news very much.'

Dexter sometimes found Blanche's frankness irritating. 'That's no reason for her to be topped, ma'am.'

'Don't be so sure. People care about these things more than you think,' sighed Blanche with a smile of gallows humour. Dexter knew the pretence of indifference was the superintendent's way of covering up the sickness churning in her stomach.

Nicola Sharpe looked very different now from how Dexter remembered her on the TV screen. The beauty of her face — and she had been beautiful — was destroyed by a jagged wound across her right cheek and a purple swelling under her left eye. A trickle of blood ran from her pert, upturned nose down to her mouth. Her thin lips on the other hand seemed untouched by death, which had set them in a slight pout, exaggerated by the liberal use of glossy lipstick. They were slightly apart, revealing a teasing glimpse of a front tooth.

Blanche left the viewing room so as to give Attwater a few minutes' peace and called across the lab liaison officer. The man's face was a plate of freckles and he ran a pudgy hand through his head of curly hair. He told Blanche in his nasal, Birmingham accent that the murder had probably taken place in the viewing room: there were no bloodstains outside. And he confirmed that so far no obvious foot- or fingerprints had been discovered, only some faint smears of blood on the carpet near one of the televisions.

The superintendent listened intently, her eyes hardly leaving the officer's face. She was a good listener except, Dexter had noticed, when she was bored. The superintendent squinted with concentration for a moment before asking whether the dead girl had a briefcase or handbag. The lab liaison officer walked across to one of the desks by the windows. On it, lying on a bed of old newspapers, was an expensive draw-string handbag made of black leather. The exterior was scratched and battered, the interior cluttered with newspaper cuttings, a small zip bag crammed with make-up, two packets of Polos and a diary. Blanche flicked through the cuttings and then opened the diary to the day of the murder. The only entry was '8.00 p.m. Farewell Party 6th Floor'. Thrown carelessly across the back of the chair at the desk was an Aquascutum ladies raincoat. Blanche asked one of the constables to take it along the corridor and see if Ken O'Mara, who had discovered the body, could identify the coat as belonging to the dead woman. The superintendent swung back to the freckled lab liaison officer. 'Did you check the videos in the viewing room to see if they've got any tapes in?'

The officer gave a broad grin of satisfaction. Blanche had not caught him out. 'I've already done it, ma'am. They're both empty.' Dexter knew that Blanche had the gift of bringing out the best in most of the officers who worked for her. Many began distrustful of her reputation – not only as a graduate 'flyer', selected to shoot up through the ranks, but as the only female detective superintendent in the Force. Her detractors said she had simply been lucky and been over-promoted. But in Dexter's experience these were people who relied on prejudiced gossip and had never actually worked with Blanche on a case.

The superintendent was about to stride off in her purposeful, but slightly knock-kneed way, when she stopped and turned. 'Have you had a chance to check the basins yet, by the way?'

'Basins?' The freckles on the forehead of the lab liaison officer drew together in puzzlement.

'The wash-basins. The murderer might have wanted to wash his hands.'

The man opened his mouth as if to say, 'I hadn't thought of . . . ' But he stopped himself in time and said he would get them checked as soon as possible. After Blanche had turned away, Dexter shrugged at the officer as a gesture of solidarity. He smiled back.

The pathologist glanced up with tightened lips. Dexter guessed it was was the closest Dr Attwater ever came to showing satisfaction. Wearing thin rubber gloves he had unbuttoned and then peeled back the dead girl's blouse. The white, pasty skin above and below her bra was peppered with wounds, each like a scarlet mouth ready to speak, the wounds linked by dried blood smeared across her chest. 'I'd say she died only – ' the doctor glanced down at his watch – 'a couple of hours ago. Say between half eight and half nine.' His voice was flat and expressionless, his eyes shutters of pale blue as they blinked behind his spectacles. Dexter realised he was wrong to think Attwater might faint when he saw a dead body. The pathologist simply displayed no human emotion at all: it would be the same to him whether he was handling a bag of potatoes or a human corpse.

'What about the weapon?' asked Blanche. 'What sort of knife was it?'

The pathologist blinked frantically. 'Can't say yet, I'm afraid. You'll have to wait until I've done the post-mortem.'

'Can you give me any idea of what it was like?' Dexter caught a faint note of exasperation in her voice. She wanted sharp observations and a willingness to hypothesise.

Attwater sighed. 'Well, the wounds don't look like normal knife wounds to me,' he began hesitantly. 'They're too narrow. It's as if they were inflicted with a . . . a stiletto, but a blunt one with a wide blade.' His small, washed-out eyes held Blanche's gaze for a moment. 'Also some of the wounds are different. There are subsidiary cuts in the flesh parallel to the main incisions.'

'Meaning two different weapons were used?'

Attwater looked alarmed. 'Oh no, I mean there might

24

have been a sharp hilt or something. But I'm not sure yet, Superintendent.'

Dexter remembered one thing Blanche had taught him over several years' working together: if you are given any set of facts you should always move them around like letters in a game of 'Scrabble', to see if they make more sense in a different order. So the sergeant asked what he thought was a reasonable question. 'No chance of her topping herself, then, Doctor?'

Attwater gave him a withering look: the sort that respectable, middle-class people reserve for a meths drinker slumped on a park bench. 'Absolutely not, Sergeant. Not with facial wounding like this.'

Dexter shrugged away his irritation with a smile. 'Only asking.'

Blanche's attention wandered to the door handle, a twisted tube of red plastic that was pushed down to open the door. Pulling on a transparent glove, she flicked it a couple of times thoughtfully. Back in the main office the superintendent asked Dexter to 'set up a special' – a post-mortem – first thing the next morning. After Dexter had roused a drowsy coroner's officer and set the time for nine o'clock, he loped down the corridor to join Blanche for the first interview.

CHAPTER
THREE

'I'd walked into that viewing room thousands, it must be millions of times, Superintendent. But to find Nicola there . . . dead. I still can't believe it, you know.' Dexter had heard such words many times before. The eternal surprise of violent death in the midst of life. Human beings would never get used to it, and nor should they, the detective thought. The terror. The injustice. It could happen to any of us in the twinkling of an eye.

Ken O'Mara reminded Dexter of a pear, with all the flesh concentrated in two places: his face and his stomach. Whenever he spoke in his quick, darting way, his chin quivered like a bowl of jelly. O'Mara's rotundity had one compensation, however, that Dexter noticed with a twinge of envy – his face was surprisingly unwrinkled for a man in his mid-forties. Pale with shock, O'Mara none the less sat slumped back on the sofa with an incongruous air of self-satisfaction.

Dexter used the pause to survey the office they had commandeered for a temporary interview room. A mahogany-veneered desk stood in one corner while the two opposite walls were lined with rather uncomfortable sofas covered in a knotted, oatmeal-coloured material. The only decoration was provided by photographs of windswept reporters in exotic locations and well-groomed studio presenters, sporting the sort of unblemished faces that made Dexter wonder if they had all undergone a course of cosmetic surgery. When he had first come into the room, the sergeant had scrutinised one particular photograph with a tuck of fascination in his lips, for hidden away in the smirking quartet of faces was Nicola Sharpe.

O'Mara began by confirming how he had found the body. He said his successor as editor of *Inside Out* had taken over a couple of days before but it was decided to delay O'Mara's farewell party until the TVL boardroom could be booked for the event. The party had begun about eight o'clock and the journalist described it as 'bloody dire' at the start, with stragglers congregating around tables groaning with full wine bottles. But an hour later it was 'going with a swing', the boardroom crammed with a hundred people or so.

Blanche asked whether O'Mara had seen Nicola at the party.

'Oh, yes. Nicola was there all right. She even dragged her husband along.' The husband, O'Mara said, was called Jim Lancaster. Nicola always used her maiden name at work.

'And where's her husband now?'

Dexter was pleased to note Blanche looked much fresher now. He had whispered in her ear about the television make-up before the interview with O'Mara had begun and she had cleaned it off in the ladies' toilet.

'I don't know. He must have sloped off early. I think he hated coming to parties like this anyway. Jim didn't know anyone and he wasn't in on the gossip.'

Blanche asked what time Jim Lancaster had left.

O'Mara flopped his heavy shoulders. 'I didn't see him go. All I know is that he'd gone before I raised the alarm.' Dexter turned to Blanche and raised his eyebrows slightly: they might have stumbled on their first suspect. She did not acknowledge his glance. She did not need to. The sergeant knew from the elaborate way Blanche took time to clasp her hands in her lap that the same thought had already occurred to her. 'Jim got pretty drunk, you know. He was knocking back the wine as if it was Perrier water. He even tottered across to me at one stage and asked if I knew where the hell Nicola was.'

Dexter enquired what time this happened. He was

27

becoming confused already by the chronology of events and guessed from the crease in Blanche's forehead that she felt the same.

O'Mara sported a cheery smile of apology that did not spread beyond his delicate mouth: the small, dark eyes always remained aloof and watchful. He hoisted his arms for a moment and held his hands behind his greasy brown hair. Under the armpits of his blue shirt were two circular stains of sweat. 'Sorry, I've been confusing you. I'd better start properly at the beginning. You see, I had a brief chat with Nicola and Jim at the party. That was around nine o'clock I suppose. And while I was talking to them, one of the waiters came across and said Nicola was wanted on the phone.' The former editor paused and scratched the back of his head with a stubby finger. 'She didn't seem at all surprised, as if she was expecting it. Anyway, she went off towards the door where the phone was and that was the last time . . . ' His voice trailed away as if an arresting and powerful image had flashed up in his mind. 'The last time I saw her alive.' O'Mara sniffed and, with a grunt, drew out a white handkerchief from his trouser pocket. He wiped the sweat first from his hands and then his forehead.

O'Mara said he had no idea who it was who had phoned Nicola. He explained that after the TV reporter had scuttled off to answer the telephone, he had chatted for a second or two with her husband and then been swept away by some new people arriving at the party. The journalist had not registered Nicola's absence until about twenty minutes later when Jim Lancaster had staggered across and asked drunkenly if he had any idea where Nicola had gone. 'I hadn't even noticed she'd left the room,' groaned the former editor, puffing himself into an upright position on the sofa. 'For all I knew she was in the loo or just gone off for a walk.' Jim, O'Mara continued, had limped away and he had not seen Nicola's husband since.

Blanche asked if O'Mara had registered anyone else in particular leave the party between nine and ten o'clock. The Irishman heaved his shoulders and sighed, his pasty flesh threatening to burst the seams of his shirt. 'There were people going in and out all the time, Superintendent. I can't say I remember anyone specially.'

'Are you sure?' The heavy lids over Blanche's hazel eyes lifted a fraction. When he was at the receiving end of such a look, Dexter sensed nothing could escape it – no gulp, no moistening of the lips, no flicker of the eyelid. It was like being stared at by the unblinking eyes of a cat.

The journalist's small, dark eyes drifted away to the photograph of Nicola on the wall. 'As I say, I can't remember anyone in particular.' Dexter thought O'Mara had injected just a little too much relaxation into his voice, tried a little too hard to make his response appear casual and off-hand. Dexter's suspicion that O'Mara's memory of the party was clearer than he pretended was sharpened by the speed with which the former editor began declaiming about the photograph on the wall, perhaps as a distraction. 'That's how I want to remember her, you know. Nicola was such a beautiful girl.' He gave Blanche a crooked smile. 'And then to find her in the viewing room, her face all cut up like that. Whoever did it must be a . . . lunatic, a complete madman.'

The sense of loss seemed genuine enough to the sergeant, although centred more on Nicola's pulchritude than on her personality. Dexter guessed that deep down O'Mara did not actually like Nicola Sharpe very much. He admired her, possibly even feared her, but Dexter sensed that when O'Mara had invited Nicola out for a quiet drink, as he undoubtedly had, it was less for the pleasure of her company as a journalist than for an opportunity to ogle her body.

There was a tap at the door and a woman police constable appeared, saying that Ken O'Mara's wife wanted to bring in some coffee. A dumpy woman with dyed blonde hair rolled in, bearing a tray laden with polystyrene cups and a plate of biscuits. She was probably ten years younger than her husband but did not look it, Dexter reflected bitchily. She kept nervously touching her hair as if to check it had not moulted and handed a cup to her husband, enquiring how he was. O'Mara grunted but did not bother to introduce his wife formally to the police officers. Mrs O'Mara did not seem offended but Blanche did. Dexter saw a glassy look of annoyance in her eyes that he often detected when the superintendent disapproved of someone's behaviour. Mrs O'Mara simpered by the door for a moment to remind her husband that he was on a diet, and that he should not put any sugar or milk in his coffee and certainly not touch the biscuits. After she had left and Blanche and Dexter had served themselves, however, the journalist slopped some milk and four lumps of sugar into his cup with a knowing grin. 'I'm a hopeless case, no self-discipline when it comes to food, I'm afraid.' He eased himself back into the sofa, stirring his cup with a sliver of white plastic.

Blanche asked O'Mara to fill her in as best he could on Nicola's background. The journalist pulled on his watchful smile. He said Nicola had 'come up the hard way'. Born in a small Yorkshire town, she had left school early and worked for the town's newspaper before moving across to local radio. It was then, O'Mara explained, that she had met and married Jim, a teacher in the local comprehensive. Nicola had been given an audition by regional television and became a presenter and reporter in Leeds before being offered a contract by TV London. O'Mara delivered his short recital with a fluency and succinctness that underlined to Dexter that the former editor might be fat but he was no fool.

Blanche paused and scratched her chin with a newly manicured nail. To an outsider the gesture would have meant nothing, but to Dexter it signified impatience and frustration. 'But what was Nicola like as a person? Why did you offer her a job, for example?'

O'Mara clasped his pudgy hands on his stomach and interlaced the fingers, his jaw already masticating his second biscuit. 'She looked good on screen and she was a good operator. It was as simple as that. Once she got the job, she never looked back.'

'Was she popular in the office?'

O'Mara's eyes widened as he turned away again to stare for a moment at the photograph on the wall. 'Is anyone saying she wasn't?' he asked with a frown of boyish innocence. He looked down at the signet ring on his left hand, which he twisted round and round between the thumb and middle finger of his right. He struggled, because the ring was as tight a fit as the waistband of his grey flannel trousers. There was something very suburban about O'Mara, Dexter thought. He probably bought all his clothes at Marks and Spencer and loved the lacy curtains Dexter imagined his wife had strung up across the windows at home – the sort of curtains that made the sergeant's stomach turn like sour milk.

O'Mara's beady eyes looked up. 'Is this interview off the record?'

Blanche nodded. 'For the moment.'

The retired editor sipped some coffee and one of his hands crept out to close round another chocolate digestive. Dexter noticed that as O'Mara absorbed the energy from the biscuits his natural ebullience returned. 'It's quite simple really. Nicola was very sexy, very flirtatious and very ambitious. And when you're like that, you're not as universally popular as the Virgin Mary is in the average nunnery.' He looked mischievously from Dexter to Blanche. 'I'm not saying this has anything to do with the murder, but you ought to know that the top management decided a month or so ago to revamp *Inside Out*. Give it a new main presenter. Someone who'd also host some of the chat shows. It'd be a big opportunity for somebody to break into the big time.'

Blanche crossed her legs and smiled to hide her impatience with O'Mara's indirectness. 'Somebody like Nicola?' Dexter caught the man's piggy eyes flicker across the superintendent's elegant calves.

O'Mara grinned and revealed a line of regular but yellow teeth. 'Exactly. Somebody like Nicola – young, enthusiastic – and, let's face it, easy on the eye.'

O'Mara said the only other serious contender for the job was Hugh Parnham, a rising star at TV London who presented its consumer affairs show. Dexter remembered seeing Parnham in the gossip columns a few times: the sort of handsome man with sculptured good looks he would have liked to bump into in a dark alley. O'Mara confirmed, however, that Parnham was in Scotland working and had not come to the party. 'Nicola and Hugh were desperate for the job. But of course, I had no idea what was going to happen. Jane Pargeter might even have got to keep it.' O'Mara patted his tapering fingers on the side of his cup, not feeling the need to explain. After all, Dexter thought, almost everyone had heard of Jane Pargeter. She was the main studio presenter of *Inside Out*, as well as other special TVL programmes, and had become celebrated for her aggressive, even rude, interviewing style. Many politicians sat squirming in the studio during her interrogations as if, rather than asking questions, she was kicking them in the groin. It was Jane Pargeter who had drawn the big audiences to *Inside Out* and so made herself the subject of many newspaper and magazine profiles.

Dexter decided to ask O'Mara about her, a person with something to lose rather than something to gain. 'Jane Pargeter must have been pretty desperate to keep her job, right?'

The former TV executive parted his lips to speak and Dexter heard the click of his tongue breaking free from the roof of his mouth. But he said nothing immediately, munching his biscuit. O'Mara stretched forward with a grunt and dropped another sugar lump into his coffee. 'She was at the beginning – when the rumours started. She was in a rage, storming round the place and looking daggers at Nicola in particular. But then she seemed to calm down, almost to accept it, you know.'

The sergeant knew Blanche would have liked to ask O'Mara outright whether Jane Pargeter or Hugh Parnham could have been desperate enough to kill Nicola. But in real life police officers do not gad about accusing people of murder. Dexter knew how professional a detective Blanche was: listening, observing, waiting. Waiting for people to reveal secrets they should have kept hidden, waiting for people to impart things whose significance they did not understand, and above all waiting to pounce, waiting for the moment of arrest.

The superintendent sat back in her armchair with a sigh. She raised her eyebrows sceptically, as if to signal to Dexter that she did not consider any job in television worth killing for. Dexter, however, disagreed. He found it quite possible for a human being to take the life of another through ambition or wounded pride, especially if there was another motive that had not yet come to light.

'Had anyone already been promised the job?' Blanche murmured, watchful for the smallest twitch of evasion. 'You know the way these things are.'

O'Mara chuckled, uncrossed his chubby legs and reached out for another biscuit. 'Not by me. But Nicola was going round saying she had it in the bag, and that she had backing right at the top of the company.'

'And did she?'

O'Mara respired deeply. 'The head of the department, Mike Slide, certainly rated her. And from what he told me once, even the chairman – Stephen Blufton – was keen on a new face to front the programme.'

'And did either of them make any promises?'

'God knows. Nicola was desperately ambitious and quite happy to twist the truth if it suited her. Sometimes I think *she* would have killed someone if they were standing in the way of *her* career.' O'Mara chewed off half his digestive and masticated greedily, waving the other half as he spoke through a full mouth. 'That was why she'd started this investigation into drugs a couple of months back – show she was extra keen, sharpen up her hard news credentials.' Dexter sensed the superintendent tauten with interest. 'Nicola was obsessed by it for a few weeks. Said she'd found this deep throat in the Drugs Squad at Scotland Yard who'd told her all about heroin trafficking or something. But then she let it all drop. Said the story didn't stand up after all.'

Dexter's forehead crinkled with disbelief. He knew most officers at the Yard only released titbits to journalists, and then only when it was in their interest to do so. O'Mara caught Dexter's look with surprising quickness. He pushed up his lumpy shoulders. 'Well, that's what she told me.'

Blanche scribbled in her notebook. 'And what was Nicola actually working on when she was murdered?'

'She was finishing a piece on homelessness. And then I was keen on her doing a story about child porn. She liked the porn story – she'd been working on it for a few weeks. Said she'd heard of an MP who deals in the stuff.'

Blanche yanked on what Dexter called her vicar's tea party smile. Not that he had ever been to a vicar's tea party, or was ever likely to. But he knew the sort of smile that such an event demanded – all teeth and no sincerity. 'Any idea of the MP's name?'

O'Mara shook his head. The journalist's pudgy hand closed round yet another biscuit. 'To be quite frank, I wasn't that interested. It was my last few weeks in the office and I was up to my ears in thinking about my new company.'

Blanche sat, hands in her lap, in a pose of relaxed boredom. During interviews she alternated between this attitude and one of rapt concentration. Dexter studied O'Mara's pale, hairless face. He thought the journalist was telling the truth – most of the time.

After a pause the superintendent spoke again, but Dexter was surprised she did not ask further about Nicola. Instead Blanche enquired about Jane Pargeter.

O'Mara blew his breath out as if it were cigarette smoke. A few biscuit crumbs adhered to his lower lip. 'Jane's a tough woman. And she's good at what she does. One of the very best. I was amazed when the management said they were thinking of replacing her – but then that's TV for you.' O'Mara shrugged. 'Didn't worry me, mind you. As soon as I heard Jane might be for the chop, I told her she could come and work for me.' O'Mara lifted his narrow eyebrows and a mischievous glint shone in his eyes. 'You see there's another reason why this job business hit Jane quite hard. She'd been the mistress of one of our best-known reporters for a long, long time before he met another woman about a year ago. And then he threw her over. I think the prospect of being elbowed out of her job as well, all in the same twelve months, hit her much harder than she pretended.'

Blanche asked coolly for the name of the reporter.

O'Mara drained his cup of coffee and began to pick away pieces of polystyrene from the rim with his fingers, placing the white flakes in an ashtray on the table. He glanced up and asked if the police really had to know, because the man was a close friend. Blanche nodded and said she did. The reporter's name – David Parkin – caused her eyebrows to rise. Parkin's face was well known, a correspondent of the old school. Tall, white-haired, and authoritative, he was blessed with the sort of voice that would have made even a supermarket shopping list sound thrilling, the sort of growling, bass timbre that made Dexter envious every time he heard it.

'Jane didn't like Nicola very much,' O'Mara went on, 'but she wouldn't have killed her, you know.' He slid the mangled remnant of his polystyrene cup on to the table and glanced at the plate on the table. The former editor puffed out a stoic sigh. Only crumbs remained. All the biscuits had been eaten.

Blanche and her sergeant sat in an adjacent office and munched their way through warm pizza, licking the tomato and anchovy from their fingers. The superintendent ate quickly but delicately and did not say a word until the cardboard box and its circular polystyrene mat lay empty on the desk. She was studying a statement that had just been taken from one of the waiters at the party. He said he had answered the telephone by the door of the boardroom and a woman who sounded Scottish had asked to speak to Nicola Sharpe. The waiter had not bothered to ask the caller's name and had simply elbowed through the crowd and brought Nicola across. He had then turned away to serve some drinks and when he glanced round a few seconds later he saw Nicola standing by the phone, the receiver back in its cradle, her face flushed with

35

excitement. She waved to a couple of people at the party, picked up her briefcase and coat, and walked out.

Blanche tossed the statement across to Dexter. At least, as she said, they now knew when Nicola had left the party and that they needed to find a woman with a Scottish accent. Blanche patted her lips with a paper napkin and sat back in the executive's chair. Dexter knew the eating of food was part of Blanche's ritual preparation before undertaking any particularly unpleasant task. She was about to set out for Nicola Sharpe's home in Kentish Town to find Jim Lancaster and break the news of his wife's murder. 'I sometimes think this is the worst part of the job,' sighed the superintendent. 'Knocking on a door and telling a stranger that someone they love is dead.'

Dexter thrust out his bottom lip and nodded sympathetically. He had been forced to do it a few times for accident victims and remembered how the disbelief turned to shock, and the shock turned to something else, perhaps hysteria, tears, a torrent of swearing or just complete silence. 'Mind you, if it was the husband who knocked her off, he'll be expecting you, won't he?'

Blanche trained her eyes on the sergeant. 'Don't worry, I'll keep a careful eye on him.'

Dexter sipped his coffee and asked her what she made of O'Mara. Dexter knew his boss sometimes valued the chance to think aloud, although he understood it was too early to draw conclusions. The case had only just begun. But Dexter asked her none the less.

'He's hiding something. But I don't know what.' Blanche eased herself up and gazed out of the window, her reflection a black mask in the glass. A glance at her watch, showing it was a quarter past midnight, seemed to act like an electric shock, making her brisk and businesslike. The superintendent asked Dexter to go and talk to the security guards on the front door while she was away and to sift through the other statements taken from people at the party. Then the superintendent reached for her raincoat and headed for the door, saying that she wanted to be picked up from home at seven o'clock the next morning.

36

'Sleep well,' shouted Blanche, her words floating into the room from the corridor.

I'll do that all right, thought Dexter, but there won't be enough of it. Another of the ubiquitous television screens was in the corner of the room, projecting silent images. It was strange that Blanche should investigate a murder in the world of television, Dexter considered. She rarely watched it, and then only to relax. She was not interested in television personalities and the stories about them in popular newspapers. Usually when he had visited the superintendent's maisonette in Ealing the television stood blank in the corner, whereas his was left switched on for most of the day. He liked the comfort of mindless chatter. The table in her flat was spread with police papers, documents and letters. A guilty conscience, ambition, and a nagging loneliness after the end of her marriage always fused to drug Blanche into an obsession with her latest case.

Dexter scratched his cheek and looked up again at the photograph of Nicola Sharpe on the wall. She was a beautiful girl, he thought. She looked so innocent, certainly very different to the rather bitchy picture Ken O'Mara had painted. Was the photograph lying, or her former editor? The sergeant crumpled up the cardboard wrapping from the pizza and tossed it into the wastepaper basket.

It was the last thing Dexter wanted to do of course. He was tired. He recalled his bed back in Shepherd's Bush – empty of a lover but none the less inviting with the prospect of sleep – and yawned. But loyalty to Blanche and years of police training made him shuffle automatically towards the lift. Besides, he remembered the unhealthy combination of digits at the bottom of his latest credit card statement. No harm, Dexter thought, in a bit of overtime.

In reception the sergeant felt hemmed in by the ubiquitous mirrors and veneered oak, the glass lampshades cast like seashells, and the six television sets, all flickering silently. Dexter half expected a gangster in a trenchcoat, like the ones he saw in late-night movies from the forties, to emerge from behind one of the pillars and strike a Swan Vesta on the sole of his shoe. Instead there were two constables hotly disputing Arsenal's prospects for the Cup and a night security man behind the counter who looked like Louis Armstrong with toothache. He told Dexter, in an irritable growl, that he had come on duty at midnight and that his two mates who had been on duty earlier were waiting in a room at the back.

One was short and wiry and an air of secret violence clung about him – the sort of man who might knock on a door, Dexter thought, and when the person inside said 'Come in,' might still kick it down for fun. In a flat London drawl the man said his name was Bill Southgate. Under his rag of damp ginger hair, the security man's eyes widened with surprise when the sergeant introduced himself before they dimmed to a twinkle of disguised contempt: Dexter sensed he was a racist. Southgate put on such a show of being relaxed and calm, however, that the sergeant guessed he was feeling vulnerable. His mate was Asian – a giant of six feet four, whose paunch was already popping the buttons of his grubby white shirt. Both men had loosened their ties and placed the jackets of their uniforms across the back of the tubular metal chairs.

Southgate smiled ruefully. 'I might 'ave saved 'er, you know, if only I'd gone on patrol as normal.' He sucked at his teeth and stared at Dexter. 'She was a smashin' girl. Always said 'ello to you.' His colleague nodded sadly in agreement.

With exaggerated politeness, Southgate told Dexter what he knew of Nicola's movements. She had come into work as usual that morning about ten, gone out to do some shopping at lunchtime and then spent time in the local pub drinking with colleagues before coming back for the farewell party around about a quarter to nine. The security men had not seen her after that. Since the rear door was locked at six o'clock and the front entrance was the only exit from the building, it looked clear to Dexter that

Nicola Sharpe had left the party and gone straight to her death.

The sergeant asked if the security men had a list of visitors who had entered or left TV London during the evening.

'No problem,' drawled Southgate, fixing the sergeant with his pale but strangely bright green eyes. He flicked his head to the right. 'Postie, can you go an' get it for the sergeant?' Dexter registered the flash of white at the edge of the Asian's eyes when his name was pronounced, and wondered whether it was caused by surprise, irritation or fear. Southgate turned back to Dexter with a smile tugging at his narrow jaw. 'That's our private joke – know what I mean? His real name is Goel. So I call 'im Goel Post. And that turned into Postie. Gettit?'

The sergeant smiled vacantly in reply. He felt like telling Southgate to stop being an arsehole and call the Asian by his real name. But he could not be bothered: it would only start a row.

The sergeant sponged up the atmosphere of utilitarian grubbiness in the room. The brick walls were painted cream and lined with lockers, except by the door where there were two calendars featuring women with breasts like Zeppelins. The carpet was frayed and dirty.

Goel returned from the counter outside with a black exercise book in his huge paw. Dexter registered that there were about thirty names to be checked, and said he would have to keep the book as possible evidence.

'I've got something else that might interest you, Sergeant.' Southgate reached down to the floor and picked something up. His stubby, nail-less fingers trembled as they held out another black exercise book. 'Nicola Sharpe was meant to be meetin' someone at nine o'clock tonight.'

Dexter heard his heart thump in his ears. He told himself to calm down and examine the evidence methodically. The book was labelled 'Expected Guests' and fell open at a page marked by an elastic band. A series of lines had been ruled down the grubby paper with a blue biro, the first column for the name of the guest, the second for the name of the person expecting them, the third for the time of arrival and the last for the telephone extension to ring when the guest arrived. The last entry was written in messy capitals: 'Mr Kennedy – Nicola Sharpe – 9.00 p.m. – Ext 7486'. When Dexter looked up the Asian was examining a carpet tile as if it were a brain-teaser.

Southgate stared at the sergeant intently, ready to speak. 'But the thing is, the geezer didn't turn up, you see.'

'And did Nicola ring down to find out if this bloke Kennedy had arrived?'

'No, we didn't get any call down here.' The security man shuffled on his chair.

The Indian looked across first at Southgate and then at Dexter without a hint of expression. He nodded agreement, his eyes round and gentle like a cow's.

'And where's extension 7486?'

'It's the boardroom where they were holding the party, isn't it, Goel?'

The fat giant nodded again. He wiped a film of sweat from his wide, chubby face with a handkerchief. The only sounds in the room were the Indian's wheezing breath and the distant whine of some air-conditioning plant. Dexter fought to suppress his elation. This man Kennedy must have had some connection with the murder. It was too much of a coincidence for Nicola Sharpe to receive a phone-call at the party at about the same time as she was supposed to have a rendezvous with him. 'And no one called Kennedy turned up?'

Southgate nodded vigorously. 'That's right. No one we saw anyway.'

The image of Nicola standing in a corner of the boardroom haunted Dexter, perhaps glimpsed through a whir of wine-glasses, the receiver crushed against her left ear to hear better. 'And you didn't put any phone-calls through to Nicola?' he asked with mock innocence.

The security man paused as if it were a trick question, a comma of suspicion on his thin forehead. 'What d'ye mean?'

40

'Did you put any calls through to her at the party?'

Southgate relaxed. 'Oh, no. People can ring in direct from the outside.'

Away in the bowels of the building a lift thumped and whined into motion.

Dexter asked if the guards had seen anything out of the ordinary during the evening. Goel glanced expectantly across at his colleague. Southgate ran a pale, muscled hand through his hair. Although he had an air of covert dissipation, he looked clean and neat, as though he had just come on duty in a new uniform. 'No, me and Postie were down 'ere all night – except for him doing a check round the building about seven.'

Dexter asked the Asian if he had gone anywhere near the *Inside Out* office during his patrol. He said he had passed but not entered it. He had no reason to.

'Would the office have been locked?'

Goel squeezed his lips together thoughtfully. 'No. People often work late. The office is locked up by the night shift at one or two in the morning.' The Indian leant forward on his chair and grunted as he picked up a half-finished mug of coffee from the floor.

'Did you bump into anyone?'

The security man looked away to the lockers, his eyes unfocused, as he tried to remember what he had seen. 'No. I didn't see anyone at all.'

Dexter sensed the contempt half-hidden in Southgate's eyes and the face of the security man became disturbingly familiar. It was the face of white people he had met who assumed all blacks are stupid. Not that Southgate made much of an effort to conceal his contempt. The sergeant preferred this relative openness to the closet disdain and fake friendliness of many in the white middle class. At least he knew where he stood.

'And can you remember anybody leaving the building between, say, nine o'clock and ten fifteen?'

Southgate picked at one of his upper canine teeth with a thick, muscly forefinger. 'Well, I can't, I'm afraid, because I was lying down out the back 'ere, you see. I had a dose of

41

food poisonin' or something. And I was lying on my back for a couple of hours.' Looking at his sallow skin, Dexter had no trouble believing him. Goel expressed sympathy with a bovine nod. 'I feel a lot better now I've been sick.'

Dexter turned to the Indian, who pondered for a moment before speaking. 'I saw a man come down around half past nine. I think it was Nicola Sharpe's husband – I'd seen him once or twice before.'

'What did he do?'

'He asked me to get him a taxi. He looked in a real state.'

'Drunk?'

'Yeah. Drunk.'

'Anyone else?'

Goel shook his head. The giant Asian shuffled his weight from one buttock to the other, causing his chair to make a sharp, cracking noise. A pout of unhappiness had set on his lips.

Dexter sucked on his cigarette with relief, the night breeze tingling cold on his cheeks. Before him, on the other side of the pavement, the headquarters of TV London loomed up into the blackness, seven storeys of smoked glass, reflecting the lights strung along the Embankment. He turned and faced the river. It was low tide and the heavy smell of mud and rotting vegetation rolled up to his nostrils. A stray car accelerated away from the traffic lights at Chelsea Bridge. It did not seem real but a ghost, doomed to vanish with the first peachy flush of dawn.

Dexter had toyed with bleeping the superintendent so that he could tell her what he had learnt from the security guards. But he decided there was nothing that could not wait until the morning. He felt the bulk of the two exercise books in his hand for reassurance. Blanche's idea of talking to the guards had certainly paid off.

The TV London building reminded Dexter of something, scratching at his memory like a familiar name that had been forgotten. A groove had been cut vertically down the centre and to soften the outline the front corners had been sliced away from the fourth floor upwards. The glass slab rose up like a tombstone of black marble. Except it was not a tombstone or a name he was trying to remember. It was something else. The soft, curly hair bristled on the back of his neck and a sour taste welled up in his mouth. Dexter shook his head and loped back to his car.

CHAPTER
FOUR

The road in Ealing where Blanche lived was just yawning into life the next morning at seven when Dexter double-parked outside her flat. There was a parking-space fifty yards back but he could not face the walk. After all, he had only got to bed three and a half hours before. Through sore and bloodshot eyes, the sergeant watched a man with slicked-back hair toss a briefcase into the back seat of a Volvo and drive off with a roar down the tree-lined street. A fat woman with enormous spectacles wheeled past a child in a buggie. Middle-class suburbia. White, clean and neat. No graffiti here. One part of the sergeant aspired to it, another yearned for the clapped-out cars, the yelping children, the animation, of his shabby street in Shepherd's Bush. He waited a few seconds for a little energy to seep back into his limbs.

Overnight a tarpaulin of grey cloud had been dragged across the sky. The air was warm and close for early April and the first pin-pricks of drizzle brushed the sergeant's newly shaved cheeks as he pressed the buzzer marked 'Hampton'.

Dexter did not like the way Blanche had decorated her maisonette. Plain carpets and plain walls were set off by expensive, flouncy curtains. After each of her rapid pro-motions, a few more antiques had appeared, mingling with the other restrained, modern furniture. Blanche was not naturally tidy. She found domestic chores tedious. So she had hired a cleaning lady to come once a week to keep the seeping chaos under control. Dexter guessed the woman had probably been the day before because the books and papers were in tidy piles and there were no clothes slung over the chairs in Blanche's bedroom. Although the superintendent was rarely there, the maisonette always oozed the warm, cluttered feeling of being lived in. Ever since Blanche's husband had walked out on her a couple of years before, Dexter knew the flat had become very important to the superintendent, her bolthole from the world, a place of escape where she could try to relax with her books and her cats over a glass of malt whisky. She had been given the two tabbies by a friend and Blanche looked after them devotedly, especially the sickly one who had been born with only one eye.

The superintendent checked her briefcase while draining off the last dregs of her black coffee, the cats rubbing against her ankles. Blanche glanced down. 'Damn, I forgot to put their food out.' She scuttled into the kitchen, opened a can of cat food and scraped it into a plastic bowl. She ushered Dexter towards the door, prodding the button on the answerphone as she passed.

The sergeant's eyes narrowed with concentration as he drove towards Belgravia with his usual disregard for the speed limits, weaving rhythmically from lane to lane and dredging his muddied brain for what Bill Southgate and Goel had told him the previous night. Blanche sat on the front seat beside him, listening intently as he went through their story, occasionally posing the odd question for clarification.

'I wonder what happened to Mr Kennedy?' she sighed, when Dexter had finished, and was accelerating along Kensington Gore past the Royal Albert Hall.

Dexter flicked up an eyebrow. 'He didn't bother to turn up.'

'That's certainly one possibility,' Blanche murmured.

Dexter did not have a chance to ask what she meant because a van suddenly screeched to a halt in front of them in the outside lane, its indicator flashing to turn right. Dexter calmly moved his right foot over to the brake and the car slid to a gentle stop with two inches to spare

45

between their bumper and the one ahead. At least that was how it appeared to him. Blanche was thrown forward into her safety belt and then tossed back into her seat as the car shuddered to a halt. Flushed, she whipped round to him and spoke through gritted teeth, 'So help me, Dexter, one day I'm going to book you for dangerous driving.'

Dexter summoned up his most winning smile, the sort he flashed at men with big pectorals down at the gym. 'Sorry,' he pleaded, and ordered himself to drive the rest of the way at a speed that would have allowed them to be overtaken by a paraplegic slug.

Blanche summarised her meeting with Nicola Sharpe's husband. She said the couple lived in a small modern house in Kentish Town and that the husband was still awake when she arrived at about one o'clock. Blanche said she could smell the alcohol on Jim Lancaster's breath as soon as he opened the door, although he seemed to sober up quickly when the superintendent announced that she had come with some bad news about his wife.

A queue of cars stretched back from Hyde Park Corner like a line of glistening shells. 'Do you mind if I have a quick fag?' Dexter asked as casually as possible, hoping that Blanche would agree without thinking. A cigarette would help to keep him awake.

Blanche sighed with mock annoyance. 'If you really must . . .'

Her companion blew the first gasp of delicious smoke out into the strengthening drizzle. The clouds above looked like cotton wool soaked in black ink. 'What is he like then, ma'am – Nicola's husband?' Dexter knew Blanche sometimes liked him to use the formal way of addressing her as reassurance that he knew his place, that he was not becoming too familiar. He did not mind. It did not affect his loyalty to Blanche or hers to him.

Blanche breathed in sharply, as if about to plunge into a swimming pool. She said he was in his early thirties, about five feet ten, and clean-shaven, with black, curly hair. He wore a pair of John Lennon spectacles. 'He's a bit of a wimp, I think. He keeps brushing the side of his nose with his finger, as if there's a fly on it.' Blanche demonstrated.

Dexter asked how he had taken the news of his wife's murder.

The superintendent thought for a moment. 'His face crumpled. Then he started to clean his specs with his handkerchief. I got the impression he wasn't really that upset.'

The car finally broke free from the tangle of traffic along Kensington Gore and Dexter eased it right into the tunnel of Sloane Street. He was about to slam his foot on the accelerator and surge past a dawdling Porsche on the inside lane, when he caught a meaningful glance from his boss. His right foot hung suspended for a moment before it came down to caress the accelerator pedal like a glass of chilled white wine – the sergeant's favourite tipple when his finances could afford it. The Ford crept up to thirty-five miles an hour. 'So do you think it was him who did her in?'

Blanche nestled back in her seat. 'Too soon to say. But he's definitely a suspect. He left the party at around the right time. And also their marriage was a bit rocky.'

Dexter glanced round with raised eyebrows.

She was silent as they passed by the greenery of Cadogan Place, the trees dimmed by the rain. Dexter guessed she was pondering her own marriage that had petered out in divorce a few years before. 'Lancaster told me he and Nicola had had a lot of rows recently. He wanted to go back up north – buy a house, start a family and so on. But Nicola wasn't interested apparently. She said she was on the point of making it really big and that her career came first.'

The rain was steady now, the spots of water growing heavy enough to splat against the windscreen before streaming down the glass. Dexter adjusted the windscreen wipers so that they swung back and forth regularly like pendulums. In the damp gloom, odd muffled figures scurried across the pedestrian crossing that barred the way to Sloane Square, collars turned up against the downpour.

Blanche said there was an empty bottle of red wine on

the coffee table when she arrived and another one beside it that Jim Lancaster had just opened. 'He told me they'd had these quarrels but he was sure they'd have patched things up. He said he loved Nicola very much. Then he looked across at me suddenly and said he was sure the phone-calls were something to do with it.'

The rain slapped across the windscreen like a flock of birds falling out of the sky, drumming on the roof and flapping down the windows. The wipers skidded ineffectually from side to side. A couple of cocktail sticks would have done as good a job. A flash of lightning flickered across the clouds. Distorted and hazy, the mansion flats of Chester Row loomed up through the rumpled sheet of water on the windscreen.

'He told me they'd had some threatening phone-calls. It started three or four weeks ago with the phone ringing a couple of times in the middle of the night. As soon as they picked it up the line went dead.'

'Did the caller ever say anything?' Dexter almost had to shout over the rumble of the rain on the roof of the car. He felt alert now, awakened by the taste of nicotine on his tongue and the scent of another possible suspect.

'Only in the last few days. And then she spoke a couple of times – it was a woman apparently. They didn't know who it was. She said something terrible would happen to Nicola if she didn't get out of London.'

'Sounds as if someone wanted her job.'

Blanche flopped her head to one side and squinted thoughtfully. Her voice, clear and well articulated as ever, jumped in volume to be heard above the drumming on the roof. 'Somebody certainly wanted something. Lancaster said they were on the point of calling the police when Nicola was murdered.'

Dexter swung left through the black archway at the side of Chester Row police station and parked among the tangle of vehicles in the car park. He switched off the engine and tapped the steering-wheel.

The superintendent rubbed her round but firm chin. 'Nicola told him that someone was coming to TVL to meet her for a chat about a story – she didn't go into details. Possibly that Kennedy character. He assumed that was what the phone call to Nicola was about. Anyway, Lancaster said he waited for a quarter of an hour or so and when she didn't come back to the party, he said he thought it might be fun to find out who she was meeting. So he started looking for her.'

'He can't have looked all that hard.'

Blanche smiled grimly. 'If his state at one o'clock this morning was anything to go by, I don't think he could have searched his own pockets, let alone a building. He said he looked in Nicola's office but couldn't find her.' The superintendent leant forward and started collecting together her things from the floor of the car. 'So he said he just went straight home.'

Dexter yawned and stretched his arms. 'His story stinks if you ask me.'

'I didn't actually, Dexter. But as it so happens I think you're absolutely right.' The superintendent edged her door open and contemplated the sodden, oil-stained tarmac. 'He said he was sure David Parkin was mixed up in it somehow. When I asked why, he just said he didn't trust him an inch.' Blanche slammed her door shut and splashed her way through the puddles to the back entrance of Chester Row police station.

The incident room down in the basement had already been unlocked by a duty sergeant who was so chirpy for twenty to eight in the morning that Dexter felt an almost irresistible desire to kick him in the stomach. The room smelt damp and musty from lack of occupation, the desks powdered with a layer of dust. The duty sergeant said the cleaners were due to arrive in half an hour. Blanche disappeared to finalise details of the local officers who would be attached to her murder squad, the sergeant putting in a good word for the constable he had met in the lift at TV London.

Dexter groaned when Blanche told him who was to be the other detective sergeant on the enquiry: Sandy

49

Wootton. Blanche had never criticised Wootton in front of Dexter. She was too clever for that, knowing that Dexter was as generous with gossip as he was with his affections. None the less Dexter knew Blanche distrusted Wootton: there was a prickliness in the air when they talked. And as for Dexter, he simply hated him. The sight of greasy, balding Wootton waddling into the office was as enticing to Dexter as the prospect of swimming in raw sewage.

Dexter watched the action boards on the walls being wiped clean, the computer engineers arrive in their over-alls, the gabbling detective constables carve out territory around their desks. The cleaners arrived and hoovered between the legs of the officers gathering for the briefing Blanche had announced for half past eight. Although he had been through the routine several times before with Blanche, the sergeant was pleased to discover the same air of excitement galvanising the incident room.

Blanche established her office in one corner: a small cubicle formed from partitions of glass and veneered mahogany. She sat there, scribbling notes, thumbing through polaroids of the corpse and reading various statements that had been taken the previous night. She rested her chin in her hand, a knot of concentration in the middle of her forehead. The detective glanced up with a distracted smile as Dexter slid the polystyrene cup of freshly brewed coffee on to her desk. She scribbled one last note, stood up, and straightened her suit. 'OK,' she said, respiring deeply, 'let's hit the road.'

The men in the murder squad – there was only one woman constable – murmured expectantly as Blanche strode in her faintly knock-kneed way to the far end of the room. She placed her cup of coffee delicately on the cor-ner of a desk nearby and summarised what was known so far. Then she allocated various tasks to the squad – mak-ing a list of people at the party, taking statements, checking which staff had access to the viewing room, elim-inating fingerprints, a call to lab liaison to discover if anything important had been discovered overnight. The list built up on the action boards on the wall. Each constable knew that most of his enquiries would, in turn, have to be laboriously entered on the carbonised pages of the 'action book'. Murder spawned its own special paper-work, its own bureaucracy.

Towards the end of the briefing a phone rang on one of the desks. Blanche snatched up the receiver, heard a few words and raised her eyes to the fluorescent light on the ceiling. 'No, I'm sorry I didn't ring you, John . . . yes, I know . . . I know . . . I've had so much to do getting the enquiry started my feet have hardly touched the ground.' The female detective mouthed the words 'Press Bureau'.

She paused. The press officer was obviously not going to be fobbed off. 'No, I've got no plans for a press conference just at the moment.'

The superintendent was forced to break off again. When she resumed, her voice was warm with false charm. 'Look, I understand perfectly the pressure the tabloids are putting you under. From their point of view it's an amaz-ing story – '

She paused and scanned the ceiling again. 'No, I'm sorry, we don't even have details of the weapon yet. I'm just off to the post-mortem now.'

Pause. Blanche sighed, a trapped look in her eyes. 'OK. I'll phone you around twelve and give you a full briefing then. 'Bye.' The superintendent reached for her raincoat. 'God, I know we need PR but that doesn't stop me hating it.' A wave of chuckles rolled across the incident room.

CHAPTER
FIVE

Dexter glimpsed the corpse out of the corner of his eye.
He preferred it to remain that way. He had the impression
of a long scar stretching from abdomen to chest surrounded by a human body. Bottles full of cloudy liquids
and strands of flesh were on a trolley next to the galvan-
ised slab. The smell of antiseptic was so pungent that it
sliced through the haze of the sergeant's powerful *eau de
toilette* and made his nostrils twitch. For some strange
reason the sight of a murder victim when first found,
however bloody, never made him gag as much as the sight
of the same body on the mortuary table. Blanche, he knew,
had steeled herself over the years to hide any signs of
sickness in case the men she worked with undermined her
reputation by labelling her a 'plonker'. But that did not
stop her showing other emotions. Looking into her eyes as
they scanned the corpse beside his shoulder, Dexter
thought he detected fleeting signs of horror and compassion – horror at the extent of Nicola Sharpe's injuries
and compassion for the agony of her death. The superintendent took a rumpled handkerchief from her bag and
blew her nose. The glitter disappeared from her eyes,
replaced only by polite attention to what Dr Attwater was
saying. Blanche was right to distance herself, Dexter
thought. Investigating a murder is like falling in love: it
never pays to get too involved.

The pathologist peeled off his rubber gloves and confirmed there was no evidence of any sexual assault. Dexter
had forgotten how quietly Attwater spoke: he had to strain

to catch his words. The superintendent nodded, shifting her weight from foot to foot to restrain her impatience.

'We can't be absolutely sure about the weapon of course,' Attwater went on, blinking through his spectacles, 'but I'm pretty convinced now it wasn't a dagger. I think it was a pair of sharp scissors.' Blanche and Dexter exchanged a glance of pensive surprise. 'The woman was stabbed with them when the blades were both open and closed.' His voice hardly rose above a whisper but in the silence of the mortuary his words seemed to resound against the cold, white walls. Attwater turned to the corpse and pointed hesitantly with his forefinger. 'I should say the initial wounds to the chest and neck were made with them closed, so that the scissors were a bit like a knife, about four inches long. Then the scissors were opened up for more stab wounds. These other ones are smaller and shallower, about three inches deep.'

Blanche asked how many wounds there were altogether.

The pathologist flicked through the pages of his notebook. He looked happier now that he was back on the firm ground of scientific fact. He said there were six of the bigger, single wounds and seventeen of the smaller, neater ones.

'So it was a frenzied attack?'

Attwater turned his colourless eyes to the corpse. 'Oh, yes, Superintendent. I think we can safely say that.' He looked back to Blanche, sensing an unasked question. 'I'd guess she died quickly. One of the stab wounds went straight into the heart.'

'Do you think the murderer would have got much blood over himself?' asked Blanche. Dexter was relieved the superintendent was turning the conversation away from the corpse to the person they were seeking.

Attwater rubbed a finger across his acned cheek. 'Some. Certainly over his hands or gloves. But probably not much over the rest of his clothes. There were no arteries cut.' He glanced across to the corpse again. 'She lost a lot of blood through her chest but much of that was probably after she was dead.'

53

Blanche squinted at the doctor, concentrating like Dexter, so as not to miss what was said. She asked if the murder could have been committed by a woman as easily as a man.

The pathologist blinked through his spectacles as he pondered the question. 'It's perfectly possible, yes. If the woman was fired up and the victim wasn't expecting the attack.' He paused, his lips tightening into Dr Attwater's pale imitation of a smile. 'And victims rarely do.'

Blanche bustled along the hospital corridor, her raincoat flying out behind her. She turned to Dexter and thought out loud. 'I know this is a bit of a long shot, but I want Wootton to check out as many pairs of scissors at TVL as he can find. You never know, the killer may have dropped them somewhere.' The superintendent swerved to avoid two hospital porters pushing empty bath chairs.

Fat chance, thought Dexter, groaning inwardly on behalf of the poor sods who would have to make the search. The sergeant accelerated his loping stride to keep beside his boss. Blanche's whole rhythm speeded up when she became excited by a development in a case. Dexter knew that the stimulus was not caused alone by the stirring of hope: Blanche was motivated as much by fear of failure, by her sense of personal responsibility for a case. The superintendent was the only superior Dexter had come across in the police who did not so much pass the buck as smother it in kisses.

'The scissors don't make the murder look premeditated, do they?' commented Dexter, pushing open a swing door at the end of the corridor. 'Someone who'd planned it in advance would have brought a knife or a gun. Or else a man might have strangled her.'

Blanche stopped abruptly and her heavy-lidded eyes swung round to meet Dexter's. 'I agree – it *does* look as if it was done on the spur of the moment, doesn't it?'

'Perhaps she met someone there and they had a row.'

'Perhaps.' The female detective shrugged. 'What we do know though is that there's no evidence of sexual assault.

54

So we can probably rule out sex as the direct motive.' She pursed her lips and turned to start walking again. 'But I've got a feeling sex is mixed up in there somewhere.'

Dexter thought Simon Franks held his cigarette between thumb and forefinger as if he was smoking as much for the image it created as for the comfort the nicotine gave him. He was in his late twenties and had a long, smooth face shaped like an egg with skin the colour of polished oak. His hair was slightly greasy, flipped into a parting on his left side, his nose so sharp Dexter wondered if it might open a can of baked beans. It was an interesting face, with more than a hint of sensuality about it, the sergeant decided, but not the sort he found attractive.

Simon Franks perched nervously on the edge of a chair in the interview room. He stubbed out his half-finished cigarette in the ashtray and lit another. 'I've never been in a police station before, you know. I always wondered what they looked like on the inside.' He looked about with the edgy friendliness of the professional classes when they first enter a police station – delighted that the police are doing their job but secretly fearing and even despising the men who carry it out.

Franks was the producer on *Inside Out* with whom the murdered woman had last worked. He told Dexter he had spent the previous day with Nicola at a facilities house in Soho, completing her film about homelessness and the video for Ken O'Mara's farewell party. Nicola played an important role in the video and the idea, Franks explained, was to screen this mock report at the end of the evening for entertainment. Nicola had left Soho at about six o'clock, saying she would see Franks later at the party. A smile tugged at the producer's thin lips. 'The farewell party was more a celebration than a wake, if you ask me – we finally got rid of him. Lazy. Fat. O'Mara was more interested in lining his own pockets than providing any sort of – how shall I say? – creative leadership.'

Dexter took a slow pull at his cigarette and made an inventory of how Franks was dressed. The sergeant who, unlike Blanche, took an abiding interest in fashion, sucked in the expensive leather blouson, green open-necked shirt with silk burgundy tie, and corduroy jeans in one glance. He hated the tie in particular. It reminded him of a slice of raw liver.

The producer's eyes clouded with suspicion for a moment while he decided whether to pass on a morsel of gossip that might be of interest to the police. Most journalists, Dexter knew, distrusted the police as much as the police distrusted journalists. 'O'Mara spent the six months before his resignation using TV London time and facilities to set up his own independent production company, you know. What's really pissed off the management is that he's taking some good staff with him.'

Franks said he was at the party from the beginning. He saw Nicola and her husband arrive and spoke to them briefly, but he did not see the TV reporter leave the boardroom. When asked by Dexter about the phone-call to Nicola, the producer shrugged and professed ignorance, saying she had mentioned nothing to him during the day about meeting anyone. He rested his smoking cigarette on the rim of the ashtray to free both his arms. He looked cramped, Dexter noticed, when his hands were not able to echo all his words.

'Do you remember noticing anyone in particular leave the party between say a quarter to nine and a quarter to ten?'

Franks pondered for a moment. 'Only one – Maggie Parkin.'

'The wife of *David* Parkin?'

Simon Franks turned to Dexter with a faint sneer on his lips. 'That's right. The once famous David Parkin.'

Dexter's eyebrows lifted slightly in reaction to Franks' dismissive comment. '*Once* famous? You mean he's not any more?'

Franks shifted uneasily and tensed his cheek muscles as if someone had just squirted neat lemon juice on to his tongue. 'Well . . . he's not the man he used to be, is he?'

'You tell me.'

56

'No, it's just a – ' the producer waved his right hand airily – 'feeling that perhaps David's done his best work. It's time for him to hang up his boots. That's all.'

Dexter sensed the urge to defend the celebrated TV reporter against Franks' vitriolic tongue but decided life was too short. 'Why do you remember Mrs Parkin in particular?'

The producer smiled puckishly, revealing a line of white, brittle teeth. 'Well, it was more a case of how on earth could I miss it. You see, Maggie and David had a row at the party.' He leant forward and tapped some ash from his cigarette. 'I heard a sort of muffled scream and then the party went silent – you know how it is when a room just goes quiet all of a sudden. I turned round and Maggie was standing there with the front of her dress soaked with red wine.'

'And what had happened?'

'God knows. Maggie mumbled something about an accident and then walked out. But someone nearby told me he'd heard them having a quarrel and then seen David throw a glass of wine over her.'

Dexter nodded slowly. This was one thing O'Mara had chosen to forget when telling them about the party the night before. Perhaps it was quite innocent. An attempt to protect a friend from embarrassment. Or perhaps there was more to it. 'And she came back?'

'Yeah. About ten or fifteen minutes later, I'd say.'

'Wearing a different dress?'

'I think so, yeah.'

The detective rubbed a forefinger over his lips and asked what time this happened.

The producer lit another cigarette with a flourish of his gas lighter and said he thought it was around nine fifteen. He leant forward and parted his lips as if about to reveal a secret. Instead he shook his head and spread his hands with disbelief, Dexter watching the smoke curl from his cigarette.

When Dexter spoke again, his tone was softer and more confidential. 'Any idea what the row was about?'

Franks inhaled and blew out the smoke over his right shoulder. 'I could make a pretty shrewd guess. But I don't know for sure.' Dexter stood up. He liked to walk around when conducting interviews. It was an outlet for his nervous energy. He waited for Franks to continue. 'David Parkin had been having an affair with Nicola. People at work have known about it for a while. It started last year at the Labour Party conference.'

Dexter tried to disguise his interest. He remembered that Jim Lancaster had told Blanche that he believed David Parkin was involved in some way with the murder. The sergeant sidled back to the table. Franks looked theatrically hesitant to Dexter, pretending to seem guilty about breaking a confidence whereas in truth he was relishing it.

'Nicola was upset though, because David had said he was going to break it off. Nicola herself told me about it a week ago after she'd had a few drinks.'

Dexter wanted to bring the conversation back to his favoured suspect, a man who now had a credible motive for murder. He asked if Nicola's husband had found out about the affair.

Franks said he did not know. 'Even assuming Jim *had* found out, he wouldn't have done anything about it anyway. He's a real wimp,' the producer sneered.

That's what you think, Dexter told himself. Sometimes it's the wimps who are the most dangerous, letting their hatred boil up inside until it spills out in an act of murderous violence. The sergeant sat down again and asked if Nicola had any enemies.

'She wasn't popular with everyone in the office – especially the women – if that's what you mean. Nicola was good at back-stabbing.' Dexter smiled to himself at the unintended irony. 'I think it was because deep down she wasn't very sure of herself. She was . . . ' He paused for a moment while he groped for the right words. ' . . . out of her depth on a network show. She didn't have the intellect. But there's no one who hated her enough to kill her.' Franks narrowed his eyes slightly. Dexter guessed he was

58

deciding how much to say. 'And then Nicola was a big flirt, especially with the bosses. She used to tickle them like trout.'

Dexter sat back in his chair, wondering if Nicola's sexual conquests were limited to David Parkin. 'And did she catch any?'

The producer narrowed his eyes. Dexter noticed for the first time that he had thick, long eyelashes – the sort that normally disappear with the onset of puberty but which make young boys so beautiful. The sort of eyelashes, he remembered, that Georgie had. 'She didn't catch any of the bosses from what I gather, although there was a rumour going round that even the chairman of the company fancied her.' Franks chuckled. 'That's hardly surprising, mind you. Most normal men would like to have known her as well as David Parkin.'

Down in the incident room Blanche listened intently as Dexter told her about the interview with Simon Franks. Jim Lancaster now had a reason to murder Nicola. So indeed did David Parkin: the lovers may have met in the viewing room and quarrelled. Or Mrs Parkin, or Jane Pargeter, or . . . Blanche brought the shutter down on their whirring thoughts, murmuring that it was too soon to decide anything. 'Sherlock Holmes,' said Blanche finally, turning to her sergeant with a crease of worry in her forehead, 'used to say that the more bizarre a thing is the less mysterious it proves to be.'

'Well this murder is bizarre all right. But it doesn't stop it being bloody mysterious. Sherlock Holmes was talking a load of cock if you ask me.'

Blanche smiled vacantly and once again shuffled through the polaroid photographs of the corpse on her desk. 'On this one occasion, Dexter, I have to say I think Sherlock Holmes was wrong and you're probably right.'

CHAPTER
SIX

She spoke with some pride, throwing her head back and stretching her neck. It was a pink neck, with the same glassy sheen as the skin on her cheeks. Thick with moisturiser, Dexter thought cynically, scared of the crow's-feet scratching at her bright blue eyes. 'I left work at about half past six, I suppose – having phoned the nanny and checked that Jack was OK.'

'Jack?' asked the superintendent.

Maggie Parkin sighed with irritation and then suddenly relaxed into a smile. 'He's our son – almost four months old now. We have a live-in nanny to look after him.'

Blanche smiled back. Talk of children easily melted her heart, for Dexter knew she would love to have some herself. It was over a couple of years now since her divorce and she had not found a new husband. It was not through lack of trying, Dexter knew, but most men found Blanche's mixture of self-confidence and vulnerability, her commitment to her career, even the idea of going out with a woman police officer, hard to stomach.

Maggie Parkin took a deep breath, before galloping through her words in a clipped, 'no nonsense' voice. 'Well, I had a drink with a tedious author of ours in South Ken, then I drove across and met David in the pub just round the corner from TVL, then about eight thirty, we went up to the party. Ken O'Mara is an old friend of David's, you know, from their BBC days.'

'Were you and your husband drinking alone, or were you with some others?' Blanche had to cut in sharply to ask the question.

Mrs Parkin ran her fingers through her wavy hair. It was the same glistening black, Dexter registered, as the cap of Blanche's biro. He wondered if she dyed it to conceal the first grey hairs of old age. Maggie Parkin confirmed that a few other people from the programme were there.

'Including Nicola Sharpe?'

Her mouth fell open and her tongue flickered across her teeth. 'Yes, she was as a matter of fact.' The tone was cold and distant, inscrutable.

'Who was she talking to?'

Margaret Parkin sighed theatrically. 'My husband actually, when I arrived. But I fail to see what this has to do with Nicola's murder.' With a flushed face, Maggie Parkin rustled in her handbag for a cigarette, which she lit with trembling fingers. She had high cheekbones that narrowed to a non-existent chin, a small, round mouth with prominent lips, and big, round eyes that were too far apart. She reminded Dexter of a camel, but no sooner had he thought of the unflattering comparison than he rejected it as unfair. For although she was not a classic beauty, Maggie Parkin was the sort of woman who was attractive because of her energy and breathless charm. She was a strange combination, Dexter thought: veering from edgy suspicion, as though she had something to hide, to seeming indifference.

Blanche waited. A drunken shout echoed down the corridor outside. A phone rang and rang in the interview room next door. 'How well did you know Nicola?'

Mrs Parkin's eyes seemed to flash as she blew out the smoke. 'I'd said hello to her at the odd party – and that's about it.'

The superintendent's eyes focused on the interviewee's face as if they were looking down the barrel of a gun. 'She had a reputation at the office of chasing after men.'

'I'm afraid I don't know anything about that, Superintendent.' Dexter found the response unreadable. Mrs Parkin held her cigarette palm upwards between the forefinger and middle finger of her right hand and breathed in the smoke. Blanche was getting nowhere. Either Maggie Parkin did not know of her husband's affair or else was a good liar. Dexter could not decide between the two.

Blanche moved her chair back. The screech of the tubular leg scratching over the plastic floor tiles echoed round the room. Blanche watched the smoke curl up from Mrs Parkin's cigarette for a moment and asked the woman sitting opposite her what she and her husband had done at the party.

She said they had chatted to various people and enjoyed themselves very much. She admitted she visited the ladies' toilets once about nine fifteen and had bumped into Simon Franks tittering in the doorway like 'some stupid schoolboy'. They were about to go home when Ken O'Mara ran into the boardroom, shouting that Nicola had been murdered. She shrugged her velvet padded shoulders. 'That's all there is to it really.'

Blanche contemplated the mist of cigarette smoke hovering under the ceiling, seeking inspiration for her next question. When she found it, her eyes dived down to Maggie Parkin's face. 'Was that visit to the loo before or after the row with your husband?'

Maggie Parkin breathed in, tautening her lips. Her eyes narrowed as she drew on her cigarette, flapping a bejewelled hand across her face to dissipate the smoke. Caught you, thought Dexter. Up shit creek without a paddle. Now, how are you going to get out of this one, Mrs Parkin? 'There wasn't a *row* with my husband. We had, it's true, one of those heated discussions in a loud whisper that husbands and wives sometimes have at parties – but there wasn't a *row*. God, those people at TVL wouldn't recognise the truth if it bit them in the leg.' She was cool, the sergeant considered. Too cool.

Blanche paused. 'And what was your "heated discussion" about?'

Maggie Parkin sucked greedily on her cigarette for comfort, like a baby hungry for the teat, and waved her hand to dismiss the question. 'Oh, it seems silly now. It was about our nanny. I want to sack her and . . . David doesn't.'

Mrs Parkin smiled patronisingly, although with a flush on her cheek. 'There was nothing to it really – David was a bit tipsy and he spilt some wine on my dress. That was why I had to leave the party. I had to go and change.'

'I thought you said you went to the loo – '

'Well, I went to the loo *and* I went down to get a new dress. It only took a couple of minutes.'

Blanche looked bored again to Dexter, as if her eyelids were about to close. She was wondering why the woman in front of her was lying – whether she had any motive other than marital pride in trying to conceal the quarrel with her husband. 'And you happened to have a spare dress with you, Mrs Parkin?'

The woman smiled and breathed out through her nose with mild amusement. 'Yes, I did, as a matter of fact. I was very lucky. I'd picked it up from the dry cleaner's at lunchtime.'

'As you say, that was very lucky,' said Blanche without malice, like an old friend commenting on Maggie Parkin's good fortune over a friendly lunch date. 'You wouldn't by chance still have the dress you were originally wearing last night, would you?'

Mrs Parkin's eyes were suddenly empty and cold. 'I'm afraid not, Superintendent. I took it to the cleaner's first thing this morning. Stains come out much better, I find . . . ' Her voice died away for a moment. 'Wine stains come out much better if they're washed out quickly.'

Maggie Parkin stubbed out her cigarette in an aluminium ashtray on the table and glanced at her watch. She said she had to return to work for a meeting. Blanche smiled and stood up. 'How long have you been married to David, Mrs Parkin?'

'Just over a year,' she said, catching the suspicion in Blanche's eyes. 'David's my second husband. We have a very happy marriage.' Dexter smiled cynically at her: he was always suspicious of people who boasted of their marital good fortune. Maggie Parkin glared at Blanche and her sergeant: a look of defiant pride.

'And is your husband happy at work?'

63

Maggie Parkin's eyes widened. 'He's been under a lot of pressure recently – there was even some silly talk of his contract being terminated. But that's all been sorted out now.' With these words Maggie Parkin shook out her skirt and glanced towards the door. A look of uncertainty flitted across her face. 'Have people been whispering things behind our backs, then, Superintendent?' She asked the question with exaggerated casualness.

Blanche looked back quizzically but said nothing. It was amazing, Dexter thought, how powerful a weapon silence could be.

'I suppose they've dragged up the old story of David's affair with Jane Pargeter,' Mrs Parkin mumbled, while picking some fluff from her skirt. She stared at Blanche, irritated by her self-possession. 'Did they?'

'Someone did mention it, yes,' the superintendent nodded. Her face was unreadable.

Maggie Parkin shrugged and spoke in her tight, staccato way. 'The affair ended just after David met me – I told him it was a straight choice – her or me. I'm not one of these women who lets herself be walked over like a doormat, you know.'

Dexter and Blanche watched her swagger off down the corridor, heels clicking on the tiled floor. Once again the sergeant could not help but admire the cut of Maggie Parkin's expensive skirt. He decided he quite liked her – despite her outward show of confidence, she carried with her the air of a victim. The black detective turned to his boss, lifting an eyebrow quizzically. 'Why do you think she was lying, ma'am?'

'Because she's trying to cover up her husband's affair. But I'm damned if I know why yet.' The superintendent rubbed her chin and smiled. 'Perhaps the famous Jane Pargeter will give us a clue.'

At that moment a detective constable clattered into the corridor to summon Dexter to the phone.

It was the lab liaison officer at TV London. He had found traces of human blood around a wash-basin in one of the lavatories on the fourth floor. There were no fingerprints.

'Gents' or ladies'?' asked the sergeant breathlessly. After all, he thought, the murderer would not want to attract attention to himself by using the wrong toilet to clean himself up.

'Neither, I'm afraid,' crackled the man's voice. 'Either sex can use it.'

CHAPTER
SEVEN

Two packets of sandwiches snuggled up to each other on the back seat of the car, tumescent in their cellophane wrappers. Dexter had snatched them from the canteen just before he and Blanche had set off. The superintendent started eating hers as soon as they had turned out of Chester Row, peeling back the clingfilm with one hand while shuffling through the sheaf of papers she held in her lap with the other: formal, typewritten statements from people at TV London who had something relevant to say about Nicola Sharpe. As they had stumbled out of the incident room, new names were already being scribbled up on the action boards with blue marker pens – yet more people to be trawled by the team of detective constables.

As they crossed Chelsea Bridge Blanche sank her teeth into her third sandwich, flicked over a sheet of paper and slotted a cassette into the tape machine. She never ceased to amaze Dexter with her ability to do several things at the same time – perhaps too many things, he thought, regarding her dishevelled hair and the flush of stress in her cheeks. Heroines, at least the ones he saw on television or in the cinema, were not supposed to look like this. They were ageless, unwrinkled and calm. Success fell into their laps like ripe fruit from a tree. Blanche had been doomed to fight for her promotion, watch her weight, and fret over her childlessness. And doomed to be one of the best detectives in the Met.

When Dexter had first worked with Blanche he had not

liked her. He was unable to relax. She seemed to misunderstand deliberately everything he said. When they travelled together in a police car they had driven around in silence. But one day he made the mistake, at least from his point of view, of bringing along a few tapes of his favourite soul and reggae music. He started to play one and a look of pain flickered across Blanche's face as if someone was trying to shave her legs with a blunt razor. She said nothing. The next day she appeared with a box of her own tapes of classical music which she thrust endlessly into the cassette machine with a distracted smile. Nothing was said. After a few days, burning with a sense of injustice, Dexter plucked up courage and asked Blanche about her double standards – what right had she to make him listen to her type of music, when he could not force her to listen to his? She thought for a moment and turned to him with flushed cheeks. 'You're right, Sergeant. I've been doing it without thinking. I'm sorry.' She sounded genuinely regretful.

An embarrassed silence hummed on the air. Dexter was stunned. A superior officer had never apologised to him before. 'That's all right, ma'am,' the sergeant gulped, suddenly wishing he had not said anything. 'I didn't want to make a big thing of it.' From that moment he had had respect for Blanche: he knew it took a rare combination of self-confidence and courage to admit she had been wrong. Nothing more was said, but ever since Dexter had brought along a selection of his own tapes and there had been an informal division of playing time on the cassette player in the car.

Dexter hadn't heard the tape Blanche was playing before. He let the opening float over him: undulating strings, like someone stirring from sleep, which rose to one crashing climax, followed by another. Finally a man began to sing in the muffled distance, as if from the bottom of a lake. 'What's this then, guv'? Not more bloody opera?' he asked through a yawn.

'I'm afraid so.' Blanche glanced up. *'La Cavalleria Rusticana.'*

'What's that mean then?'

'Rustic chivalry. One Sicilian peasant kills another one for seducing his wife.'

'Sounds a good laugh.'

'Not much of a good laugh in this opera, Sergeant. It's all about love, hate, jealousy and revenge.' Blanche squinted thoughtfully. 'A bit like the murder of Nicola Sharpe.'

'Would you like a drink?' Jane Pargeter said, nodding towards her open drinks cabinet, even before Blanche and Dexter had time to sit down on the black leather armchairs in her sitting-room. A cut glass tumbler sat on the coffee table beside a bottle of gin and a bottle of tonic water. Both were half empty. Dexter's immediate reaction was to say yes, but he declined the offer: he was on duty after all, and even the detective constable's iron constitution wilted under the influence of alcohol at half past three in the afternoon.

In the flesh Jane Pargeter was familiar but different to how Dexter had imagined her from the image on television. The voice was the same: clear and authoritative, sure of itself, although faintly slurred by alcohol. He also knew the face – the firm jaw, the wide mouth that sagged slightly on one side as though supporting an invisible cigarette, the pert nose, the dark blue eyes: the constituent parts of beauty. Other things were a surprise. The sergeant had expected her to be taller, instead of a good nine inches shorter than Blanche. He also thought she would have looked younger and fitter. Dressed in a pair of designer jeans that were stretched over her buttocks like clingfilm, and with blotchy skin without a trace of make-up, she looked closer to fifty than the forty Dexter knew she really was. Jane Pargeter was one of those lucky people who looked better on television than in ordinary life, a woman transformed by the camera.

She kept up a flow of nervous chatter from the kitchen while she brewed up two cups of instant coffee. Everyone at TVL was just stunned by the murder, she said. People were stopping outside the office where it took place and whispering to each other – someone had even placed a bouquet of flowers at the door that morning. She'd gone in first thing but couldn't face the idea of working.

Blanche stood in the centre of the room and suppressed a yawn, her eyes absorbing the surroundings. Jane Pargeter's flat was in a huge and expensive mansion block on the north side of Clapham Common. The apartment itself was enormous and, as if she were scared of the space, Jane Pargeter had crammed it with expensive furniture. All of it was modern – whether reproduction antiques, like the bookcases and table, or high-tech, like the light fittings. It was a confusing hotch-potch, bought on impulse over a number of years without considering how it would all fit together. Dexter rather liked it but he knew from the indifferent look on Blanche's face that she did not: she was very classic in her tastes.

Jane Pargeter poured herself another slug of gin and slopped in some tonic water, spilling some on the coffee table. She did not bother to wipe up the puddle. 'I'll obviously do what I can to help,' she began, sipping her drink. 'But I really think you're wasting your time coming to talk to me. I mean I was at the party but I didn't see anything suspicious.'

Blanche sat down on the sofa and folded her hands in her lap. She said it was a routine enquiry and the police were interviewing everybody who had been at Ken O'Mara's farewell. Someone was playing rock music in the flat above and the faint throb hovered in the sitting-room.

Jane Pargeter blinked her watery eyes. 'I turned up at the party pretty much at the start, I think, around a quarter to nine. I drank quite a lot. Ate a lot. Talked a lot. I enjoyed it.'

'Did you go out of the room at all between the time you arrived and, say, a quarter to ten?'

'Yes. I popped out to the loo.'

'What time would that be?'

She pulled on a wan smile. 'I thought you might ask that. Just after nine or so, I suppose. And then I went

69

straight back to the party. I didn't go out again until Ken stormed in and said he'd found Nicola.' She said anyone at the party could confirm her story.

'Did you see Nicola at all?'

'At the party?'

Blanche nodded.

The TV presenter pondered for a moment, running her chubby fingers through her hair. 'It's funny you should ask because I bumped into her just as I was coming back from the loo. She was leaving the party. That was the only time I saw her.'

Dexter assumed this happened just after Nicola had been called to the phone. He asked Jane Pargeter to describe how Nicola appeared.

'She looked quite normal. She just nodded, walked past me and that was it. I didn't think twice about it.'

'And you had no idea where she was going?'

The presenter stopped fingering the amber necklace she wore round her neck and crossed her arms. The movement made her look more self-contained and masculine. 'No. Why should I?'

It was as though a chapter in the conversation had finished. The only sound in the room was the continued throb of rock music from the flat above. Dexter stretched his long legs. If Pargeter was telling the truth and did not leave the party until the body was found, she could not have murdered Nicola. The only point in ekeing out the conversation was the hope that she had seen something curious. The superintendent seemed to share his thoughts. She drew her hands together, fingertip to fingertip, and raised them to her nose. 'Who did you talk to at the party?'

The TV presenter shrugged her shoulders. 'Lots of people. Ken. Mike Slide. Simon Franks. I even bumped into Nicola Sharpe's husband – a tedious man called Jim something.'

'Lancaster,' added Blanche.

'That's right. Lancaster.'

'What did you talk to him about?'

70

Jane Pargeter drew back her lips in a gesture of uncon-cern. 'I can't really remember. Education, I think. The only interesting thing about him was to speculate why on earth a sparky girl like Nicola should want to marry him.' Jane Pargeter threw her head back and contemplated the ceiling. The TV presenter looked across at the sergeant, as though registering his presence for the first time. She looked down at the carpet.

Blanche asked if she had seen Jim Lancaster leave the boardroom at any time.

'I did actually. I know he was looking for Nicola at one stage because he asked if I knew where she'd gone. I said I didn't but I'd passed her coming in to the party.'

The superintendent's voice was calm. 'What time was that?'

'Oh, I don't know. Some time between quarter past and half past nine, I suppose.'

Dexter tried to hide his excitement. They had found a witness who confirmed that one of their prime suspects had left the party at the right time to murder Nicola. Lancaster had even told Jane he was searching for his wife. It was perfect. The sergeant glanced across at Blanche but her face betrayed no emotion at all. He remembered how she had reluctantly sat down to play him and a couple of other men at poker a few years before. Her face had been just the same then – interested but inscrutable – and she had taken a fiver off all of them.

'Did Lancaster seem calm or was he in a bit of a state?' enquired Blanche, brushing her front teeth with the tip of her thumb.

The presenter drained off the last of her gin and tonic and clinked the ice in the bottom of her glass. 'He seemed in a bit of a panic. He just asked me if I knew where she was and then I watched him disappear out of the room. It was only a matter of seconds.'

Dexter's instinct was to drive round to Lancaster's house and interview him straight away. But he knew he had to be patient. Blanche was not in a hurry. She was still trying to win the woman's confidence.

71

The superintendent asked Jane Pargeter whether she had seen anyone else leave the party. The presenter said she could only recall a few people, and volunteered the story of David Parkin throwing a glass of wine at his wife and how she had watched Maggie Parkin stalk out of the room trying to pretend that nothing had happened. She told the anecdote with a glint of relish in her eye, revelling in their embarrassment. Dexter remembered she had once been David Parkin's lover. When pressed she also said she remembered catching a glimpse of David Parkin going out of the room.

'You seem to have had a good view,' commented Dexter.

The TV reporter chuckled and tossed her head back. 'You've got to keep your eyes open at parties – for the gossip.' Dexter decided he rather liked Jane Pargeter. She seemed to have a proper regard for the frivolous things in life.

The rhythm of the rock music thumped relentlessly. The sitting-room suddenly felt claustrophobic. The cast-iron window framed the trees of Clapham Common under a darkening sky. Flecks of drizzle brushed the window. Jane Pargeter stood up and switched on the standard lamp beside her chair, standing with her arms akimbo, self-contained yet vulnerable.

'I'm sorry to intrude on your personal affairs, Miss Pargeter, but didn't you have an affair with David Parkin?' Blanche's question seemed to resound round the room with its impertinence.

'What's that got to do with this bloody murder?' Jane Pargeter slumped down in her armchair and crossed her legs angrily. 'I thought you came round here to ask if I'd seen anything suspicious last night, not grill me about my sex life.'

Dexter caught a glance from Blanche: she was always intrigued by conflict or displays of strong emotion. 'I'm sorry to intrude. But you see, if – as I've been told – David Parkin . . . ' She paused to choose her words carefully. Jane Pargeter looked up, her eyes watchful. 'David Parkin had had an affair with you and then started one with

72

Nicola. I just wondered whether the timing of the two affairs overlapped, that's all.'

Jane Pargeter's blue eyes grew chill with anger or sadness. Dexter could not decide which. Perhaps it was both. 'Well, I'll answer the question, but only because I don't want to give the impression I'm hiding anything. We were lovers on and off for three years. Then David met Maggie Parkin about eighteen months ago and we split up.'

'Were you very angry about it?'

'Of course I was at the time. But not now.' She smiled, as if recalling some secret happiness. Dexter guessed that she had found a new man. 'I don't still hate his guts – if that's what you're asking. David seems very happy and he's got a lovely little son.'

'If he was so happy why did he start an affair with Nicola?' asked the superintendent, leaning forward in her seat.

Jane Pargeter sniffed and prodded with her toe at an imaginary stain in the carpet. 'It just happened, from what I can gather. They were at the Labour Party conference together last year and that's when it began. They tried to keep it a secret but you can't keep secrets long in television.'

Dexter believed Jane Pargeter was more interested in David Parkin's affair than she pretended: you can't be someone's lover for three years and then cast them off with the same indifference as an old pair of socks. He knew. He had been through the same mill a couple of years before. Jane had probably watched rumours of the affair harden into fact with an amalgam of loathing, sadness and jealousy.

The superintendent squinted at Jane Pargeter for a moment. 'Did Maggie Parkin know about the affair with Nicola?'

'I haven't the faintest idea. But she should have done unless she was completely blind.'

'What about Jim Lancaster? Do you think he knew about Nicola's affair?'

'Pass. It's not the sort of thing I ask people at parties.'

Her stare was cold and unreadable for a moment before she broke into a smile. 'I don't know. He probably did. Ask him.'

Blanche sipped her coffee, now lukewarm after sitting untouched on the low table for a few minutes. Jane Pargeter walked self-consciously to the kitchen to make herself a cup of tea: she had obviously decided she had drunk enough gin for the afternoon. Dexter tapped his fingers on the tubular arms of his chair, thinking how much more comfortable his sofa was at home. Pargeter intrigued him. She was the first television celebrity he had met in the flesh, and he still could not quite believe the woman who had been sitting in front of him was the same one he had watched so regularly on the box. It was rather like when he had gone to Paris for the first time when he was eighteen. He had seen the Eiffel Tower so many times in photographs or on television he did not think it really existed. And yet it did. He had stood in front of it and pinched himself, observing the intricacy of the ironwork with the wonder of a child. He observed Jane Pargeter come out of the kitchen – the neck of her shirt folded up, her forearms freckled but brown from a recent holiday – with the same attention to detail.

The last piece of territory he and Blanche needed to explore was one the superintendent had not yet entered – deliberately, Dexter suspected: Nicola Sharpe's drive to take over Jane Pargeter's job. Even though Blanche's first question was innocent enough, Dexter knew immediately that the superintendent was thinking along the same lines. 'How did you get on with Nicola, Miss Pargeter?'

The blue eyes, bloodshot but penetrating, held the detective's face for a moment. 'Call me Jane, if you like, Superintendent. As one professional woman to another.'

'OK. My name's Blanche.' The superintendent paused and flicked up her eyebrows. 'So how did you get on with Nicola, Jane?'

The presenter cradled her cup in her hands, staring down at the tea. Dexter noticed her fingernails were long and primed with pink varnish. 'All right.'

'Really?'

Jane Pargeter flopped back in her chair and threw an arm across the back. She smiled. 'No, to tell you the truth, I didn't like her at all. She was a jumped-up little bitch.' There was little emotion in the way she spoke, merely a statement of fact. Dexter was surprised that the TV presenter revealed her true feelings towards Nicola so quickly: most people in his experience, when first interviewed by the police, tried to hide extremes of love or hate. Jane Pargeter was determined to look relaxed, Dexter thought, even though the number of times she kept bobbing her mouth down to sip her tea showed that she was not. She stared first at the superintendent and then at Dexter without blinking. 'She was after my job, you see. She even had the cheek to go around saying she had it.'

Blanche probed, her voice husky with mock concern. 'I gather there was some silly talk about you being replaced?'

'"Silly talk" is precisely what it was. No more than that. I've been at the top in television for a decade, you see, Blanche. Nicola could hardly tell one end of a camera from the other.'

The matey use of Blanche's name struck a false note with Dexter, like interviewees he had seen on chat shows who kept tossing in the name of the host every thirty seconds to make it appear they were bosom pals. Jane flopped forward on her chair and sighed heavily. Her stomach edged up over the waistband of her slacks. There was a hard edge of arrogance to Jane Pargeter – the same self-confidence she displayed on the screen.

'So what was behind all these rumours that she'd got your job then?' Blanche asked. 'Are you saying Nicola made the whole thing up?'

Jane Pargeter sipped her tea again. She suddenly pulled herself up short and injected some huskiness into her voice, like a politician who wants to convince you of his sincerity. 'Yes. I think she did for the most part. That's why I stopped worrying about it.'

Blanche tightened her lips in polite disbelief. 'But surely someone must have told her something.'

75

The TV presenter looked hard at Blanche, her eyes focused with suspicion. 'Not as far as I know. She was taking a lot for granted.'

'Apparently Nicola was going round saying she had the backing of top management.'

'Who exactly?'

'Someone mentioned Mike Slide, the head of the department, and even the chairman of the company, Stephen Blufton.'

'Well, there you are. I'd always guessed Nicola had a rich fantasy life but I'd never guessed it was quite that rich,' she snorted derisively. 'Nicola was bullshitting. That was one thing she *was* good at. Mike Slide certainly rated her – although God knows why. And as for Stephen Blufton – well, he sticks his oar into programme-making a lot but he's got no interest in promoting the career of an inexperienced regional reporter.'

You did not like Nicola Sharpe, did you, thought Dexter, listening to the verbal stiletto slip between the dead woman's ribs. Jane Pargeter certainly had a fine line in bitchiness. The sergeant thought he should offer his boss some support in her battle to prise a little truth out of the woman they were interviewing. 'Come on, Miss Pargeter, *someone* must have had an interest in giving Nicola a leg up?'

The presenter smiled. 'Only Nicola herself, as far as I can make out.'

Jane Pargeter was lying. Dexter was sure of that. And he was sure Blanche shared his opinion: she was squinting at the TV presenter as if she were a small but fascinating object in a museum. Jane Pargeter had come much closer to losing her job than she pretended.

The superintendent sighed and sat back in her chair, asking Jane to tell her side of the story.

'I suppose it started about a month ago. People were whispering about me behind my back – smiling to my face of course – but whispering behind my back. I've been round long enough to realise something was up. It didn't take long to find out Nicola had told them that she was in

76

line to take over my job.' She leant forward in her chair as if to make the facts clearer, cool and in control, as if reading from autoscript in the studio. 'I stormed round to see Mike Slide – he's the new head of Topical Features – and asked him outright if it was true. He just sat there jiggling his bloody spectacles and saying that as far as he knew it wasn't.' She drank off what remained of her tea. When she spoke again it was with a sneer. 'That clinched it. I'd been in this business long enough to know he was lying and that something was going on.'

'So what did you do then?'

'Stormed around for a few days, lobbied as hard as I could and got on with my job. What else could I do?' The spark in her eyes suddenly died. Her hands, like claws, clutched her cup and she looked sorrowfully at the luke-warm tea. Her hair, Dexter noticed, was matt and streaked with grey, no longer glistening with the aid of a back light in the studio. Her right cheek twitched faintly. 'I'd given the best years of my life to television. And sometimes I wonder whether it hasn't all been a complete waste of time.'

It was a maudlin performance fuelled by the gin in her blood, but none the less powerful for that. Dexter, and he was sure Blanche as well, was left wondering whether Pargeter believed what she was saying.

The presenter sighed and rubbed one palm across the other. 'People in television take it so seriously. I've seen people burn themselves out. Marriages break up. And at the end of the day hardly anyone remembers the pro-grammes they did it for.' She looked across to a bureau on which stood a framed certificate for TV Presenter of the Year Award.

'I've seen just the same in the police,' murmured Blanche.

A smile flickered on the presenter's lips. 'I suppose you're right. Television's no different.'

The rock music above suddenly stopped, although its rhythmic throbbing seemed to linger in the air. It was as if the neighbour had sensed that the police officers were

77

about to leave and wished to honour their departure with silence. Blanche eased herself up.

Having asked Jane Pargeter to come and give a formal statement at Chester Row, Blanche halted just outside the open door to the flat. 'Do you think Nicola's work might have put her in danger?'

Jane Pargeter asked what she meant.

'I gather she'd been looking into drugs a few weeks back and then into child porn. I wondered if she might have stumbled across something.'

The TV presenter reclined against the door-jamb, a crinkle of suspicion on her forehead. She shook her head. 'I think you've been watching too much television.' She proffered her hand in farewell.

As his boss turned away and began to stride down the corridor, Dexter noticed a wary look slither into Pargeter's eyes. He glanced over his shoulder when they were twenty yards along the carpet and was surprised to see her still leaning thoughtfully against the door. Ten yards further down the corridor, he heard the door slam with a resounding crack.

CHAPTER
EIGHT

The bleak greenery of Clapham Common slipped from sight as they headed east towards Blackheath. Dexter had been stationed in Brixton several years before and he inhaled the familiar atmosphere as he wound along Coldharbour Lane towards Peckham: the dilapidated shops selling second-hand furniture and televisions, the handsome couple posing against a car as though for a fashion magazine, the parked cars tumbling over the pavement. He felt comfortable now watching the black faces on the pavement, screwed up against the drizzle, but remembered his resentment when he had first learned of his posting. How stupid the Met could be, he had thought. Brixton was a black area. PC Dexter Bazalgette was black. Send Bazalgette to Brixton. The pasty-faced bureaucrats at New Scotland Yard were not to know he felt about as much at home there when he first arrived as a Martian.

The Street Duties sergeant at the police station had given him a hard time. Dexter wondered at first whether it was because he was black or a probationer, but after a few months he was sure it was because of his Jamaican origins. Dexter had seethed silently for a few weeks and mentioned his anger to a priest during confession. The soft, educated English voice floated through the dark grille. It advised him to forgive the man and pray for him to have a change of heart. Dexter did neither. He whispered 'bollocks' under his breath and started going to another church. Dexter did not forgive easily.

There were fun times of course when he got his

revenge. He used to be stopped frequently after work and normally he just told the constable he was a policeman straight away. But on one occasion, when he was waiting to meet a girlfriend, a constable came up and was so rude Dexter decided to play him along.

'This your car, mate?'

'Yeah.'

'Makes a change, dunnit.' He turned round and smirked at his squad car with a woman police constable in the front. 'What are you doing here then?'

'Meeting someone.' Just then Dexter's friend came up – a white girl he had kept in contact with from his schooldays.

'White slag, eh?' Dexter let him continue. 'You got a job?'

'Yeah.'

'You must be the one in a million then. What do you do?'

'Work for the government.'

The constable started to go round the car, examining it minutely, occasionally glancing up at the WPC to confirm the impression he was making. 'So where are you off to?'

'Work, actually.'

'Where's that then?'

'In the police station down the road. I'm a copper.' Dexter flourished his warrant card. The constable flushed red and apologised, causing the WPC in the squad car to rock with laughter.

Dexter smiled to himself as he remembered that incident. He edged the car he was driving into Peckham High Street. Parades of shabby shops, gathered like mongrel dogs on a street corner, were parted by a grim council estate, and then reassembled. Pedestrians scampered blindly across the road to catch waiting buses, the cars jerked ahead a few yards every time the traffic lights turned to green. The drizzle fell steadily, dribbling across the pock-marked tarmac, forcing forlorn figures at bus-stops to huddle together even closer under the shelters. Dexter watched the lights of a garage or a garden centre slide by, glistening damply through the mist. He accelerated up a dark and steep hill and finally they emerged on to the flat expanse of Blackheath.

The Parkins' house stood in a drive marked at the entrance with a notice restricting access to residents only. The sergeant bumped over the sleeping-policemen and gazed at the neatly trimmed lawns and hedges with aggrieved jealousy in his eyes: the private estate was a symbol of a world from which he was excluded, a world of privilege and snobbery, a world that had turned its back on the poor, the sick and the unfashionable who had been swarming round their car only ten minutes before. Once again he thought how privileged he was as a policeman, given a special dispensation to walk into other people's houses – whether rich or poor, criminal or victim – and ask intimate questions that would have led anyone else to be punched on the nose.

Dexter remembered occasionally seeing David Parkin's face on television: handsome, weathered and topped by a shock of prematurely white hair. He smelt of good-quality *eau de toilette*, his grasp firm as he shook them by the hand and strode ahead, waving the nanny and his young son towards the sitting-room. For a man whose lover had been brutally murdered the night before he seemed cheerful and composed. Although ten years older than Jane Pargeter, he exuded health and energy, as well as the same self-confidence. Everyone in television seemed to have a sense of their self-importance, Dexter reflected.

Parkin gave a brief account of the previous night in his bass voice, saying that he had spoken briefly to Nicola at the pub outside TV London before the party started, and had spotted her in the boardroom. But he had not seen her leave. He did not mention the quarrel with his wife. When David Parkin sat back on his armchair, tossing aside a copy of the *Guardian*, Dexter sensed a sneaking admiration for him. Even Blanche, the sergeant thought, seemed to share it. She was not immune to the charm of a handsome man.

When Parkin finished speaking, Blanche smiled. 'Mr Parkin, just how well *did* you know Nicola?' The gentle

81

stress on the word 'did' made it clear Blanche expected there to be more to their relationship than a glancing acquaintance at work.

His tongue flickered over his lips. And then he smiled back – revealing a perfect set of small, white teeth – taking care to include the sergeant in the gesture. The reporter's eyes narrowed, the flesh puckered up as if he was staring at the sun. 'Very well indeed, if you must know. I was having an affair with her. There's no point in lying about it.' He spoke without conviction, as if he believed the last phrase was something he was obliged to say rather than genuinely believed. Parkin lounged back in his chair. The sleeves of his pale blue shirt were rolled up over his muscly forearms. The light from a standard lamp caught the hair bubbling up through the open neck of his shirt and on the backs of his arms. The man was very conscious of his own image, Dexter reflected, like an actor measuring his every movement on the stage.

Blanche sighed. 'Did your wife find out about it?'

Parkin's eyes narrowed again. Dexter noticed that white hairs were even bristling from his ears and above the line on his cheeks where he shaved. 'What's my wife got to do with it?'

'I've no idea. That's why I'm asking.'

A quiver of tension flickered through Parkin's hitherto relaxed body. His grey eyes turned frosty. 'I think I need a drink. Do you want one?'

They said no and Parkin went out. Dexter was sure the TV reporter's motive for leaving the room was more to check the nanny was not listening at the keyhole than a raging thirst. He returned with a can of lager and a glass, shutting the door carefully behind him.

'My wife did know that Nicola and I were having an affair.' He made great efforts to include Dexter in the conversation, the sergeant noticed, embracing him in his replies. He was probably the sort of liberal, Dexter thought, who boasted of the number of blacks he knew but whose acquaintance was limited to inviting them round to show off at trendy drinks parties.

'So why didn't your wife tell us about it?' asked Dexter.

'She phoned me after you interviewed her and said she guessed you'd found out about the affair – to warn me. She said she played innocent to try to protect me.'

'Protect you from what?'

Parkin shrugged. 'She thought you might see a link between the affair and the murder.'

Blanche sat forward in her seat. 'And is there?' The question was posed in a flat tone, seeking information rather than accusing. From long experience Blanche knew it was pointless to confront most interviewees, foolish to drive them into a corner.

Parkin sipped some beer, leaving a crest of foam on his upper lip, which he wiped with the edge of his hand. For a moment, he seemed apprehensive to Dexter. 'There's nothing to cover up. I didn't do it, Superintendent.'

Blanche adjusted her skirt. She asked when Maggie Parkin had found out about her husband's affair.

Parkin sighed with exasperation. 'A couple of weeks ago, if you really must know. It was all pretty sordid. She found a receipt for a hotel in Hampshire in my suit. I'd told her I'd been away filming in Scotland that night.' Blanche said nothing. Dexter knew that she preferred to wait and let the interviewee be sucked back into the vacuum of silence. 'We had a flaming row. I said it was just a fling. That I wasn't in love with Nicola – which was true – and that I'd give her up.'

Blanche waited but Parkin was not going to say anything else unless prodded. 'And had you given her up?'

The TV reporter swung his eyes back from the window and trained them on the superintendent in a long, calculating stare. 'No. That's to say I was going to – but . . . ' He swigged his lager. 'I had to wait for the right moment to tell Nicola. I couldn't see the point of rushing into it. I'd made the decision. That was the important point. It was just a question of – how shall I say? – implementing it.'

In other words, thought the sergeant, Parkin was either a coward or a liar, or both. A coward because he did not have the courage to tell Nicola that he was ending their affair, or a liar because he made a false promise to his wife to give up his young lover. Dexter suspected Parkin's indecision was a mixture of the two. Maggie Parkin was infatuated with her husband and only too willing to believe his promise. Pulled between a trusting wife and a beautiful young lover, David Parkin had decided to delay an unpleasant confrontation with Nicola as long as possible. He was only human.

'So you hadn't actually ended the affair with Nicola before she was murdered?'

Parkin made a long sigh to give himself time to think. 'That's right.'

'But you told your wife you had?'

He stared down at the carpet. No one, Dexter reflected, likes to admit to an act of cowardice. 'Yes, just to keep her quiet.'

'So when *did* you intend to tell Nicola?'

'When I was ready.'

'And were you ready last night at the party?' Parkin looked puzzled, trying to fathom the point of the question. 'I was wondering whether you'd arranged to meet her for a talk – to break the news to her?'

Parkin glowered back. 'No. I did not.' He articulated each word with precision.

'You had the opportunity, after all. You were seen to leave the party after Nicola had gone out.'

The reporter's eyes flickered down to the floor. 'I *did* leave the party for a few minutes, it's true. But that was simply to get a breath of fresh air. I popped out on the sixth-floor roof and had a cigarette.'

Blanche rubbed her chin and stared at Parkin thoughtfully. She asked if he had left the boardroom before or after the altercation with his wife at the party.

The reporter picked up his empty lager can and contemplated it as if it were a work of art. After a few seconds, he crumpled the aluminium with a sudden grip of his fist, as though he had taken an important decision. 'It was a stupid row really. It was about Nicola. You see, I had a chat with Nicola at the party and Maggie became hysterical. She told me I was never to speak to Nicola again.' Parkin rolled the crushed can round in his palm. 'Maggie started going at me about whether I really had finished the affair yet. Her voice was getting louder and louder. So, to calm her down, I threw my glass of wine over her.' He laid the can down on the teak coffee table and spread his hands. 'And that's it. That's the truth.' He said his wife was probably out of the room for about fifteen or twenty minutes.

'And that's presumably when you went for a smoke on the roof?'

'Yes. I needed to calm down myself and think it all through.'

Dexter sensed a prickly atmosphere in the room – a chill on the hairs at the back of his neck, an almost eerie silence. For some strange reason the image of the corpse of Nicola Sharpe floated up in his mind, and it brought with it a breath of foreboding, a sense that he was in the presence of evil. It was nothing to do with David Parkin and nothing to do with the room – warm and comforting, the walls cluttered with Victorian paintings and prints, the antique furniture gleaming spotlessly. The sensation had come from Dexter's imagination, a reminder that murder often had a smiling face and was just at home in bourgeois drawing-rooms as in seedy bed and breakfast hotels.

Blanche's voice suddenly became quiet and insinuating, without a trace of hostility. Her relaxed manner was the reason, Dexter had concluded, why she often coaxed answers to some of the most prickly questions. 'I don't like prying into people's private lives, Mr Parkin. But I'm afraid it's my job. I want to ask you about Jane Pargeter.' Blanche's deep brown eyes held Parkin steadily. The reporter uncrossed his legs and sat back in his chair. 'Jane told us she hated Nicola. I was just interested in whether you thought she disliked Nicola so much because she'd started an affair with a man who'd recently been her lover – you.'

Parkin spread his hands in a gesture of uncertainty. Dexter wondered if the idea appealed to his vanity. 'I

85

think the fact Nicola was after Jane's job was far more important.' The TV reporter rubbed his cheek. 'But Jane wouldn't have murdered her, if that's what you're getting at. She's a hard woman but . . . not as hard as that.'

Dexter watched Blanche shuffle into a more comfortable position in her chair. Her eyes glanced round the room before coming to rest on the lithe and handsome man sitting opposite. He guessed she was mulling over what Parkin had told them and garnering any remaining questions. 'Who was it, by the way, who told Nicola that she had the presenter's job?'

'She said Stephen Blufton was behind it all. He's the chairman of TVL, if you didn't already know.'

'I've seen his name in the papers a few times,' murmured the superintendent, whose forehead creased with puzzlement. 'And why would he promise her the job?'

Parkin curled his lips into a sneer. Somehow it appeared undignified to Dexter because the TV reporter's face was so classically handsome. 'Because he wanted to sleep with her. That's why.'

'And did he?'

'Not as far as I know.'

'What do you mean?'

Parkin picked up the crushed lager can and turned it round and round in his hands. 'Nicola had met him once or twice at various parties. And then a few weeks ago she told me she'd been invited to go and see him at his house – or "castle" as Blufton prefers to call it.' The sneer scarred his lips again. 'She went, because Nicola was never one to miss out on a chance to push herself forward. Anyway, she said he made a pass at her and she almost had to fight him off.'

'But he promised Nicola that she'd take over Jane Pargeter's presenter's job?'

'Apparently. He told Nicola the programme was looking tired and the job was hers for the asking.'

Blanche asked if Blufton had been at the farewell party the night before.

Parkin pondered for a moment. 'No, he wasn't. He only

comes to the odd party. He sometimes likes to mix with the troops – especially the good-looking female ones.'

Parkin added that although Nicola had become his mistress, she was keen to avoid gossip in the office and maintain her independence. She insisted that they were not seen often together at TVL and that she kept what she called her professional distance. 'Nicola was known as a chatterbox at work but she was very good at keeping the secrets that really mattered.' David Parkin placed the crushed lager can back on the coffee table and examined it regretfully, like a faded photograph.

Dexter saw Blanche gaze at Parkin with sadness. Whether it was to share his moment of regret at the passing of time, or to express disillusion with Parkin himself – she had made some comment in the car about how he was one of the few television reporters she knew and respected – Dexter did not know. After a second or two she glanced down at her notebook: although the detective had a retentive memory she sometimes scribbled the odd reminder. 'One last thing, Mr Parkin. Nicola's husband told me that he thought you had something to do with the murder. Why do you think he should say that?'

Parkin looked worried but then snorted a laugh through his chiselled nose. 'Well, it's obvious, isn't it? The little creep was trying to get his own back on me for sleeping with his wife.'

Blanche nodded thoughtfully as though Parkin had made a profound point rather than a cheap jibe at a cuckolded husband. As they rose to leave, Dexter wondered why.

As he was waiting for the barmaid to pour the drinks, Dexter could not resist temptation. He slid a coin into the slot of the juke-box and let a long, chocolate finger trip over the buttons. He made his choice and watched fascinated as the arm jerked across and laid the record on the turntable. The throb of the music swelled into the pub in Peckham, thumping the thick varnish that smothered the bar, the Formica-topped tables and the stained, velvet

87

curtains. Although many London pubs seemed to look the same when he first walked in, Dexter enjoyed collating the differences that set one apart from another. Sometimes it was the people, sometimes the decor, sometimes the smell. In this pub it was the dark emptiness, the isolated figures clutching their half-empty glasses, eyes transfixed by the jumble of images on the television screen high on the wall. The sergeant made a mental note never to come to this pub again.

The barmaid took the money wordlessly and Dexter swaggered over to the corner where Blanche was sitting. She took the double whisky he offered her and greedily took a gulp. Dexter knew that she was not always as relaxed as this in pubs. Blanche enjoyed social drinking with her officers but Dexter sometimes noticed she was ill at ease. Pubs could become for her extensions of the office, places to put on a good show for the Yard, swilling pints of bitter with the lads to enhance her image. It was then Dexter detected an underlying tension: Blanche became bored and wanted to leave, but was reluctant to do so in case she gained a reputation as a straight-laced bore.

'People like you are a menace, Dexter,' she scowled good-naturedly. 'Noise polluters. There I was revelling in the murmur of drunken conversation from the bar and you go and spoil it by sticking the juke-box on.'

'Getting my own back,' Dexter smiled, 'for all that bloody opera you were playing in the car today.' The sergeant gnawed hungrily at his cheese roll and sipped from his glass of bitter. He said nothing for a moment, watching Blanche with his wide eyes, the black lashes curling back on themselves.

'The trouble is,' murmured the superintendent, wiping a crumb from the side of her mouth with a paper napkin, 'we've just got too many suspects. And credible ones at that.'

Dexter pretended to nod agreement. He often believed Blanche saw cases as more complicated than they really were. It was almost as if she wanted the intellectual stimulation, the fascination of the difficult.

'Lots of people with a motive, and lots of people with an opportunity,' continued the superintendent morosely. 'It could have been Jane Pargeter, who was about to lose her job.'

'Remember she didn't leave the party though when Nicola was out of the room.' This was a good example, Dexter thought, of Blanche being unwilling to exclude someone from their investigation at an early stage so that they could concentrate their efforts. Besides, he rather liked her boozy self-confidence – and her style of interior decoration.

'True,' replied Blanche, unconvinced. 'Or it could have been Maggie Parkin – '

'She's certainly suspicious, trying to cover up her hubby's affair.' There were other things as well, Dexter recalled. The convenience of a change of dress in her car. Even the row with her husband could have been provoked.

Blanche twirled her glass, sending the ice-cubes inside racing round. 'Or it could have been David Parkin.'

'I thought you said you had a lot of respect for him as a reporter?'

Blanche laughed gently, allowing the whisky to roll over her tongue. 'Until I met him in the flesh. He's too charming by half.'

'What's puzzling me is that phone-call Nicola had at the party. I'm sure it's got something to do with the murder.'

'It could just be a coincidence. Or from someone connected with the mysterious Mr Kennedy – perhaps his secretary saying the meeting was off.'

'At nine o'bloody clock. Come off it, guv'.' Dexter shrugged with disbelief. 'Based on what we know so far, I think it's the husband.'

Blanche laughed. 'You haven't even met him yet and already you've put him behind bars for life.'

The sergeant tapped the side of his nose. 'Instinct, ma'am. Instinct.' Dexter ignored her friendly chuckle and explained the reasons why he thought Jim Lancaster was the prime suspect, counting off the points on his fingers.

First, he had the opportunity. They knew he was out of the boardroom at the right time. Second, Jim Lancaster had a good motive. His wife was having it off with another man. 'That's enough for me. He's the man to watch for the moment – until we can point the finger at somebody else.'

'Yes,' said Blanche, 'in a case like this there's always a husband, isn't there?' Dexter was unable to decide whether her wistfulness was caused by sympathy for the victims of adultery or knowledge that the majority of murders were committed by close relatives of the dead. Blanche drank off the last of her whisky, leaving a few pebbles of un-melted ice in the bottom of her glass.

Dexter was glad to get back to Chester Row. He enjoyed the camaraderie of police life and spent several minutes going about the murder squad office, exchanging pleasan-tries with officers he did not know and catching up with the latest news. He saw one of his jobs as keeping his ear to the ground on Blanche's behalf, trying to catch discontent while it was no more than a distant rumble and to spot which detectives needed encouragement and which a gentle kick up the backside. Blanche's antennae were very sensitive at gauging the progress of an investigation but she relied on Dexter to hoover up male gossip that was beyond her reach, idle chatter in the canteen or the gents' toilet that sometimes hardened into hostility or resentment at some way a case was being handled. It transpired that nothing dramatic had happened since they had left: tests on pairs of scissors at TVL headquarters were getting under way and Hugh Parnham, the third candidate for the *Inside Out* presenter's job, had phoned from Scotland to say he would be back in London the next day for an interview.

Dexter sat with the superintendent while she dialled the head of the Press Bureau, who told her his phone had not stopped ringing all day: press and television news editors were demanding to know why Scotland Yard was keeping such a low profile on the Nicola Sharpe story. They were desperate for solid information rather than rumour, and a few made veiled threats to scale down their coverage of another case for which the Yard was desperate for publicity unless there was a press conference. The head of the Bureau said the pressure had become so intense by the end of the afternoon, and Blanche had proved so elusive, he had been forced to phone her boss for advice. Commander Brian Spittals had ordered a press conference to be called at ten o'clock the next morning so that it could catch the lunchtime news bulletins.

The superintendent slipped the phone back into its cradle and a crease of worry tucked itself into her forehead.

Dexter asked what aspect of the investigation was causing her concern. Blanche took a second to focus on what he had said and then laughed. 'Oh, it wasn't the case I was worried about. It was something far more important. I was wondering where the hell I can get my hair done first thing tomorrow morning.' She heaved out a great sigh and did not move for a full fifteen seconds: the sergeant watched them tick past, marked by the flick of the thin red hand of the electric clock on the wall. Dexter guessed she was starting to share the same nagging sense of depression that had afflicted him since the end of the interview with Parkin. The sergeant was buoyant and resilient but sometimes a dark mood ambushed him. It might last a minute, an hour or even go on for days and there was nothing Dexter could do to fight it.

Dexter explained how he was wavering about the list of suspects: one moment thinking it consisted of only a handful of people and then believing almost anyone in the building could have done it. Perhaps it was this very indecision that made him depressed. Blanche listened patiently, like the elder sister Dexter had never had but always wished for.

The superintendent sat back, shoulders slumped, her eyes bleary with fatigue and thoughtfulness. She peered out into the office, winding down now at the end of the first day: at the two constables scribbling notes at their desk, at another sitting at the HOLMES computer, at a

91

WPC glancing through the actions book. 'We mustn't fall into a trap, Dexter.'

'What do you mean, ma'am?' the sergeant grunted suspiciously, over-sensitive in his present mood, and fearful the superintendent was blaming him for some unknown misdemeanour.

'I mean that someone, somewhere, might want us to look at things in a particular way.' Dexter could not be bothered to ask her to explain. She chewed her bottom lip. 'After the press conference tomorrow, I want to cast our net a bit wider.'

That's not the problem, the sergeant groaned inwardly, tightening his lips to hide his irritation: the net was wide enough already.

'In the meantime,' Blanche said, 'I want to have another chat with our prime suspect.'

CHAPTER
NINE

Dexter was puzzled when the man answered the door. He did not fit the description of Jim Lancaster that Blanche had given him in the car that morning. But the superintendent did not seem surprised. She showed her warrant card and when she explained that they had come to see Nicola's husband, the man invited them in. He was dressed in a shabby olive-green pullover and jeans. 'Jim's in the sitting-room,' he said, leading them along the corridor. Dexter caught a look of suspicious surprise from the man as the sergeant followed Blanche in, a glance that said, 'Crikey, the black is a policeman too; I just thought he was her driver.' As the years went by, Dexter saw the look less frequently but when he did it irked him as much as ever.

'I'm Derek Beasley, an old mate of Jim's from college,' the man murmured. And then, realising that his presence needed further explanation, he added, 'Jim asked me to keep him company until his sister gets here tomorrow.'

Dexter felt there was something strange about Beasley but could only place it when Lancaster's friend raised his right hand to tug at his beard: the last two fingers were no more than withered stumps. 'Jim's still very shocked. The doctor gave him a sedative this morning but he's spent most of the day slumped in front of the box.'

Jim Lancaster seemed to shrink when he saw Blanche. His rounded shoulders collapsed further and his timid eyes quested to right and left to avoid her gaze. He reminded Dexter of a panic-stricken mole who had suddenly found himself trapped outside his burrow. But Nicola's husband recovered himself and padded over from the settee to switch off the television. With the chatter of the sitcom dead, the room seemed unnaturally quiet.

Dexter watched the husband's eyes grow watchful and his hand rise to brush the side of his nose. The sergeant remembered it was one of his characteristics Blanche had mentioned. He struck the black detective immediately as a man trying to hide something, although Dexter knew that timidity often aroused unwarranted suspicions.

It was a modern house and everything in it was modern: the low ceilings, the plaster on the ceiling scumbled in circles like icing on a cake, bare walls, the woodwork all deal and varnished. The furniture was also modern and marked by a northern love of cheap glamour – polished brass, smoked glass and white crocheted curtains flirting at the windows. Dexter felt cold.

'Do you mind if I take a seat?' began Blanche.

Lancaster grunted, as if suddenly waking from a reverie. Dexter wondered if his vagueness was due to the shock of his wife's murder or an attempt to gain time. Nicola's husband sat down on the sofa, rubbing his hands on the knees of his brown corduroy trousers, blinking through his spectacles.

Blanche asked him how he was. The enquiry seemed to take the school teacher by surprise. He mumbled that he was still in a state of shock and had been walking around in a dream all day. His comments were guarded, as if he feared they might incriminate him. Dexter found his brevity a refreshing contrast to the self-conscious talkativeness of most of the people who worked at TV London.

'Look, I'm terribly sorry,' continued Blanche, 'to have to come back and see you at a time like this, Mr Lancaster – '

'Call me Jim, Superintendent. I get enough surnames at school,' said Lancaster wearily. His voice was marked by flat northern vowels and was so soft Dexter felt the muscles in his cheeks tense as he strained to hear.

'OK, Jim,' replied Blanche with a smile. Dexter noticed his boss did not suggest Lancaster address her by her

Christian name in return: she only encouraged such informality from the victims of crime rather than its possible perpetrators. 'A few things have cropped up that I didn't have a chance to talk to you about last night.' Lancaster scratched his nose. Blanche sighed. 'For a start, we've learnt Nicola was having an affair with another man.'

'Yes. I know,' he groaned.

Blanche's eyes widened slightly, as though she had been irritated by the reply. 'Why didn't you tell me last night?'

Jim studied the carpet like an ashamed schoolboy. 'I don't know. Shock, I suppose. It was something I was trying to forget.' He glanced up when he finished speaking to gauge the effect of his words.

Blanche gazed at him fixedly. 'But you can understand how suspicious it looks? You learn your wife's having an affair – but you don't tell the police about it.'

'Look, I may have been angry when I found out but . . . ' Lancaster flared, before trailing off in mid-sentence. He shuffled in his chair. 'But I didn't want to see Nicola dead.'

'Why didn't you mention it last night?' Blanche repeated.

The school teacher snatched his breath, as though about to snap back. But he thought better of it and slowly breathed out the air through his nose. When he did finally speak it was with a studied calm to smother his irritation. 'Shock. It didn't seem relevant last night. Anyway, I've told you now,' he exclaimed, glancing up and blinking wildly. 'So you can't accuse me of hiding anything.'

'I'm just trying to get at the truth,' soothed Blanche.

Dexter was glad they had come back to see Lancaster at the end of the day. And God, it had been a long one: Simon Franks, Maggie Parkin, Jane Pargeter, David Parkin. Twenty-four hours before, Nicola Sharpe was little more than a bloody corpse, a name, a glossy image on a television screen. But as the day had passed, and Dexter had started to picture her personality, he had come to realise how deceitful that image was. Nicola was not just a simpering and empty-headed blonde with a pleasant voice.

95

She was calculating and ambitious, and by all accounts at least a competent journalist. Dexter guessed she was deeply in love: not with her husband, with whom she was trapped in an unsuitable and corroded marriage; nor even it seemed, although no one knew the secrets of the dead woman's heart, with her older lover; but she was certainly in love with herself, Dexter believed, and with her image on the screen. The sergeant wondered what he would have thought of Nicola if he had met her when she was alive. He imagined she would have been charm personified if she wanted something from him, but offhand and dismissive if she had not. Like many journalists, he concluded cynically. But although she may not have been popular at work she was not evil. She did not deserve in that tiny viewing room to have been stabbed by a pair of scissors through the heart.

'Who was she having the affair with?'

Blanche's question woke Dexter from his reverie and he cast around for a photograph of Nicola in the room. There was none. The only photograph was of an elderly couple on top of the television, grey-haired and sporting smiles of false teeth.

A groove of concern chiselled itself down the middle of Lancaster's forehead. 'David Parkin.'

'Is that why you told me he had something to do with the murder?'

'I suppose so.'

Blanche paused. 'You only suppose so – have you got any other reason?'

Lancaster slipped off his spectacles and began to clean them meticulously with a white handkerchief, scouring the rims with his fingernails. 'Look, Superintendent, he's the shit who's been screwing my wife. I was so upset last night that his name just slipped out. I've got no evidence against him – I was just . . . ' He glanced round the room, grasping for words. 'Speculating.'

He could have done it, Dexter saw suddenly. Lancaster could have murdered his wife. And the sergeant was sure Blanche agreed with him, from the way she was scrutinising the man in front of her. The anger was there, the bitterness of betrayal, the sickness that came with the understanding that another man had been caressing his wife's nakedness. Dexter had been betrayed by lovers once or twice. He knew what it was like. But he realised that for a man like Lancaster − trusting and timid − the betrayal would have been much, much worse.

Blanche respired steadily to allow the tension to subside and asked Lancaster why David Parkin might want to murder his wife.

Lancaster waved his hands vaguely. His normally flat voice was tinged with desperation. 'Oh, I don't know. Perhaps they'd had a row or something. You see, one of the reasons I mentioned his name last night was that he wasn't in the room when I came back − the boardroom, you know, where the party was being held. You remember I said I went off looking for Nicola?' Blanche nodded. 'Well, I didn't find her. So I went back up to the party to see if she'd come upstairs again. But she wasn't there either. Nor was David Parkin. It was more than I could stand, you know. I had an image of them having it off together in the same building where I was. I felt sick. So I just went home.'

This must have been when Parkin said he was out on the roof having a smoke, Dexter concluded. All very convenient if Jim Lancaster had killed, or was about to kill, his wife.

A rap on the hall door echoed round the room. Although fully furnished it had an air of emptiness and desolation. Beasley's apprehensive face appeared. 'Everything all right? I wondered if you fancied some tea or coffee?'

Blanche's lips set into a pout of annoyance. Dexter guessed why: Lancaster had been ruffled by her questions and the interruption would allow him to regain his composure. 'Not for me, thanks, but I don't know about Jim or Sergeant Bazalgette.'

Dexter was gasping for a drink but decided thirst was the better part of subordination: he did not want to annoy

Blanche by prolonging the interruption. Jim Lancaster looked around with predictable relief and asked for a coffee.

Blanche waited for the door to click before she asked the next question. 'And when you discovered Nicola and David Parkin were missing from the party, you didn't go down to the office again?'

He shook his head. 'No. I couldn't face it. I just took the lift straight down to reception and went home.'

Blanche sighed and squinted at Nicola's husband, summoning up all her powers of concentration. 'What do you mean – you "couldn't face it"?'

Lancaster looked alarmed for a moment. Dexter just caught a flash of white in his eyes behind the gold-rimmed spectacles. 'I just meant . . . the whole thing. Her and Parkin together. The party. I just wanted to escape.'

The superintendent nodded slowly, pretending to be satisfied by the reply. Dexter knew it was tempting to ask Lancaster whether he was lying and that he really meant that he couldn't face the idea of seeing his wife again, a wife he had murdered and left a bloody corpse on the floor downstairs only a few minutes before. But he realised they needed much more evidence before they could arrest him for murder. Nicola's husband sat quietly on the sofa, his only movement the whisper of his hands rubbing on the knees of his trousers and his eyes blinking wildly behind his spectacles. Dexter understood why Blanche had described this shy, finicky man as a wimp.

'When did you first find out the affair was going on?' the superintendent asked.

The pause before Nicola's husband spoke again seemed long to Dexter. 'I found out a couple of weeks ago. Through a letter.'

'From Parkin?'

Jim Lancaster nodded.

'Have you still got it?'

'No, I burnt it,' he replied, so softly that Dexter had difficulty hearing what he said. When he spoke again it was with more confidence. 'I showed it to Nicola, you see, and she confessed. She said it had been going on for a few months.'

Blanche leant forward in her chair, alert and watchful, but her tone sympathetic – playing the marriage guidance counsellor, Dexter thought. 'And what did you decide to do about it? Get a divorce?'

Lancaster stared at the superintendent and gulped. Dexter watched his prominent Adam's apple rise and fall. 'No. Nicola told me she didn't want one. She said she loved me and the affair had been a big mistake.' He looked down at the carpet and folded his arms in a protective gesture.

'Is that what she really said?' asked Dexter, speaking for the first time, not believing a word of what Lancaster had said. He was sure that when confronted by the letter Nicola would have told her husband to get lost.

Before the school teacher could answer, there was another rap on the door and Beasley scampered in like an overgrown puppy, casting inquisitive glances at Jim Lancaster and the two police officers. As he passed across a cup of coffee, he asked Jim if it was 'going all right'. The husband smiled nervously and said he was fine.

The sergeant's eyes surveyed the room: the prints of countryside scenes in aluminium frames, the meretricious chandelier, the knick-knacks accumulated from various holidays, including a *bouzouki* on one wall. 'I see there aren't any photos of Nicola anywhere.' It was more a statement than a question.

'I threw them all away a couple of weeks ago as soon as I came across that letter from Parkin,' Lancaster murmured. 'I was so angry. I had to do something.'

His words hung on the chill, stale air. Dexter yearned for a cigarette and squeezed his ballpoint tighter to quieten the urge. Outside his ears picked up for the first time the rustling of invisible leaves and the rattle of window-frames: the wind was rising.

When Beasley finally skipped out of the room, Dexter posed his original question again. 'Are you sure about that? Nicola said she was going to give Parkin up?'

Jim Lancaster nodded and a dim look drifted into his

eyes. 'That's right. She said she'd been stupid. She said she'd give up her job and we'd go back up north. Start again.'

Dexter pursed his lips with disbelief and turned to Blanche, who was examining her fingernails thoughtfully. 'Can you remember who you talked to at the party?'

'Not really. I was pretty drunk. They were just faces. Hardly any of them can be bothered to talk to me anyway.'

'Do you remember talking to Jane Pargeter?'

'Yeah, just about.'

'Anyone else?'

'Not really.' Jim looked away and focused on the solid glass ashtray on the coffee table.

The sergeant lounged back in his chair and gnawed the end of his pen. He asked if Nicola had ever mentioned a man called Kennedy. Lancaster shook his head. He also denied that his wife had given him any details of who she was supposed to be meeting at TVL at the time of the party. She said only that someone was coming to see her.

Dexter gnawed his pen again. He was hungry. It was a good job he had filled his mini-freezer with chilled meals from the supermarket a couple of days before. The thought of a hot lasagne at home cheered him up and helped him ignore the throb of a headache that had begun during the drive up to Kentish Town. 'Did you have any idea what the story was she was meant to be meeting this person in connection with?'

'She didn't tell me and I didn't ask.'

'She didn't say it was drugs or child porn?'

Lancaster looked slightly shocked when the sergeant mentioned child porn. 'She mentioned both stories to me. But she didn't go into any detail.'

Blanche leant forward and Dexter automatically deferred to her. 'You don't think she could have come across something that put her in danger?'

'Doubt it. I didn't see much of her recently anyway. She was always working so hard – or so she said.' The last words were suffused with a whining bitterness.

'Someone told us she'd got hold of the name of some MP

100

who's mixed up in child porn. Do you know who it is?'

'No idea. There are probably hundreds of them mixed up in it anyway.' It was a dry, harsh humour, born of trusting no one in authority. Lancaster sighed and brushed an imaginary fly from his nose. He looked away, his eyes blank like old coins.

Blanche eased herself up and Dexter watched the tension start to drain from Lancaster's body. Outside a car revved up its engine as it changed up a gear only to screech to a halt at the corner and roar off again. Probably a group of youths returning from the pub, thought Dexter. Next door, through the partition wall, some shouts were audible, so muffled it was impossible to tell whether it was a violent assault or someone asking for his bath to be turned off. London, meditated Dexter – so many people crammed together, yet knowing so little about the others standing only a few feet away.

'There's just one last point,' said Blanche, 'the clothes you were wearing last night when I called round. Have you still got them?' She posed the question as casually as possible but the school teacher recognised its significance.

His eyes clouded with suspicion. 'No . . . I haven't actually. I took them to the dry cleaner's this afternoon.'

Dexter noticed that Blanche hid her surprise, although her eyelids parted slightly. Nicola's husband was after all, thought Dexter, the second suspect they had seen that day who had decided to dry-clean the clothes worn at the farewell party. 'Why such a hurry?'

Lancaster was tense again, his thin hands clasping each other. 'I wanted them cleaned, that's all. They were mixed up with what happened last night.' Blanche wrinkled her forehead. Nicola's husband caught her look. 'It was a kind of psychological thing – a sort of purification, I suppose.'

Blanche turned her biro slowly round in her fingers, meditating on the patterns created by the octagonal tube of plastic, and asked for the name of the dry cleaner's.

The superintendent slipped her notebook and pen back into her capacious handbag to indicate the interview was over. Jim Lancaster's lips twitched into a smile of relief and he led them towards the hall. There, much to Dexter's amazement, Blanche strode down some steps to the kitchen, where Beasley sat at a pine table nursing a glass of wine. The superintendent thanked him for his help and bade him goodnight but with a distracted air as though her attention were elsewhere. She reappeared a moment later and the police officers walked out to their car.

'What was that about then, ma'am?' probed Dexter, once they were out on the pavement, puzzled by his chief's foray into the kitchen.

'Just drive slowly round the block, Dexter, and you'll find out.'

The pavements were deserted, a kaleidoscope of patterns as the light from the streetlamps was fragmented by the wind-whipped trees. Nicola's house was one of a block of three modern ones squeezed into a gap in a row of substantial Victorian villas. Most of the houses were well maintained with the few rooms that were still lit disclosing the appurtenances of middle-class living: paintings and prints, a piano, a music-stand, crammed bookshelves. As the police car hummed round the block, one or two other houses caught Dexter's attention because of their air of dirt and dilapidation: divided into bed-sits, they had batteries of bells by the main door, broken windows mended with brown tape and unkempt front gardens crammed with junk. Kentish Town just before midnight, thought Dexter.

Dexter stopped the car about fifty yards down the road from Jim Lancaster's house. Blanche glanced up and down the empty pavement, slid on her leather gloves and loped off into the night.

A few minutes later she slumped back into the front seat of the Granada. Her right hand held a mangled silver photograph frame about eight inches by six. The glass was smashed. Within was a colour photograph of Nicola that had been taken several years before: her face was chubbier and her hair, although still a remarkable blonde, was straight and parted down the middle. A cheeky innocence was imparted to the ruined photo by Nicola's prominent front teeth: her vanity and the ambition to succeed in television must have made her pay later for cosmetic dental work, concluded Dexter, who had an acute eye for wigs worn by men and corsets by women. 'Where did you find this then, ma'am?' asked the sergeant, taking the photo from Blanche and studying it by the map-reading light.

'The dustbin. I left two others there,' murmured Blanche. 'But one would have been enough.'

'Yeah. At least he's not lying about one thing. He *did* get rid of his wife's photos.'

The superintendent's face, softened by the glimmering light, nodded gently. 'Yes. But not when he said he did.' Her car seat squeaked as Blanche reached up to switch out the light. Her face was plunged back into shadow. Dexter watched as his boss stared out into the night, no more than a black profile: her full lips, rounded nose and firm chin silhouetted against the wall behind. 'The photos were on the top of all the other stuff in the dustbin. And the rubbish bin in the kitchen was empty when I looked in it as we left.'

As Dexter adjusted to the dark, he saw that Blanche had turned back to him, her heavy-lidded eyes trained on his face. 'So that's why you trooped off to say goodnight to that bloke Beasley in the kitchen. I didn't think you'd be interested in his home phone number.'

Blanche chuckled. 'Don't worry, Dexter, I gave him yours.'

'Thanks, guv',' joked the sergeant. 'Don't get me too excited.' Dexter sensed Blanche's eyes on him, excited and expectant. He paused and thought through the implications of her discovery. 'So . . . if the kitchen bag had just been changed and the photos were on the top outside, it can only mean he threw out the photos in the last couple of days.'

The superintendent nodded vigorously. 'Yesterday probably because the photos weren't in the house when I called to see him last night. I should have spotted it then, but I didn't. So well done you.' She rubbed her chin slowly with her forefinger. 'Now, it's perfectly possible that he *did*

103

discover Nicola was having an affair a couple of weeks ago but only threw out the photos last night. But why would he bother to lie about it?'

'Search me,' grunted Dexter who, having met Lancaster, was increasingly convinced of his guilt. And as his conviction grew so his depression and associated headache began to fade. Dexter was by nature impatient. He was sometimes irritated by what he saw as Blanche's deductive ramblings, her obsession with the power of reason. He liked to decide who was guilty early in an investigation – after gulping down his own potent brew of intuition and prejudice mixed with the available evidence – and then squeeze a confession from the suspect. He hated cases that required painstaking enquiries over months and months and had little prospect of solution. The sergeant was irresistibly drawn towards activity. Whether in choosing the pattern on his wallpaper or deciding what to do next in a murder case, Dexter wanted action. 'I think we should arrest him,' said the sergeant simply. 'Lock him up in an interview room. Make him sweat a bit.'

Blanche turned to her sergeant with a weary smile. 'You really do need some sleep, don't you?'

'What do you mean, guv'?' replied the sergeant resentfully.

'Come on, Dexter, he's not going to come voluntarily, is he? So as soon as he's in the station the clock begins to run and he'll be screaming for his brief.'

Dexter sighed. She was right of course. Under the law a suspect had to be charged within twenty-four hours of arrest or else released. And Lancaster was just the sort of geezer to know his solicitor's telephone number off by heart. Dexter held up the mangled photograph frame. 'You've got this.'

'And what am I expected to do with it? Hold it up in front of him like a cross in front of Dracula? Sometimes, Dexter, I think you're a real – what do you call Wootton sometimes behind his back?'

'Dickhead, ma'am?'

'Yes, dickhead.' The expletive sounded strange to the

104

sergeant on Blanche's lips, as if she were hearing it for the first time. Her voice was edged with irritation. Dexter realised that she was tired and frustrated too.

The sergeant decided to beat a tactical retreat. 'Well, I didn't mean arrest him just at this minute. You could go back and confront him with the photo now. See what he's got to say.'

'We need some proper evidence, Dexter. Not smashed photos from dustbins. You can start first thing tomorrow morning by going to that dry cleaner's on the Kentish Town Road.' She yanked back her sleeve to peer at her watch. It was midnight. Dexter yawned and she smiled. 'I want you there at eight o'clock, please. I should just about have finished at the hairdresser's by then.'

CHAPTER
TEN

Things started to go wrong from the moment Dexter got up. As usual he had planned his early morning routine with almost military precision. Not a minute was to be wasted. The electronic cheep from the alarm chiselled into his skull at precisely a quarter to seven. He waited two minutes to focus his thoughts, threw back the duvet – its stale scent reminding him yet again to visit the launderette soon – and staggered into the bathroom. He turned on the shower and waited for the hot water to flow through so that he could adjust the temperature. He waited and waited. And waited. His fingers kept dipping into the torrent but the water remained chill. 'Shit,' he murmured under his breath, goosepimples plucking at his naked skin. He ran the pink insides of his fingers along the radiator. It was as cold as a glass of lager. 'Fucking shit,' he said, 'this is just what I need.' The central heating was not working.

He tore open the cupboard door and peered at the tiny porthole of glass on the front of the central heating boiler. It was black. The comforting blue flame of the pilot light was dead, blown out by the gusting wind of the night before.

Still swearing under his breath, Dexter pulled off the cover from the bottom of the boiler and relit the pilot light. At least he would have hot water that night when he returned home – if he had the time to return home. Now what was he supposed to be doing that morning? Dexter recalled the meeting with Jim Lancaster and Blanche's order to visit the dry cleaner's. There was some hope, he supposed, that the clothes had not yet been laundered. He certainly hoped so. Having met him, Dexter was convinced Lancaster was their prime suspect. He was evasive and weak. And he had lied. Only in small things so far but Dexter was sure, thinking back to the taut image of the man sitting on his sofa the previous night, that he was lying about bigger things as well. Flicking the side of his nose, the spectacles, the feeble and whining voice – all irritated the sergeant. As a boy Lancaster would have been the natural victim of bullies – punched, thumped and insulted. And it is often those who suffer abuse who are capable of horrendous acts of violence, storing up their hatred for release in an act of revenge against the world. The sergeant paused, pulling the electric shaver away from his chin with an angry buzz, and cut short his flight of fancy. Blanche was right. They needed evidence against him. They needed it quickly and they needed it badly.

A dark curtain of cloud hung over the horizon to the north as Dexter weaved his way through the clotted traffic on the Kentish Town Road. The dry cleaner's lurked in a short terrace of shops, penned between an off-licence and a café. The door was secured by a hasp and a heavy padlock and the windows were protected by grilles. Dexter pressed his nose against the grid of cold metal but all he could make out in the shadowy interior was a counter and the shimmer of clothes hung up in plastic bags. A rectangle of cardboard hung on the door announcing that the shop was due to open at nine o'clock. Dexter had woken up early only to find himself with forty minutes to kill. The sergeant swore good-naturedly at Blanche under his breath. He did not resent her visit to the hairdresser's. He would have done the same in her position if he had to appear at a press conference – appearance was important to Dexter. But he would have preferred to spend the extra time in bed none the less.

He ordered a cup of tea and a bacon sandwich in the café a few doors down and sank his weary limbs down to wait, revelling in his first cigarette of the day. A price list drooped listlessly on the back wall, the letters and numbers formed from rectangles of clear plastic slid into horizontal grooves. Although the wall was originally orange, a brown shadow in the shape of a fan stretched up to the ceiling above the frying pans on the hob. A handsome Irish youth with ginger hair squirted some boiling water into the tea-pot and swilled a cup of dark brown liquid into a chipped cup. Dexter threw him a glittering smile but there was no response. He felt like one of those astronomers who pumped radio waves out into the galaxies in the hope of finding intelligent life elsewhere in the universe but never heard anything back. Vaguely disappointed, the detective sat by the steamed-up window, attracting the occasional glance from the groups of sullen men at the Formica tables, his nose prickling with pleasure at the smell of frying bacon.

Both newspapers he bought had big articles on the murder of Nicola Sharpe. It was their first opportunity to treat the murder in detail. The lead story on the front page of the *Daily Mail* blazoned a colour photograph of the dead girl under the headline 'TV GIRL MURDER MYSTERY'. The *Daily Mirror* devoted a whole inside page to the story. He scanned the newsprint greedily while his teeth sank into the bacon sandwich, the melted margarine dribbling over his fingers. Unlike Blanche, he enjoyed the cases he worked on being in the public eye.

Both newspapers gave fairly accurate accounts of what had happened the night before last. They said Nicola had been found brutally stabbed to death in her office – although neither newspaper disclosed that the murder weapon was a pair of scissors. Both gave glamorised sum-maries of Nicola's rise in the space of ten years from being a cub reporter on a local newspaper in Keighley to 'star-dom' at TV London. Both also gave prominence to the fact that Blanche happened to be at TV London at the time of the murder and had taken charge of the case. The detective superintendent, despite her dislike of publicity, was now quite a celebrated figure in the media. Dexter smiled to himself as he imagined his boss's grimace when she saw herself described in the *Mirror* as 'Scotland Yard's female supersleuth'. He knew Blanche would be much happier with the file photo the same newspaper had used of her. It was probably three or four years old and Dexter clicked his tongue with the realisation that Blanche had aged.

'Do you own this place then, mate?'

The man swung round, fear flashing in his eyes. He was about fifty, Dexter supposed, with great soulful eyes and brown leathery skin. Every movement he made was slow and deliberate, as if designed to conserve energy. 'What if I do?' he grumbled with a tremor of his sculpted lips, his accent indefinably foreign.

The sergeant produced his warrant card and said he wanted to ask some questions. The man examined the card quizzically as if the rectangle of plastic was a conundrum. Then he beckoned Dexter in. The fluorescent tubes on the ceiling flickered into life. The air stank of chlorine.

The proprietor thrust aside the plastic tassles that filled the doorway through to the back of the dry cleaner's and dumped his shopping bag on the floor next to an ironing board. Dexter explained why he had come.

The man gave a sigh of resignation. He started to run a gnarled forefinger down the receipt stubs. 'You said this Mr Lancaster come in yesterday?'

Dexter nodded.

A few seconds later the finger stopped moving and the man turned round the book to face Dexter. 'There you are – one jacket and one pair of trousers.'

'And have you cleaned them yet?'

The man shrugged his shoulders apologetically. 'Yes. My son did them last night. They're hanging up over there.' He nodded towards the rack on Dexter's right.

'Shit, what a bloody morning,' groaned the sergeant under his breath. First the central heating. Then having to kill forty minutes when he could have been in bed and now this: the delay in visiting the dry cleaner's meant a vital piece of evidence might have been destroyed.

The proprietor lumbered over and dumped the clothes on the counter. The sergeant flicked up the plastic film and scrutinised the tweed jacket and brown trousers with a faint sneer: he wouldn't be seen dead wearing such clothes. With such dreadful taste Lancaster deserved to be the murderer, Dexter told himself with a smile. But the detective saw nothing suspicious. 'Did he give any special instructions when he handed these in? You know – get rid of any stains?'

The man ran a calloused hand through his thick, curly hair and stretched his lips into a look of uncertainty that presaged a loud belch. He touched the right cuff of his pullover. 'There were a couple of stains here he wanted us to get rid of. And on the knees of his trousers. My son had a job doing it.'

'Blood?'

The proprietor stared back over the great, sagging pouches under his eyes. His skin was sown with little black spots. 'Might have been. He just used the normal stain stuff, you know.'

Dexter took the jacket to the window so that he could scrutinise the cuff by natural light. The tweed was completely clean. 'Well, there's nothin' there now.'

The proprietor beamed behind the counter, revealing a row of yellowed teeth. 'They come up real well, didn't they? He's a hard worker, my son.'

Dexter detected a glimmer of pleasure, as if the man felt instinctive sympathy for Lancaster and took personal satisfaction in thwarting the police.

Fuck you, thought the detective.

Dexter arrived back at Scotland Yard just in time for the press conference. He knew Blanche was nervous by her uncharacteristic air of distraction and tried to calm her with compliments about her appearance. Her hair had been cut shorter than usual round her neck, accentuating the elegant curve of the nape and softening the slight masculinity of her features. She had applied more make-up than usual but with her habitual restraint. Dexter

110

decided once again that Blanche's attraction did not lie in any classical beauty. It resided in her peculiar amalgam of irregular features, dull when separate, but irresistible when brought together and animated by her intelligence and energy.

While he and Blanche hummed up in the lift to the conference room, Dexter told the superintendent what he had found out at the dry cleaner's. Although she did not seem to be listening, Dexter knew from experience that she would remember everything important he had told her. Her only reaction was a sigh of disappointment.

Dexter stood at the back of the conference suite behind the video cameras and serried ranks of reporters. The room hummed with an expectant murmur which heightened and then died away when Commander Brian Spittals, followed by Blanche and the head of the Press Bureau, strode out on to the platform. The veneered desk where they sat was suddenly drenched in light as the languid television crews jumped up and took their positions, communicating with each other by harsh whispers or frantic sign language. Trust Spittals not to miss a chance to get into the papers, thought Dexter with a snort.

Spittals made great play of tapping the microphones and checking that they worked before he introduced the superintendent. Blanche blinked into the glare and began to speak from her notes in a well-articulated voice. As she spoke the pens of the newspaper reporters seemed to take on a frantic life of their own, skipping across the lines of their notebooks. Their television colleagues were more patrician, only occasionally deigning to nod down at the page and scribble the time of an important section of Blanche's statement. Four photographers scampered round the podium, halting to squint through their viewfinders and freeze the scene with their flashlights.

A murmur crossed the room like a wave when Blanche revealed she was seeking a man called Mr. Kennedy, who had been due to meet Nicola Sharpe at nine o'clock on the night she was murdered.

When she had finished, Blanche sat back with evident

111

relief. Dexter noticed that she had made no mention of the murder weapon being a pair of scissors or of the discovery of blood in a wash-basin near where the body was found.

A flurry of hands whisked into the air, accompanied by chaotic shouts.

'Quiet, please! Gentlemen, a bit of hush, please!' Spittals' voice rose above the chaos with the natural authority of one who was used to being obeyed. 'If you'd care to raise your hands, we'll take questions one at a time. Reg?' The commander nodded down to a middle-aged man with a florid face and crinkly, Brylcreemed hair. The face was familiar: he had been the crime correspondent of a well-known tabloid newspaper for many years and was guaranteed to give the Yard a favourable press.

The man smiled gratefully at the commander. 'Super-intendent, do you know anything about this mysterious man, Kennedy – why he was meeting Nicola Sharpe, for example?'

Blanche leant forward towards her microphone. 'I'm afraid not. All we know is that Nicola was due to meet him at nine o'clock and that he didn't turn up. For all we know he was a complete stranger.'

The reporter's bloodshot eyes did not leave Blanche's face. 'I gather you've been interviewing some of the well-known faces down at TVL, Superintendent – like David Parkin and Jane Pargeter. Can you confirm that?'

The room was silent with expectation. Blanche coughed and responded that the police were talking to everyone who had been at the farewell party on the sixth floor, including Parkin and Pargeter.

'And are they suspects?'

'It's much too early in the investigation to talk about *anyone* being a suspect,' exclaimed Blanche curtly, pointing to a waving hand several rows back. She cut across Spittals who was about to signal to another of his cronies on the front row. Dexter smiled: Blanche had obviously decided to show some independence now that the press conference had begun.

A young, blond man with a high forehead and loosened

tie jerked up. He asked with a pronounced Welsh accent whether Blanche had interviewed Nicola's husband.

Blanche winced as a cameraman's flash exploded in front of her. 'Yes, I have. In fact it was me who had to break the news of the murder to him.'

'How did he take it?'

The superintendent looked at the reporter coldly. Dexter guessed that if the conversation had been in private, Blanche would have said, 'He sat down and opened a bottle of Bollinger '59 actually – what do you think?' Dexter remembered the name and vintage from a description Blanche had reluctantly given him once of a feast at her old Cambridge college. But the detective superintendent was only too aware of how double-edged a weapon irony could be when deployed against a bunch of journalists. Their sympathy had to be cultivated not abused. So she contented herself with giving the reporter what he wanted. 'Nicola's husband was obviously very, very distressed. He's still in a state of severe shock.'

'You said Nicola was brutally stabbed to death, Superintendent. Presumably it was a knife, was it?'

Blanche paused for a fragment of a second, calculating how to mislead the press without lying to it. 'That's a fair assumption, although we're still waiting for the full results from the post-mortem.' The superintendent told the lie fluently, looking the reporter full in the face.

'Superintendent,' began a woman TV reporter a few rows back, who wore artificial eyelashes like black combs. 'You've talked about Nicola's husband. But was Nicola romantically linked with anyone else? I mean could that have been a motive for the murder?'

One man a few yards ahead of Dexter turned to a colleague and muttered, 'Bonking in the viewing room, eh?' with a smutty chuckle.

The superintendent grimaced as though her nostrils had suddenly detected a bad smell. Dexter knew she hated intrusions into the private lives of the victims of crime. 'No comment, I'm afraid.'

Whispers hummed round the room. A look of

113

puzzlement flickered on the woman journalist's face. 'So, you're confirming she *was* having an affair with someone?'

Blanche sighed. She gave a knowing smile. '"No comment" means exactly that. I'm neither confirming nor denying anything. It's simply too early to say.'

The woman journalist pressed on in her throaty drawl. 'What about personal rivalries in the office, Superintendent? Have you found out anything there?'

Dexter had always been impressed by Blanche's coolness under fire. He knew she was nervous and that this reporter was pressing the superintendent on the most delicate areas of the investigation. But Blanche gave nothing away. 'Nothing out of the ordinary.'

'What do you mean by that?' barked the woman, obviously annoyed by Blanche's laconicism.

'Just what I said. Most journalists by nature, as I'm sure you know, are back-biters.' A titter of whispered 'Ooooooos' echoed round the conference room. The detective smiled to soften the barb she had just thrown even though the tone was not hostile. 'And by all accounts Nicola Sharpe had her supporters and her detractors. But so far – and this may be what you're driving at – we haven't found evidence of anything that could explain her murder.'

A reporter a few yards ahead of Dexter turned to his colleague and murmured, 'Christ, she's tight-arsed, isn't she? Getting a story out of her is like getting blood out of a stone.'

'It's all the same with these women who think they're heading for the top. They always play it by the bloody book.'

A tall, dark figure slipped into a seat to Dexter's right. The sergeant acknowledged the man's smile with a nod.

'Are you getting any special insights 'cos you're a woman?' asked another voice. 'You know, a professional woman in a man's world?'

Blanche smiled and shook her head. 'No.'

Several reporters chuckled, one of them shouting, 'Didn't know you were editing the women's page, Charlie.' Another titter passed round the room.

After a few more desultory questions, Brian Spittals beamed and called the press conference to a halt. The journalists gathered in knots to compare notes and decide on the best angle on the story. Blanche, smiling blandly so as to appear co-operative, was ushered over to a corner of the room to record the first of a series of television interviews.

Dexter loved watching press conferences for cases with which he was involved. They served up to the public a version of events and only those, like Dexter, who were privy to the truth would be able to distinguish how close that version of events was to reality. The detective enjoyed the sense of privilege imparted by being an insider. As usual, Dexter judged that Blanche – despite her misgivings – had performed well at the press conference, providing enough information to keep the newspapers happy without compromising the investigation.

He stood up, intending to wander over and offer his boss congratulations on her performance. Blanche finished almost every press conference or interview in a state of mild depression. Instead he was confronted by the tall, dark man whose hand was extended ready to clamp on to the sergeant's and give it a hearty shake as if he were an old friend. 'DS Bazalgette, aren't you?'

'Probably.'

The man laughed nervously. He was in his mid-forties, his hair liberally splashed with grey. 'What do you mean, probably?'

'Well, I'm goin' through a bit of a personality crisis at the moment. I often wake up in the morning and wish I was Eddie Murphy.' Dexter was wary: he was using the banter to keep the man at a distance.

The man laughed loudly, too loudly for the sergeant. Dexter remembered that cackle and so the journalist who owned it: John Barry, who had helped report Blanche's last murder case for the *Herald*. Dexter guessed immediately that the man was trying to extract an exclusive story on the investigation into the murder of Nicola Sharpe. The sergeant was tempted to walk off but did not. He was intrigued and wanted to know what the *Herald* had discovered. Besides, his ego was tickled by the implicit flattery of the journalist's attention. He folded his arms, admiring the two glittering rings on his right hand.

Barry leant forward and whispered conspiratorially, his breath smelling of mint, 'Look, Sergeant, we know as well as you do that Parkin was having it away with Nicola Sharpe. The question is – did he murder her or was it the husband?'

The black detective edged away from the chairs towards the door. He had decided to play a little game and risk putting pressure on the person he was convinced had committed the murder – Jim Lancaster, the man who had taken his jacket and trousers to the dry cleaner's the day after the murder to have some stains removed. 'Work it out for yourself. Why on earth would Parkin want to kill his own mistress? Angry hubbies, on the other hand, kill double-crossing wives all the time.'

Dexter strode away to ask Blanche how the interviews had gone. He was sure no one had noticed him talking to the journalist.

CHAPTER
ELEVEN

Dexter was suspicious from the moment Blanche first shook hands with Eddy Russell. There was an unwonted gaiety in her manner as if the superintendent had spent the morning swallowing double Scotches. He knew she had not because the press conference had finished only an hour before and not a drop of alcohol had passed Blanche's lips. Dexter crimped with irritation: Blanche fancied the man she was meant to be interviewing.

It had all begun innocently enough. When the press conference was over Blanche had led Dexter down to the incident room. The sergeant thought Blanche would be tired after the tension of the previous hour or two, and he expected Blanche to sit at her desk quietly for a few minutes. But the superintendent was too excited to rest. She prowled among the desks and glowered at the action boards as if they were a bunch of football hooligans.

Suddenly she bustled over to her sergeant and motioned him into her office. 'Dexter, I think we've got to step back a bit. Approach this murder from some new angles. I'll tell the squad later. But I want you to make a start now.'

The sergeant sighed to himself. He knew what was coming: the pursuit of some clever ideas of Blanche that were totally irrelevant to the case, ideas that sprang from intuition but were justified by reason. Dexter was irritated by Blanche's love of the difficult and complicated as opposed to his preference for the simple and straightforward. He wondered if it was because a woman's mind worked in a different way to a man's or whether

Blanche simply thought too much.

The superintendent said she wanted some men to investigate the stories that Nicola was looking into before her death – child porn and drugs. They were to start by talking to the officers in the Drugs Squad that Nicola had met. She wanted another group to collect more background about TVL and its bosses, in particular about the chairman, Stephen Blufton.

'Who, the guy who's meant to have told Nicola she had this new job?'

'That's the one.'

Dexter had nodded with mock enthusiasm. He thought they were investigating a murder at TV London not whether its chairman had a casting couch. But on reflection he concluded Blanche was right. The investigation was already starting to stagnate.

Dexter began work. And for the first time since the investigation had begun the sergeant felt he had been lucky.

When he phoned up the Scotland Yard Press Bureau the woman who answered said it was she who had fixed up Nicola's first contact with the Drugs Squad. It was with a detective inspector called Eddy Russell. Russell happened to be in the office and sounded watchful when Dexter explained why Blanche wanted a word with him. The inspector, though, agreed there was no time like the present for a meeting.

An hour later Dexter found himself sitting next to Blanche on a settle in a pub near Scotland Yard with Detective Inspector Eddy Russell of the Drugs Squad perched on a stool on the opposite side of the Formica table. Knots of office workers in various poses hid the bar, girls in high-heeled shoes and heavy make-up, men in cheap suits and loud ties: only the glasses hanging suspended in a rack above their heads indicated where drinks were being dispensed. Russell was tall and slim, with a well-sculpted face, his eyes wide and grey. He gave the impression of vulnerability by sitting with his chin on his chest so that he had no alternative but to look up through his eyebrows. Dexter thought the inspector spoke with the brittle confidence of someone who underneath was not that sure of himself.

'Nicola wanted a story for her TV programme,' he began, sipping his pint of lager. 'Said she wanted to find out the latest angle on the police battle against drugs.' His voice struck Dexter as unremarkably attractive, like an actor's. Russell gulped another mouthful from his pint of beer and ripped open a bag of crisps.

'Did you tell her about any specific operations?' Blanche slid forward on her seat to attract the inspector's attention.

Russell caught the look with a shiver of panic in his eyes as if it were a wet glass that had slipped out of his hand. 'No – except ones that were finished. Why?'

It was Blanche's turn to tug her lips into a flirtatious smile. She murmured that Nicola Sharpe had told her editor that she had been given a really good story by someone in the Drugs Squad.

Russell finished munching a few crisps. 'You know the bullshit that some journalists talk.'

Blanche chuckled.

He took a swig of lager and looked up watchfully. 'Besides, if the story was so good, why didn't she do anything about it?'

'She said it didn't stand up.'

Dexter was not sure what to make of Russell. One side of him found the inspector attractive and amusing. Another whispered that the policeman was wary, unsure of what to reveal and what to hide. Blanche did not seem to share his ambiguity, flirting with the inspector. The mating instinct allied to fear of loneliness was an irresistible combination, concluded the sergeant, gazing round the pub to conceal his irritation. It was filling up with more and more people. The odd, lugubrious figure sitting on a stool at the bar was now completely hidden from view along with the half-caste man yanking the arm of the one-armed bandit a few yards away. Dexter let his eyes play over the clutter designed to bless the pub with a friendly air: two post horns slung like bombs from the ceiling, mock Tudor beams, lines of plates balanced on every available ledge, and a grubby portrait of the Queen hung in dusty splendour above the bar.

When Dexter focused back on the conversation, Blanche was laughing at some joke of Eddy Russell's that the sergeant had missed. The sergeant knew she was a tough woman and had few weaknesses. She coped well with the peculiar pressures of being only an honorary man in a male world. She did not scream and weep – at least in front of him – when things went wrong and did not have a reputation for being raucous about women's rights. She was ever watchful, and careful not to court publicity. Whatever risks she took in her career were calculated ones. But with men – and this was the reason for Dexter's apprehension – it was different. After the separation from her husband, Blanche's love life was a Russian roulette of the emotions: taking men to her heart, and sometimes to her bed, with the fateful enthusiasm of a suicide pulling the trigger of a gun. None of the relationships had survived, although Blanche had. But one day, unless she was more circumspect, Dexter feared she might not.

'Inspector,' broke in the sergeant, determined to pose some important questions that Blanche had not yet bothered to ask. 'Do you think Nicola could have got hold of something that put her in danger?'

Russell turned to Dexter with a look of surprise and irritation, as if he were a complete stranger butting in on a private conversation – which indeed was just how the sergeant felt. He had smooth bags under his eyes, Dexter noticed, puffed out with fatigue. 'Like what?'

'I don't know. She might have stumbled on to some big-time drug smugglers for example.'

Russell did not answer immediately. His eyes – matt like those of a dead fish on the slab – flickered up to the bone china model of a Suffolk Punch above their heads, the bright colours making the creature appear unearthly. 'It's funny. But when I heard about the murder I wondered just the same thing.'

The superintendent dropped her head to one side.

'Why? Because you thought she was in danger when she met you?'

Russell jerked his head defensively. 'Oh, no. I didn't have any reason to think she was in trouble. She was much too smooth for that. But if you know anyone who comes to a bad end you tend to think over what you said to them, what they said to you.' Russell smiled again but Dexter found it impossible to decide whether it was a smile of contemplation, charm or mendacity — or all three. Dexter did not trust Russell one millimetre, let alone an inch, and he made up his mind to tell Blanche at the earliest opportunity. 'I don't know. She may have stumbled across something. There's so much money riding on drugs deals . . . ' He shrugged his shoulders as his voice trailed away.

Dexter watched the conversation between his boss and Russell rattle on for several minutes. It seemed a waste of time to the sergeant and a mood of depression began to cloak him again. Blanche was right to insist that these leads were followed up but it did not look as if they were going to take them anywhere.

As Blanche and Russell chatted on about some Woody Allen film, Dexter let his eyes glaze over. He felt increasingly irritated and despondent. He wondered what had happened to handsome Georgie, the boy he was supposed to be meeting at the pub on the night of the murder. He had rung his number several times but there had been no reply. Loneliness stole across him at the strangest times.

After a few minutes, Blanche seemed to sense Dexter's baleful mood, checked her watch and stood up to go. The pub was a pullulating stew of people, swelling and bubbling behind a screen of smoke.

Russell's eyes followed her every move as if he were looking through the sight of a gun. 'I'd like to keep in touch,' he said. 'Just in case something crops up and I need to let you know.' He drew out his Metropolitan Police diary.

Blanche dictated the direct line to the incident room. She hesitated for a second and then gave Russell her home number. 'Give me a call whenever you want.' Dexter noticed that her smile of farewell was warmer than it need have been.

As the superintendent cut her way through the herd of lunchtime drinkers, Dexter followed in her wake, like a driver who glues himself to the back of an ambulance careering through busy streets on an emergency call. The sergeant was pensive. At least the interview with Russell had told them Nicola's investigation into drugs had taken place. And if it had, who knows who else she had spoken to. After all, the inspector himself admitted wondering whether Nicola had learnt or been given something that put her in danger.

Dexter looked back and saw Russell drain off the last drops of his lager. The sergeant doubted if they would need to see him again. And with an inward smile Dexter realised another reason why Blanche's flirtation with the inspector had made him so irritable. He also had found Russell attractive – battered yet handsome and oppressed by some secret worry. Dexter shrugged philosophically. He had given up years ago the delusion that all men were homosexual at heart, and that it was just a question of finding the key to unlock their repressed desires.

The two security men Dexter had interviewed immediately after the murder were on duty when the sergeant loped into the headquarters of TV London late that same afternoon. The giant Asian greeted the detective with a silent nod, his red-headed companion with a suspicious glare. Blanche had left a message for the sergeant to join her in the editor's office of *Inside Out* on the fourth floor. Dexter had no idea why, except that the superintendent sometimes found it useful to revisit the scene of a crime alone and absorb its atmosphere at different times of day or night. Dexter distrusted the whole concept, fearing that Blanche did not just operate at the rational level of searching for evidence and reassembling facts, but that she so thought herself into the mind of murderer and victim, that she communed with spirits. He had read that acts of violence can leave their imprint on a place, a shadow that some can sense for centuries afterwards. He suggested once to Blanche that she could perhaps feel such chill draughts blowing from the past when others could not. Blanche laughed. 'I thought you were a Christian, Dexter, not a spiritualist.'

'I might be a Christian, guv', but I also believe in ghosts.'

'Do you?' Blanche looked at him as if he needed urgent psychiatric treatment. 'Well, I don't. What I believe in is the power of the human imagination. That's the only thing I use to think myself back into the past.'

It was unsettling for Dexter to walk the same corridor of frosted glass and fire extinguishers at TV London again. With so many memories already jostling in his mind, it seemed that weeks had passed since the killing. He had experienced this telescoping of time before when working twenty hours a day at the beginning of a murder investigation, but the slowness of passing time still came as a shock: Nicola Sharpe had been stabbed to death less than forty-eight hours before.

The door to the main office was unlocked and Dexter walked in. The room was deserted and desolate: the arctic blue bubble of the drinking water machine looked as if it had turned to ice, two desk lights burned pointlessly above unoccupied desks and the rubbish bins were still brimming with polystyrene cups and waste paper. The office looked as if it had fallen under the same spell of passing time as Dexter, and been unoccupied for weeks rather than hours – the motes of dust, the grime of London gently settling on files, videotapes and yellowing newspapers.

A man with black curly hair and a nose like a doorknob bustled up from his desk when Dexter walked in to the inner sanctum of the editor's office. Blanche introduced the sergeant to Dave Pushell, who had taken over from Ken O'Mara as the new editor of *Inside Out* just before the murder. Pushell pumped Dexter's hand. He throbbed with nervous energy: when one of his thighs was not jigging, one of his fingers would tap or his teeth would hungrily gnaw the end of a biro.

123

'As I was saying, Superintendent,' he said, spinning back to Blanche, 'I really do understand your problems but we do have to get back to normal at some stage. There's a slot to fill this week, another one to fill next week and so on.' He talked fast and fluently: everyone in television seemed to, Dexter reflected, as if they were born with cassette tapes in their mouths rather than tongues. 'I've had to move the whole of our office down two floors into the variety shows department. I mean, there we are in the middle of some serious investigation into terrorism and some dickhead stumbles into the office dressed up as a pumpkin.'

Blanche nodded in a conciliatory way. 'Most of the interviews should be finished in a couple of days – '

'That's only the start of my problems. One of the loopier producers is going round saying the office is haunted.' Dave Pushell adjusted his bright red spectacles which had lenses the size of teacups. 'She says she won't move back in here until we redecorate the whole office from top to bottom and hold a bloody seance.'

Dexter smiled to himself, recalling his thoughts in the corridor a few minutes before. Although he had only been in his new job for a few days before the murder, Dave Pushell had already tried to imprint his personality on the office. His own journalistic scalps now adorned the walls rather than those of O'Mara – a photograph of the doorknob nose in the company of Mikhail Gorbachev, a flag of the African National Congress, and a TV award so shapeless Dexter imagined it to be modelled on a cow turd. And Pushell had not finished unpacking. Crates and cardboard boxes still littered the floor. Pushell's voice was shrill with frustration as Blanche led him out.

She strode back to the editor's room and slumped down in a chair. 'God, I'm glad I don't work for him,' she sighed. 'He thinks the whole world revolves around his flipping programme.'

The sergeant waited a moment for Blanche's exasperation to dissipate, for her attention to return to why he was there. 'What do you want first, ma'am? The good news or the bad?' He did not know why he asked the question, except as part of a ritual that reassured him Blanche had not changed. The female detective always gave the same answer.

'The bad.'

It was part of Blanche's character to want the pain first before the pleasure. Perhaps she was a bit like that as a child, Dexter sometimes wondered, always eating the pastry round the outside of a tart before she gobbled up the fruit-crammed centre. 'Drawn a blank so far on the child porn. Simon Franks told one of the DCs that Nicola had mentioned some MP in the West Midlands. We're checking out the name but nothing's come up so far.'

'And the good news?' Blanche wanted her reward, her confirmation that the world was not as unjust as she sometimes imagined.

'I've got some half-decent background on TVL and Stephen Blufton.'

The superintendent gave a snort of mock disbelief. 'Call that good news?'

'Well, you'd hardly expect Jim Lancaster to ring me up and confess, would you?'

'You never know. He might do, if you agreed to reverse the charges.'

'What, with your reputation for watching the pennies, guv'. Sometimes I think you're an accountant rather than a copper.'

Blanche laughed easily. It was true: she did have a reputation for good housekeeping. It was one of the reasons she had been promoted so fast. Expenditure on the police was no longer open-ended, regardless of efficiency.

The sergeant smiled and took out his notebook. Although they had only had a few hours, he was happy with what the squad had uncovered from newspaper cuttings and phone-calls — not that they had detected any connection with Nicola Sharpe. But he knew from experience it was often best with Blanche simply to answer a question she asked rather than seek to question why she posed it. That was one of her privileges of authority. 'TV London won the franchise to broadcast to the London area a couple of years ago. I don't know if you remember, but there was quite a punch-up over who would win it.'

Blanche nodded. 'That's right. Some of the other contenders said TV London was lying, didn't they? Saying TVL couldn't afford to pay the amount they were offering and still produce good television?'

'Yeah.' Dexter breathed in to calm his annoyance. Sometimes he wondered why the superintendent asked him to research questions to which she already knew the answers.

Blanche listened attentively as the sergeant skipped through details of the company structure and gave a thumbnail sketch of Stephen Blufton, the chairman of TV London. 'Interesting guy, Blufton,' said Dexter. 'No one knows much about his background. Apparently his mum died when he was just a kid and his dad was a confidence trickster. Spent a lot of time inside. Blufton says that's the main reason why he's into prison reform.'

'He set up his own charity or something, didn't he?'

'That's right. It helps ex-cons find jobs.'

Dexter explained that Blufton had left school in Guildford when he was sixteen and had built up a chain of antique shops and pizza parlours. He had also been registered as the owner of a number of import-export companies.

Blanche took a sip of water. 'Sounds as if Blufton's a sharp operator.'

Dexter nodded. He went on to explain that Blufton was one of the first people to start seeing how much money could be made in the independent TV sector – the little companies that mushroomed all over Soho. He set up a couple himself but also put some big money into a facilities house that hired out videotape machines, camera crews, and picture editing.

'And did he make a lot of money?'

'Oh yeah, he did very well.'

Blanche paused and chewed her bottom lip. She asked how Blufton had come to establish TV London.

'Well, when the franchise for the London area came up he put together a big consortium with him as chairman, promising a lot of money and a lot of telly. And much to everyone's surprise he won it. He built the new head-quarters by the river here and everything looked rosy. But he borrowed too much money from the banks. And now there's also been a drop in the number of people watching, so the advertisers aren't too happy either.'

Blanche squinted at her sergeant, as if trying to read his mind. 'So is the company going bust?'

'Oh no, nothing like that. TVL's got problems, but no one says it's going to pop its clogs.'

Dexter looked up and saw the superintendent's heavy-lidded eyes still narrowed with concentration. Blufton had carefully manicured his image as a man of the people over the past couple of years, the sergeant went on, preferring to give interviews in an open-necked shirt and jeans – both with designer labels – rather than wear a suit. He wanted to project the image of being in television not to make money but because it was fun. He came across in the media as being very different to the classic TV executive, relaxed and friendly and sporting a social conscience through his prison reform work.

The superintendent wandered over to the window. She gazed down at the London horizon, its tranquillity pierced by hulks of office buildings. The sun was a great cauldron of red, painting the edges of clouds that swung round ponderously in the sky like a child's mobile. Cars streamed along the Embankment, their headlamps probing the dusk; a barge slapped its way along the shimmering river. Dexter caught Blanche's eyes twinkling with curiosity for a moment, held by the magnificence of the scene, a fleeting moment when the much abused city appeared beautiful. He sometimes wondered if it was not Blanche's ability to daydream like this for a few seconds a day, the power to see beauty in apparent ugliness, that was the key to her resilience. 'What about Blufton's love life? Is he married?'

'Used to be. He got hitched fifteen years ago to some fashion model. But it didn't last more than a year. They

127

got divorced and he didn't get married again.'

'Girlfriends?'

'He used to get through them like a packet of Polo mints apparently. There are stories about him turning up at parties with various bimbos on his arm – you know the kind of thing. But now he's in his forties he seems to have slowed down a bit.'

Blanche asked if Blufton was close to any woman in particular.

'Not that's public anyway. His big thing at the moment doesn't seem to be women but some ruined castle down in Berkshire that he's getting restored.' Dexter handed across an article dated about a year before from one of the broadsheet newspapers. It was accompanied by a photograph of Blufton standing – arms akimbo – in front of a grey smudge of masonry. The photograph was in black and white and showed pretensions to art by being shot through a wide-angle lens with Blufton's face in close-up. The effect was, in Dexter's view, unflattering and vaguely sinister, like the one produced by trick mirrors at fairgrounds. Blufton's nose seemed bulbous, every pore of his skin highlighted, every hair of his spade beard appeared to bristle. Even the man's ready smile was made to appear broken and toothless. The article said the chairman of TV London had just taken up residence in the castle.

'I'm glad you dug this up,' commented Blanche, squinting quizzically at the photograph, 'because that's where you and I are going to meet Blufton tonight. I just hope he's better looking than this.' She smiled.

The sergeant nodded sagely, trying to work out how best to dissuade his boss from a fruitless trip to the country. Blufton only seemed interesting as a wicked seducer, luring Nicola on to his casting couch with the bait of Jane Pargeter's job. Dexter decided his best weapon was irony. 'So, we're gonna see where he tried to get his wicked way with Nicola, are we?'

Blanche looked at him in mock disapproval. 'Nothing's even proved about that, Dexter. It's only rumour.'

'Yeah. But rumour's more fun,' replied the sergeant

with a lascivious widening of the eyes.

Blanche told Dexter she had passed an hour or so in informal chats with producers on *Inside Out*, hoping she might learn something of significance. They confirmed Nicola's unpopularity in the office, especially amongst the women, because of her ambition and insecurity. They had also confirmed that the affair with David Parkin had been a public secret on the programme for several months, and that Nicola had whispered to several people that she had been promised Jane Pargeter's job by Blufton. It was this, Blanche said, that had pushed her towards phoning his personal assistant and arranging the interview that night.

Jane Pargeter was not particularly popular on the programme either, but several people who had been at the party supported her story that she had not left the party at all until Nicola's body had been found. 'So that seems to rule her out as the murderer,' Blanche concluded with a sigh of relief.

Dexter let his eyes wander over the crates on the floor, brimming with files and books, and on to a dusty azalea on the window-sill for which he sensed a twinge of sadness.

CHAPTER
TWELVE

Dexter thrummed his fingers on the steering-wheel as one clot of traffic thickened into another. He was no longer indifferent to the cars around him – they had become alien and aggressive, peopled by spectres whose driving was at best incompetent and at worst downright criminal. The sergeant sensed the muscles in his chest tighten with irritation as he edged along Cromwell Road, glued to the bumper of the car in front. It seemed he had been behind the same car for hours now – a Jaguar whose iridescent blue reminded Dexter of oil shimmering on the surface of a puddle. The car was driven by a man so shrunken his head hardly protruded above the steering-wheel. Dexter tried every manoeuvre imaginable to overtake. He flashed his headlights and jumped lanes whenever a gap opened up. But whatever he did, the Jaguar was always there, filling any crack in the traffic with stately inevitability.

Even when the police car was able to surge up on to the elevated section of the motorway at Chiswick, the stream of traffic moved no faster and the Jaguar continued to glow in Dexter's headlamps. The sergeant's irritation was sharpened by Blanche lying back, eyes closed, and wallowing in the same opera music she had played the morning before. The brittle hysteria of the singing heightened Dexter's mood before he finally broke free and roared past the Jaguar. He thrust up two fingers in triumph at the driver, an old man who was as indifferent as a waxwork.

Blanche opened a road atlas once they left the motorway and navigated with the diligence of a woman who did not have a natural sense of direction. They soon left the urban sprawl of roundabouts, sodium streetlights and Wimpey homes and Dexter began to speed along country lanes. Solitary oaks loomed up in the headlights, negative images on a photographic plate. With all sense of distance blotted out by the night, their car slapped over the deserted tarmac. Dexter lost all sense of time and space. He could have been plummeting down to the centre of the earth, in a submarine nudging over the seabed or flying soundlessly through outer space. The moon had risen but no sooner did it spill its silver light over the fields than it was swallowed up by cloud.

Blanche said little, her head no more than a deep blue profile against the window. Occasionally her face was illuminated by the navigation light for a few seconds. It looked grey with fatigue.

After a twenty-minute drive, Blanche spotted a notice marking the entrance to Malbis Castle. A brick wall about six feet high stretched away into the blackness of trees to right and left. Flimsy steel gates hung from two pillars. Shivering in the night air after the fug of the car, Dexter pressed the buzzer installed in one of the pillars and the gates hummed apart. A plaque had been hung on the gates: 'Fierce Dog – Beware'. Dexter drove through a small wood, emerging on to a small apron of gravel.

The superintendent slid out of the car and tried to rub the tiredness from her eyes, respiring the chill of the night like an elixir. Dexter was constantly surprised by her resilience, her ability to summon up reserves of concentration and energy. His eyes played over the building in front of them – a jumble of towers, crenellations and massive walls with a sagging flag of St George above the gatehouse picked out in the beam of a spotlight. The edifice was ringed by a narrow, black moat and the obscurity in which most of the rebuilt castle was wrapped only sharpened the impression of Gothic romance. Dexter thought it was outlandish and rather fun.

Blanche was less impressed. 'It's like something at a theme park,' she commented with a yawn. 'A bit of tourist kitsch.'

'You're too much of a snob, guv' – that's your problem.'

Dexter meant it as a joke but Blanche stared at him for a moment, as if the comment was intended as a serious criticism, before she chuckled softly. The sergeant sometimes forgot how sensitive to criticism the superintendent was under her carapace of self-confidence. 'And your problem, Dexter, is that you're not snob enough.'

Another beam splashed a pool of light over the gatehouse, revealing a drawbridge lowered over the moat with portcullis behind, while another illuminated the apron of the car park. One of the four cars parked there was a Porsche Carrera with the number plate SOB 1.

'That must be his car,' murmured Blanche. 'Stephen Something Blufton.'

'Or just Son of a Bitch,' Dexter replied with a smile.

The sergeant felt uneasy while he and Blanche stood on the drawbridge. It was nothing to do with the castle. He always sensed he was exposed in the countryside at night. The rustle of leaves in the breeze deafened him; the black water of the moat lapped against the banks with the insistence of a rising tide. He felt more at home in a city at night, comforted by strips of empty pavement, the harsh lines of concrete towers and by the ubiquitous blanket of artificial light. Even at four in the morning, if he woke during a rare, sleepless night, Dexter liked to brush back the curtains of his bedroom and marvel at the twinkling lights. It made him feel safer and less alone. But in the countryside, when there was only an intermittent moon, it could be truly black – the darkness of the blind that Dexter found terrifying.

A heavy door swung open and a figure beckoned them into a warm lozenge of light. It was only when his eyes had adjusted to the brightness that Dexter could assess Stephen Blufton properly. He bore little resemblance to the photograph in the newspaper, with wide hamster-like cheeks and a narrow chin masked by his spade beard. He stood a little below six feet and sported a warm smile beneath a curly mop of black hair liberally sprinkled, like his beard, with grey. He shook them firmly by the hand – a comforting, hearty grasp that cheered Dexter, who had a pet dislike of cold hands proffered nervously like fragile porcelain. The chairman of TVL had an engaging air of untidiness about him, symbolised by his uncombed hair and floppy pullover. Dexter had expected a bigger and taller man with the harsh glint of money-making in his eyes, rather than this relaxed, almost shambling, figure. He led them into the kitchen, chatting to Blanche and Dexter as if they were house guests rather than police officers who had come to interview him about a murder. The room was crammed with bric-à-brac – a Gothic pew, a rusty suit of armour, an umbrella stand in the form of a bear.

Around a pine table sat a beautiful girl with two men. They gave pinched, nervous smiles and said, 'Hi.' Blufton introduced the girl as Selina, his personal assistant, and the men as the producer and scriptwriter of a new film project about King Arthur. Dexter remembered that Blufton had a reputation as an executive who took a direct interest in the programmes his company made. The scriptwriter – a trim, balding man in his fifties with a moustache – squeezed Dexter's hand a little too warmly and gave him a serious smile of appraisal. It was an unmistakable pass but the sergeant had no desire to respond: the man was too camp for his taste. Dexter glanced at Blanche but she was as inscrutable as usual, diffident but assured.

With easy charm, the chairman of TVL led the police officers down a corridor past studded chests, fragments of sculpture and pottery. They passed several canvases of Dutch landscapes glowing on the walls – trees huddled under magnificent skies or minute skaters twirling on expanses of ice. Blanche listened politely but said nothing, so Dexter felt obliged to respond to Blufton's patter.

'Interesting place you've got here, Mr Blufton,' commented the sergeant politely, awestruck by the amount of dosh the man had to afford such a place. 'You must have been collecting antiques quite a while.'

Blufton smiled with pleasure, wrinkles tugging at his

133

eyes that kept searching hungrily for their faces. Dexter noticed for the first time how thin his legs were as they wandered along the corridor. 'On and off. I pick them up when I can. When I bought the castle five years ago it was just a ruin. I've had to build it up from scratch really.' His voice was an enthusiastic drawl, indeterminate and classless.

They passed through a room furnished only by a great oak table and two benches. The walls were bare stone covered with a fan of rusting swords and three flintlocks. 'This is what we call the Armoury,' bubbled Blufton. 'You know, where the sentries kept their weapons and so on. We even found a record of the castle being besieged for one day during the Civil War.'

Blufton's study matched the rest of the castle in its eclecticism – an enormous library desk strewn with papers, tin soldiers and teddy bears propped up on shelves, the walls lined with Victorian prints and paintings. A fax machine lurked in one corner and the two telephones on the desk were studded with a variety of buttons indicative of modern efficiency. He removed a birdcage containing a mechanical singing canary from his chair and sat down, gesturing for his guests to do the same. His almond-shaped eyes twinkled as they watched Blanche and Dexter absorb the room. 'It's quite a weird mixture, isn't it?' He glanced round. 'I just can't resist the junk antiques as well as the good ones, you see. I like the variety.'

'Is the castle open to the public?' asked Blanche.

'From the summer. I'm picking up the PR material in a couple of weeks. Malbis Castle has a very rich history. I think it'll soon be on the tourist map.'

Blanche flicked up her eyebrows in polite surprise. 'And will you carry on living here then?'

The chairman of TVL gave two dry grunts in lieu of a chuckle. 'No way. I'll have moved on to something else by then. I'll need a new challenge.'

Blanche scrutinised the man they were interviewing, as if he were a wasp she was trying to trap. The millionaire seemed to catch the change in mood and suddenly looked serious. The room was silent, apart from the hollow and remorseless tick of a grandfather clock in the corner. The dial had a painted face that showed a scene of rural bliss at sunset: a family sitting outside their thatched cottage while three children gambolled on the grass. It seemed incongruous to Dexter, inappropriate when he knew they had come to talk about violent death.

'I first heard about the murder around midnight, I suppose,' Blufton began with a sigh. 'I got a call from Mike Slide – have you met him?'

Blanche nodded.

The millionaire sat forward in his chair to show his concern, rubbing one hand across the other in his lap. He looked relaxed and calm. 'Mike knew I always work late, and even though there wasn't anything for me to do, he thought I ought to know.' The clunk of the grandfather clock swelled into the room.

'How well did you know Nicola?' Blanche let the question drop as softly as a feather.

Blufton rubbed a finger across the edge of his lips. Dexter wondered if it was an indication of nervousness. But the gesture was accomplished so smoothly and was finished so quickly Dexter found it impossible to judge. 'I knew her as one of my employees. I'd met her at the odd party where we'd chatted and that's about it.' His eyes, flecks of blue mixed with brown and framed by thin lids, did not waver.

Blanche's armchair squeaked as she moved her weight from one side to the other. 'Did you ever invite Nicola out here?'

'Yes, I did. On one occasion.' Although he narrowed his eyes, there was no hesitation in his reply. He gave the impression of wanting to be open and frank – perhaps even defiantly honest, Dexter considered. 'I wanted to sound her out about a job.'

The sergeant saw his opening and decided to pounce. 'So you did offer her the presenter's job on *Inside Out*, yeah?'

Stephen Blufton swung his head calmly round to the

135

black detective with a glint of watchfulness in his eyes. This was the sort of look Dexter had expected Blufton to wear permanently, the calculating glance of a businessman forced to take a prickly decision, weighing risks and benefits against a tight deadline. 'I asked her if she was *interested* in the job. I didn't at any time actually *offer* it to her.' His voice remained calm.

Dexter paused, wanting to study Blufton's face. The man's eyes did not blink. It was a poker game of honesty. 'And was she interested?'

'Of course,' he said, the conviction of surprise in his voice. 'Anyone with an ounce of ambition would have been. But I made it perfectly clear – or at least I thought I did,' Blufton added, spreading his palms in a gesture of openness, 'that I wasn't actually offering her the job. As I told her at the time there were several possibilities.'

'Like who?'

'Hugh Parnham for a start.' Blufton's eyes twinkled with mischief. 'And then there was always the possibility that we might decide to keep Jane Pargeter after all.'

'Hardly sounds like decisive management, Mr Blufton,' Blanche interrupted with a gentle smile to soften the barb.

'Since when has decisive management produced good television, Superintendent? Since when has decisive management produced anything creative?' The millionaire grunted up from his chair and opened a mahogany wardrobe to reveal a refrigerator full of bottles within. His confidence in facing the world seemed genuine enough, with little room for self-doubt. Dexter had met such relaxed optimism only once or twice before – either in evangelists or conmen. Not that there was any of the same obvious strain with Blufton to convert his visitors to his vision of the truth. He gave the impression of telling the detectives what had happened and asking them to believe it on the authority of his charm and personality.

Blufton paused by his drinks cabinet, a smile tugging at his lips. 'Who told you by the way – that I talked to Nicola about the presenter's job?'

'It's common gossip at TV London,' replied Blanche.

'Nicola spread it round the office. Except she was saying that you'd actually *offered* her the job.'

Blufton grunted again. 'I should've guessed she couldn't keep a secret. Hardly anyone can in this business.' Having established that his visitors did not want a drink, the businessman poured himself a tall glass of gin and tonic.

Blanche waited for him to sit down and take a couple of sips. 'Why did you think *Inside Out* needed a new presenter? What was wrong with Jane Pargeter?'

'Nothing's wrong with her,' he said with sudden warmth. Realising that his reaction might appear excessive, Blufton sighed and consciously relaxed. 'She does her job brilliantly. It's just that we thought the programme might benefit from a new face. To freshen it up.'

The superintendent asked if he thought Nicola could do the job better.

'Not necessarily better. But differently.'

Blanche stared hard at Blufton, her fleshy lips slightly parted. 'And there weren't any other reasons why you sounded her out about the job?'

'Such as?'

You know what she means, thought Dexter. You don't gain anything by playing innocent.

Blanche picked up the challenge. 'You wanting to sleep with her for example.'

Blufton laughed, revealing a line of white teeth, regular except for the two upper canines which had grown forward over the teeth in front. Dexter, who noticed such things, wondered why, with all his money, Blufton had not bothered to have them fixed. The sergeant could never understand rich people with imperfect features who did not spend money on cosmetic surgery. He would have corrected his flattened and crooked nose – broken in an accident when at school – immediately if he had ever had the money.

'Superintendent, I can assure you the sofa you're sitting on is *not* a casting couch.'

'Do you wish it were?'

Blufton pondered for a second and ran a strong, spade-

137

like hand through his hair. He sat forward on his chair, clasping his hands. 'Look,' he sighed, 'I gave that sort of thing up a while back. I realised I was getting too old. It's just not worth the candle.'

Blanche harried him relentlessly. 'So you didn't make any advances to her?'

The businessman stared unsmilingly at the superintendent. 'No. I invited her here on business. And that was it. Strictly business.'

Watching him sip his gin and tonic, Dexter admired the millionaire's self-confidence once again. It was the foundation on which his whole image rested: the lack of pomposity, the charm, the casual clothes. The sergeant suspected that Blufton's self-confidence sometimes crept into arrogance, a desire to treat the people around him as tools for his own gratification, although he was too in control to allow this to happen in the presence of police officers.

Blanche propped her head on her elbow and asked when Nicola came out to visit the castle.

The businessman leant across to an enormous, leatherbound diary and gave the date in early March. Blufton sipped his gin and tonic. 'She came in the morning, about half past ten I suppose. She told me how she thought the way to put *Inside Out* on the map was to do more hard, investigative stories. Like the one she said she was doing on drug smuggling.' He frowned. 'Do you know about that by the way?'

'Only vaguely.' Blanche gestured with her right hand, inviting him to continue.

Blufton respired deeply, his eyes glued first to the superintendent's face and then Dexter's. The sergeant felt uncomfortable, as if the millionaire was trying to possess them through his unwavering stare, attempting to inveigle them into doing his will. Dexter had encountered the same expression many years before in his teens. He had been in a pub in Hammersmith when a hypnotist jumped on to a low podium and put on a show. Dexter had allowed himself to be hypnotised and still remembered staring into those wide eyes, as blue as the top of a ballpoint pen, with pupils that shrank and swelled in time to the man's words. But with Blufton the spell, the sense that he was engaged in some elaborate, magical charade, was broken as soon as he began to speak. 'Nicola told me she'd found out about a couple of drug smuggling operations in this country run by the Mafia.'

'The Mafia?' The muscles of Blanche's face tightened with disbelief and surprise.

Dexter sat back in his armchair, unsure whether to laugh outright or smile knowingly at the businessman's practical joke. The Mafia was as much at home in Britain as coconut trees or rattlesnakes. London and the United Kingdom was the wrong environment – too cold, too sunless, too well policed. There was corruption, Dexter knew well, but it was not widespread, not endemic, as it was in New York or Sicily. But then it occurred to him that perhaps the joke was Nicola's and not Blufton's at all, some invention to impress her boss and ensure her succession to Jane Pargeter's job.

Blufton's eyes glittered with irritation: he had obviously expected his revelation to be treated with respect. 'Well, that's what Nicola said. She told me they were both being organised by the Sicilian Mafia. One was heroin, the other cocaine.' He shrugged dismissively. 'But if you don't believe me, you don't have to.'

Dexter turned to Blanche. He sensed a tension in the air, prickling with Blufton's bruised ego, and thought it was best for her to defuse it. The superintendent sat slumped back in her chair, cupping her chin in her hand. She eased herself up quickly. 'It's not that we don't believe you, Mr Blufton, it's just that what you said was a bit of a surprise.' Dexter wondered what sort of game Blanche was playing – encouraging Blufton rather than calling his bluff. She paused and smiled. 'Did she give you any further details?'

Blufton sighed and furrowed his brows. He seemed placated, even relieved, now that the police officers had expressed their belief in him. 'Well, not a great amount.

139

She said the Mafia loved the idea of a free market right across Europe as much as legitimate businesses do.' Blufton relaxed back in his armchair, like a dinner guest telling a well-worn anecdote. As he relaxed, his charm and humour seeped back and, to trap their attention, Blufton rarely allowed his eyes to stray from those of his listeners. Dexter found the effect comforting rather than disconcerting: he had been won over by the man's charm. 'She said the heroin comes in by what's known as the Balkans route. It arrives in Turkey from Pakistan and then it's hidden in secret compartments in lorries. The lorries drive off across Europe and with the amount of traffic there is the chances of them being caught are pretty minimal. And the Mafia have people in this country who meet the lorries at Dover and then distribute the heroin.'

Dexter nodded. 'What about the cocaine?'

'Well, Nicola said the Mafia have something going at Gatwick airport. They've bought some baggage handlers who intercept the stuff before it gets through to customs.'

Blanche rubbed her chin sceptically, staring back at Blufton. 'Did Nicola mention anything specific about these two drug smuggling operations?'

The businessman nodded and sat forward on his chair. 'She did actually. She said – and I don't know if she was just bullshitting me,' and here Blufton opened his palms in a gesture of frankness, 'that she'd found out the dates when a couple of lorries were due at Dover. She even said she'd discovered the name of the Mafia boss who's running the whole shebang.' Blanche turned to Dexter, her eyebrows uplifted in surprise for a moment before her gaze sank thoughtfully to the carpet. Blufton stood up and plunged a pudgy hand into a concertina file. 'I don't know if it's of any help but – er – I made a couple of notes at the time. It just interested me, you know.' The hand rampaged through various pockets and emerged a few seconds later with a rectangle of paper torn from a reporter's notebook. Dexter walked across to look over Blanche's shoulder. At the top of the sheet was Nicola's name and below a few scribbled notes, summarising what

140

Blufton had just told them. Lower down Dexter read: 'Two sailings expected. Dover 17 March and Dover 4 April. The boss: Leonardo Della Torre. Supposed to live at Godalming.' At the bottom of the page was the injunction: 'Good story. Tell Mike Slide.'

Blufton pointed with a stubby finger to the second date. 'As you can see, a lorry's supposed to be in tomorrow. I don't know if it's any help to you.' The rumpled millionaire stood above them, eyes narrowed to note their reaction, one hand scratching the back of his head.

Dexter shrugged. He did not know what to believe. He was inclined to think Nicola had invented the whole story, or else been told it and then discovered subsequently that it was a sham. This, at least, would explain why the murdered reporter had abandoned her research so suddenly.

Blanche scratched the underside of her right eyelid, weighing up her response. 'Did Nicola say where she got this information from?' Dexter guessed that she thought the same as him but was keen to learn as much as she could from Blufton about Nicola and her motives for giving these 'facts' to the chairman of TVL.

The tension drifted from Blufton's eyes, as if he had expected another challenge to his veracity. 'No. She wouldn't tell me. She kept going on about "confidential sources". I assumed it was someone in the police or customs.'

Blanche held the man's gaze for a second and glanced back down at the piece of paper. 'And who's this Leonardo Della Torre?'

'Nicola said he was the man sent over to organise things for the Mafia. Sent over from Sicily – or so she said. She said she thought he lived somewhere near Godalming but she wasn't sure. That's why I put a question mark.'

Dexter stirred restlessly. He was becoming impatient with the superintendent's dispassion, her willingness to fret time away on these pointless enquiries. 'All sounds silly to me, ma'am. Mafia bosses don't operate out of Godalming for Christ's sake.'

'Don't they?' She looked up at him through her

141

eyebrows and smiled. 'Ever heard of a man called Francesco Di Carlo?' The sergeant shook his head. 'He ran the Mafia's drug business in Britain for ten years until he was arrested in the mid-eighties.'

The superintendent sighed and turned the paper round and round in her hands as if it were a visual conundrum that could be solved by approaching the problem from an unexpected angle. 'Who else knew Nicola had this information?'

Blufton edged back to his seat. 'God knows. Whoever gave it to her and whoever she told, I suppose.'

'Did she tell anyone at work?'

'Probably everybody from what you were saying about her ability to keep a secret.'

'And did she intend to tell the police and customs at some stage?'

Blufton sighed and chopped the air decisively with his right hand. 'Look, Superintendent, I assumed they were the source of the information in the first place.'

Blanche shifted in her chair and rubbed a finger across her lips. 'Why do you think she told *you* all this?'

'To impress me, I think. After all, she wanted the presenter's job.' He glanced down at the mechanical bird caged at his feet.

Blanche smiled politely and asked Blufton whether Nicola had ever mentioned a man called Kennedy. The chairman of TVL shook his head and asked why. The superintendent explained about the name of the guest Nicola was expecting to meet. Blufton raised his eyebrows with interest and seemed amused to Dexter, as if the name Kennedy triggered off the memory of some private joke. 'So you need to interview this man Kennedy urgently?'

'Yes, very much.' The restful clunk of the grandfather clock echoed round the room.

The millionaire raised a hand to his left eye and massaged the lid gently as though it were sore. 'OK,' he murmured, 'I'll offer a reward. Twenty thousand pounds for information leading to the police being able to interview this Mr Kennedy. How's that?'

142

Dexter nodded. This man *was* loaded. In the past he had only got decent-size rewards for the arrest and conviction of armed robbers and known murderers, not for information leading to a mere interview. The reward would bring even more publicity to the case and, Dexter reminded himself with a groan, endless claims for the money from conmen and lunatics. It was more trouble than it was worth.

Blanche obviously agreed. 'That's very generous of you, Mr Blufton. But if I may, I won't announce the reward for a couple of days. I'll keep it back in case we get bogged down.'

The millionaire shrugged. 'Well, it's up to you, Superintendent. I'm just keen that the bastard who murdered Nicola Sharpe should be found.'

'So are we.'

The chairman of TVL did not seem offended by the implied criticism. Instead he stared at Blanche, his eyelashes remarkably long and black, his hamster cheeks plump and shiny. He pulled on a charming smile, inspired once again – or so it appeared to Dexter – by another private joke which only he could understand. 'Let's broaden it then. Make the reward for information leading to the arrest and conviction of the person who murdered Nicola Sharpe. How does that sound?' Blufton was obviously used to cutting deals and exercising the power that money bestowed.

Blanche said she would instruct the Press Bureau at New Scotland Yard to announce the reward.

She closed her notebook and stood up in her usual, brisk way. Dexter expected the superintendent to bid farewell and for she and the sergeant to roar up the motorway back to the Yard as soon as possible. Instead, Blanche asked Blufton where he had bought the mechanical canary. The millionaire proudly handed the superintendent the cage and, while winding up the clockwork mechanism, described how he had bought it at a country auction in Warwickshire. Blanche placed the antique on the library desk and listened with rapt attention to the tin bird's hollow cheep. Dexter enjoyed such distractions but was surprised by this moment of innocence in Blanche. Her puritan temperament usually allowed no quarter, little escape from the burden of an investigation. She could laugh and joke with her colleagues but Dexter often wondered how much of the crude banter she found genuinely amusing. Blufton gave a puzzled smile – the expression of a bachelor uncle who discovers an everyday object in his pocket that makes his nieces and nephews scream with laughter.

Despite Blanche's protestations, the businessman insisted on leading the police officers back to the drawbridge by a route which took in the Great Hall. It was no more than an enormous drawing-room but the combination of a log fire, wood panelling and a Jacobean table covered with a crisp, white cloth and laid with four places for dinner created the illusion of gracious living. The sight of empty wine-glasses reminded Dexter of a question he had intended to ask earlier.

'You didn't come to the farewell party for Ken O'Mara, did you, Mr Blufton?'

'No, I didn't, unfortunately – or fortunately, depending on your point of view.'

'Why was that?'

The millionaire, standing with his legs apart, breathed in to help disguise a nascent paunch. 'I didn't have the time. I had a business dinner here at the castle. Just like the one tonight.' He gestured towards the table with an amiable smile and led them to the gate.

Dexter parked the car next to the first telephone kiosk they chanced across on the way back to Reading. It stood under some beech trees, between a row of cottages and a battered church. A faint drizzle had started to fall, hanging like droplets of liquid silver in the light from the headlamps. As soon as the sergeant turned off the windscreen wipers a curtain of mist was breathed across the glass. Dexter had said nothing since leaving Malbis Castle, sensing that the superintendent was tired and wanted time

144

to think. 'Nice enough bloke, Blufton, I thought,' the sergeant began, remembering the businessman's lack of pomposity. 'I reckon he was telling a pretty fair version of the truth, yeah?'

Blanche was biting her lip in thought. She sighed. 'Probably. He seems plausible enough. Perhaps a bit too plausible.'

Dexter watched the shadows of the trees play over the panels of the door of the kiosk as it creaked shut behind Blanche. She stood in the hazy light cast by the bulb in the ceiling, looking uncomfortable and angry, as she phoned Eddy Russell of the Drugs Squad with the information about Della Torre and the lorry due to arrive at Dover the next day.

'So much for the bliss of rural life,' snapped the superintendent, as she slumped back into her seat, her nose wrinkling. 'There was stale wee all over the floor. It was like phoning from the middle of a public toilet.'

Dexter shrugged. 'Well at least the phone worked.'

'As you know, Dexter, I'm never thankful for small mercies, only big ones.' Blanche tugged a handkerchief from her bag and blew her nose violently as if to remove the smell of urine from her nostrils.

'So what did he say?'

The superintendent narrowed her eyes with puzzlement. 'Well, he sounded surprised and a bit worried – as if he'd been caught on the hop.'

'Did he pooh-pooh the Mafia idea?' Dexter asked the question with the implication that the inspector should have done.

'No, he didn't. He didn't say much at all really. Just made a note of what I said and said thanks very much. He told me he'd tell customs about the lorry straight away.' She glanced across at Dexter. 'I'm meeting him tomorrow night for a chat.'

Dexter nodded to himself as he understood what was happening. Under the cover of her investigation, Blanche was warily trying to get to know the inspector better, hoping to develop the relationship into something more

145

intimate. Blanche would never admit it of course. The superintendent's personal life was alien territory to Dexter, one that she guarded fiercely, even though it was the sergeant who suffered the consequences when Blanche emerged from it wounded. The only times she talked openly about her hopes and disappointments was when she was drunk – a state Dexter had seen her in only three times, all at parties and all after the separation from her husband. She had not been maudlin then: the tears, Dexter felt, were as much ones of laughter as of despair. But on these rare occasions the frontier posts protecting Blanche's personality had been unmanned, and Dexter had been able to wander at will through her past and her present. And each time Dexter believed he had come closer to Blanche, understood her better, and liked her more.

Dexter knew the superintendent well enough now to chance his arm occasionally and probe into her personal life when she was sober. 'This chat is purely business then, ma'am?'

'Of course, Dexter, what else?' Blanche yawned, trying to hide the flush of excitement burning her cheeks.

Blanche's favourite curry house was in one of London's most eclectic suburbs. Among red brick terraces, under grey skies and deafened by the whine of jets swooping down to Heathrow airport, a nation had chosen to found a colony in exile. Although far from the dust and heat of India, the Sikhs had come in their thousands, roosting like exotic birds on the chimney-pots and the concrete of Southall. They brought their turbans, their pride and their brown eyes twinkling at the prospect of business. They built a temple in a side-street to house their Holy Books and to dispense hospitality. They founded a little Punjab through whose gates they left in the morning and returned in the evening, glad to be back among their own kind.

The superintendent had fallen asleep during the journey, her head gently rolling from side to side against

146

the car seat, her front teeth prominent in her open mouth as she breathed through her nose. She suddenly looked tender and vulnerable to Dexter and he wondered once again how she had managed to survive the grimy and bruising life of the Met.

Dexter ate Indian dishes without relish and when he did, he preferred a curry house with a clean table-cloth, candles in yellow globes of glass and obsequious waiters. Being the son of an immigrant himself, he had no time for what he regarded as ethnic tourism. Blanche, on the other hand, loved her café with its ramshackle tables, grubby menus and her face being the only one in the restaurant that was not Asian. So on their way back from Reading Dexter had swung in to Southall from the motorway and parked in a side-street.

The heavy scents of Indian cooking however soon revived Blanche. She swigged from a pint glass of *lassi* and munched her *chapatis*. 'You're right about Blufton. He probably is OK. But I don't know . . . there's something almost too convenient about his story.'

For Dexter the issue was clear. Blufton seemed trustworthy enough and had no direct relationship with Nicola. He might have coveted her body but there was no evidence that he had ever managed to seduce her. He had not even been at the party. The only thing of real interest Blufton had passed on was the intriguing story – and the sergeant was less sceptical now – of Mafia drug smuggling. Dexter shared his thoughts with Blanche, who listened politely. 'I thought he was all right for a millionaire. Not posh or anything.'

The superintendent folded up a *chapati*. 'The castle was a bit of a con, though.'

'Seemed all right to me.'

'It's about as genuine as a Roman roof tile made of polystyrene. Didn't you notice the table in the Armoury?'

'What about it?' asked the sergeant, sipping his pint of lager.

'Well, its legs were the upturned legs of a billiard table. The whole thing was made from bits of scrap.'

147

'What about all those paintings then? They looked the real thing to me.'

'Oh, yes, they were genuine enough. But as for the pottery . . . ' Blanche twisted her lips into a sneer.

'What do you mean?'

The superintendent dipped the *chapati* into the tin bowl of *dal* and chewed off a mouthful. 'Hardly any of it was really medieval – which was the impression Blufton was trying to give. Most of it was Indian, made in little villages in Rajasthan, just over the border from where these people came from,' she added, waving towards the other diners.

Dexter shrugged. He thought Blanche was being too finicky. It did not matter two hoots to him that Blufton was not over-concerned with authentic period detail. It was the overall impression that counted.

Blanche chewed thoughtfully. 'Perhaps you're right. There's probably nothing to it.'

The sergeant called across one of the waiters to order another pint of lager. A glint of panic flashed in the boy's eyes because he did not speak English very well. He scurried across to fetch his cousin – a tall, gangling youth – who took the order with a flourish of smiles. 'On the other hand,' said Dexter, through a mouthful of chicken *tikka masalla*, one of the few Indian dishes he could stomach, 'there might just be something to this drugs thing.'

'You never know.' Blanche wiped her lips with a paper napkin. She gave a sceptical shrug. 'I'm dubious about this Mafia story. Sounds just the sort of thing Nicola would have made up to impress Blufton.'

With DI Russell not dismissing the Mafia theory out of hand Dexter had found his outright disbelief weakening. 'It might just be possible though, right?'

'Anything's possible, Dexter. I might even become a chief constable one day.' The comment was meant humorously, and the sergeant could detect no bitterness, only amused, ironic detachment. Until quite recently there might have been a sting of sarcasm in her voice, the anger of the betrayed. But Dexter knew Blanche had benefited from a growing friendship with a woman she had met on a management course at the police college at Bramshill – a former commander in the Met who had taken to lecturing after a heart attack. Dexter had met Helen Briggs only once but liked her straight away – the bubbling laugh, the enormous bosom, the trunk-like legs and, above all, the endless cigarettes that drooped from her finger. Commander Briggs had counselled Blanche to calm down and accept more of the things in the police she could not change. And Dexter had watched Blanche slowly become calmer and more stoic about the future. The ambition and drive were still there, but more tempered, more resilient than before. Blanche had increasingly come to accept that doing her best was good enough and that she did not need to measure herself against some ideal standard.

'Straight up, though, ma'am. Do you think Nicola could have stumbled on something big?'

'It's always possible. But I doubt if the Mafia is involved. London isn't New York, you know. Do you remember the Di Carlo case – the one I mentioned to Blufton?'

Dexter's lager arrived. He took a swig and shook his head.

'The Sicilian Mafia laundered piles of drugs money before Di Carlo got caught and sent to jail. But that was an isolated case. The Mafia never really got established in London. Thank God.' Dexter was always surprised by Blanche's memory: she collected facts with the passion others sought stamps or antiques. The superintendent tore off a piece of *nan* and wiped the curry sauce from her plate. 'Besides, if you're a drugs syndicate and want to murder someone who knows a bit too much, you don't do it in the victim's office, do you? Much too risky.'

The sergeant nodded agreement. He remembered the menacing phone-calls to Nicola and wondered aloud whether someone from a drugs syndicate had been trying to scare her.

Blanche made a non-committal murmur. She signalled to the waiter that she wanted the bill and asked Dexter to

149

phone in to the incident room to see if anything had happened. He was directed down a corridor faced with mud-brown wallpaper to a payphone. The air was pungent with spices; the linoleum on the floor peeped through offcuts of burgundy carpet.

'Where the hell have you been?' muttered DS Wootton breathlessly, who had been summoned to the phone by a constable. 'I've been trying to find you everywhere.'

Trust Wootton to be panicking again, thought Dexter, determined to disguise his dislike of the man. 'Why, has something happened?'

'Oh, yeah, something's happened all right. We might have found the pair of scissors that killed Nicola Sharpe. They were in David Parkin's desk.'

CHAPTER
THIRTEEN

Blanche took the plastic bag from the Scenes of Crime Officer with a grim smile. She turned the pair of scissors over with her long, slim fingers and frowned. The scissors themselves were ordinary enough, standard office issue, and shining steel: there was no outward sign that they could have been a weapon of murder, Dexter thought. The closed blades were not smeared with blood, and nothing about the scissors screamed out that they had taken a human life.

Detective Sergeant Wootton – pasty and blinking through his dirty spectacles – stood in the circle, keen to be involved. There was a hum of excitement in the incident room that had not existed when Blanche and Dexter had left earlier that evening. Two detective constables walked in and listened eagerly to the latest gossip, glancing over to the superintendent with new animation in their eyes.

As if anticipating a question from Blanche, the SOCO pointed to the screw joining the two blades. 'The blood's in there, ma'am, inside, between the blades. They were cleaned but not very well. There's a fair amount left . . . '

Dexter leant forward and saw some black marks around the rivet.

'Did you find any prints?' The superintendent looked up at the SOCO, posing the question like a doctor checking the symptoms of a sickly patient.

'There are a few partial ones on the handle.'

Blanche nodded. 'OK. Get them lifted.'

The SOCO was a woman of about thirty. Although her

face was pale it was lit by a flush of unmistakable triumph. She explained how she had continued her search for the murder weapon that afternoon. She had deliberately not revealed what she was looking for, and so insisted on evacuating every office before she began work. With the help of a detective constable, she had to sift through the papers on every desk top and the rubbish in every drawer. By early evening they had reached the documentary department offices on the second floor and in one desk, at the back of an open drawer, was the pair of scissors. The stains around the rivet had shown up positive in the test for human blood.

The desk belonged to David Parkin. Besides working on *Inside Out*, the reporter was also presenting a special documentary about forensic science. The four police officers laughed at the irony. 'Well, he doesn't seem to have learnt much from it, does he?' chuckled Dexter.

Blanche retreated to her cubicle in the corner of the room, a knot of thoughtfulness still on her forehead, her movement followed by all the constables in the office who looked up from their conversations. Dexter knew they were hungry for information so he winked at them and made a thumbs-up sign. If he could not inform he could at least reassure. Although he had been told to do this on some goddamned boring management course, the sergeant did it instinctively.

Dexter bounced along behind Blanche with renewed energy. He was buoyed by the knowledge that at last they had a clear suspect. Not someone, like Jim Lancaster, implicated just by opportunity and motive but a suspect linked to the murder by hard evidence. A murder weapon had been discovered in Parkin's desk, David Parkin had been in the right place at the right time and he had a conceivable motive to kill the television reporter. After all, he and Nicola were lovers, and from his own experience the sergeant knew violence and passion were jealous twins. Admittedly, it would take twenty-four hours to see if the blood on the scissors matched the sample from Nicola Sharpe and if the partial fingerprints could be matched against the elimination prints from David Parkin. Only then could they think of moving against him. It was essential, Dexter knew, to gather together as powerful a case as possible against the reporter before arresting him because from that moment the clock would begin to run: Parkin would either need to be charged with the murder or released within twenty-four hours. Dexter jigged his toes on the floor of Blanche's office, impatient for the night to slip away quickly.

Blanche leant forward on her desk, her hands in an attitude of prayer, her eyes unfocused with thought. 'Even if these tests on the scissors are positive we still need more evidence.'

Wootton lifted his eyebrows sceptically. 'Do we?'

'Parkin will say he lent Nicola the scissors and there was some accident. She cut herself or something. No jury will convict on that.'

Dexter's toes suddenly flopped down and stayed glued to the floor. His shoulders slumped and nervousness fluttered in his stomach. Blanche was right of course. They *did* need more evidence. And Dexter tried to calm his faint resentment against her for casting a shadow over his optimistic mood. He often told himself he was stupid to feel like this but the sensation was real none the less.

Looking back, the superintendent's solution seemed obvious to the sergeant. It was a matter of elimination. There was only one place they could scour that did not need a search warrant: TV London.

The Asian security man unlocked the door to the documentary department office and loped off down the corridor with a distracted smile on his face. The Scenes of Crime Officer walked in and the fluorescent bulbs on the ceiling flickered into life. In one corner of the rectangular office a television set had not been switched off and the title sequence of a forgotten film from the seventies flickered silently on the screen. The office was smaller and tidier than the one used by *Inside Out*, although laid out in a similar way with desks back to back.

The SOCO strutted across to one at the far end, shielded behind a panel of rough hessian. The desk was less neat than the others with a stack of yellowing news-papers on one corner and two piles of books about forensic science on the other. In the middle was a framed photograph of a woman, whom Dexter recognised as Maggie Parkin, holding a baby. The sergeant smiled to himself. David Parkin was obviously keen to preserve at work the image of a happy marriage despite, or perhaps because of, his affair with Nicola.

The SOCO indicated with her soft, white hands the drawer on the top left in which she had found the scissors. She said the drawer was unlocked and the scissors were at the back.

Dexter nodded. The desk was anonymous and modern, blockboard veneered with mahogany, the legs no more than sticks of black metal. The drawers were divided into two blocks to right and left. 'Did you check all the drawers?'

The woman said she had, and in the filing cabinet behind, but that she was searching specifically for a pair of scissors.

Dexter dragged over a chair and sat down at the desk. He pulled out each drawer on the left one by one and methodically sifted through the files, papers, pens and notebooks. After fifteen minutes' work he had found nothing of interest. The drawers on the right were locked. The SOCO drew the key from her pocket with a smile, saying she had borrowed it from the office manager. The top drawer contained a bizarre mixture of objects: a stapler, a bottle of ink, assorted keys, a leather bookmark, an empty black plastic container for film – the flotsam washed ashore in an office from any human life. Dexter drew out the second drawer with more hope. It was crammed with notebooks filled with Parkin's bold scribble as well as copies of various scripts in loose folders. Some related to the project he was working on, others to pre-vious films he had made – one on schizophrenia, another on pollution of the North Sea, another on the future of

Islam. Dexter flicked through the files with all the concentration he could muster. He began to wonder how much more time he would need to waste before phoning Blanche with the bad news that he had found nothing. After all, what could he expect to find? A signed confession? A video of Parkin engaged in the act of murder? His attention was seized by a triangle of pale blue, the corner of an airmail envelope, the two protruding edges marked by alternate parallelograms of red and dark blue. Dexter drew it out and registered David Parkin's name written on the front in ballpoint pen with the words 'PERSONAL AND CONFIDENTIAL'. The letter had been ripped open so Dexter drew out the note within, a sheet torn from a reporter's notebook. There was no date.

'My dearest David – although I don't have the faintest idea why I should still call you this after what you told me last night – I've had a long think. I'm not just going to let you throw me away. I just won't let it happen. It's up to you. But if you go ahead with your threat I'm warning you that you'll be finished. I'll tell the tax people about how you've been on the fiddle all these years over your freelance earnings *and* I've got those photos of you. Do you remember – the ones of you sniffing coke in the hotel bedroom for a joke when we first met? That would look great in the tabloids. Think about it, David. I don't want to threaten you but you've forced me into a corner. I love you too much and I'm not going to let you walk over me just because your wife found out about our affair. Think about it and let's have a proper talk. Love Nicola.'

Dexter realised his fingers were shaking as he finished reading Nicola's round, almost childish, writing for the second time. A surge of elation rushed through his body as he read the note for the third time, unable to believe the implications of what he was reading. Nicola had threatened to blackmail David Parkin if he ended their love affair. He was holding the evidence in his hand. No

155

wonder Parkin was havering, unable to assemble the courage to make the final break with Nicola. Parkin must have received the note and, in a panic, thrust it into the bottom of the locked drawer, assuming that no one would find it. 'I think we might have got the bastard,' said Dexter, taking deep breaths to calm himself. 'If only those tests work out.'

The incident room was in darkness, except for a couple of desks whose reading lights had not been switched off, a glowing computer screen and the flashing red lights of some electrical equipment. Wootton had already gone home: he had a young family and a termagant wife. Blanche stood by the door for a moment with her hand on the switch, the back of her head lit fiercely by the lights in the corridor, her face hidden in soft obscurity. Her heavy-lidded eyes were vacant with thought. 'And leaves the world to darkness, and to me,' she murmured.

'What's that?'

'A line of old poetry, Dexter,' she said with a smile. Her fingers pressed the switches and the lights on the ceiling of the incident room flickered into life. She threw herself down at her desk and read Nicola's note through yet again, the sparkle of excitement in her eyes. 'You're right. If those tests turn out the right way tomorrow – ' she glanced at her watch, remembering they were now in the early hours of the morning – 'or rather tonight, it'll be worth bringing Parkin in.' She laid the rectangle of glistening plastic down on her desk and sat back in her chair. 'Do you know, I've been thinking.'

'Always a good idea, guv'.'

The superintendent smiled. Dexter could tell she was exhilarated by the day's events. 'I'm not sure that man Kennedy that Nicola was supposed to be meeting ever existed.'

'What – you mean Nicola or Parkin just invented him?'

Blanche stared at her desk and nodded. 'Yes. And if not them, somebody else.' She studied the sergeant with a twinkle of amusement in her eyes. 'I don't know why you look so amazed. You look like a kid who's just discovered

156

Father Christmas doesn't exist.'

'You mean he doesn't?' Dexter pulled on a face of mock disappointment to cover his surprise. He had just assumed Kennedy had existed. Thinking about it again, Blanche might be right. No one – absolutely no one – had seen a man called Kennedy arrive, or known anything about a man with that name. The only evidence for his existence was a phone-call from Nicola and his name scribbled in a book. 'That's something we can ask Parkin about tomorrow night, yeah?'

'Don't count your chickens, Dexter.' Blanche coughed and ran a hand over her forehead. 'If the blood *does* turn out to be Nicola's, it does look stupid of him, doesn't it – to leave the murder weapon in his desk? And the letter.'

'It was his second office, remember, a long way away.' Dexter was deliberately sparing with his words. He was tired and wanted to go home to bed.

'But why should he keep the scissors rather than throw them away?'

'Perhaps he wanted a souvenir.'

'What, like a stick of Brighton rock – with blood running down the middle?'

'Murderers have done weirder things. And don't forget – they can be bloody stupid sometimes.'

The superintendent suddenly looked up, her eyes flashing. 'Come on, Dexter, you're meant to be giving me inspiration not falling asleep,' she snapped.

Dexter shook himself awake. 'Sorry, ma'am, but I'm knackered.' He smiled submissively. He could recognise the danger signs: Blanche was over-tired and as impatient as he was underneath for night to fall again. Every investigation was to her like a personal crusade, a quest, that she had to complete. Failure was an abdication of personal responsibility, a cause of a guilty conscience. She was more relaxed than she used to be but still, in Dexter's view, judged herself too harshly.

'We're missing something obvious, Dexter. Something that pulls all the pieces together. It's like doing one of those IQ tests and you keep going over the words and numbers again and again. And then when someone tells you the answer you kick yourself.'

Dexter levered himself up from the chair, his eyelids leaden with sleep, and murmured that he had to go home and rest.

Blanche nodded goodnight. As Dexter staggered out of the door, he saw the superintendent still pondering over Nicola's letter, her face bathed in the light of her desk lamp.

CHAPTER
FOURTEEN

The canteen at TV London was largely deserted at half past ten the next morning when Dexter and Blanche sat down at a table in the corner of the self-service section. It had just been wiped by a sullen black woman in a nylon overall, from whom the sergeant tried in vain to extract a smile, and the police officers sat back to allow it to dry before resting their elbows on the surface. The whole room breathed an air of hygienic efficiency: the walls were emulsioned so that they could be repainted at little cost, and the tables stood on plastic tiles which could be quickly wiped and disinfected. The cosy harshness was broken only by a pair of plastic houseplants and by prints of country scenes on the walls. Blanche sniffed unhappily as cigarette smoke drifted across from a table on the other side of the room occupied by a raucous group of maintenance men in boiler suits. One was hoovering up a plate of sausage and chips while reading the *Sun*. Another table was hidden by a group of young men in open-necked shirts and brown pullovers. Others were occupied by scattered individuals, some reading a newspaper, others dreaming into space or others still sipping a coffee and chatting.

Jane Pargeter stood at the counter, nervously elegant, Dexter considered, in her khaki skirt and crisp, white blouse, an antique brooch pinned to the neck. Behind her and to the right stretched a plastic canopy containing cakes and filled rolls. A man in a suit came up beside her and made some remark which caused Jane to throw her head back and cackle. Her laugh was so loud it attracted glances from people in the room. 'Did he really? You're joking?' she said with her distinctive throatiness, as she paid for the coffees.

Jane carried the tray across to the police officers with what looked to the sergeant like absurd concentration and Dexter wondered uncharitably whether she had already been drinking. She slid the tray on to the table with a jolt, slopping some of the coffee over the edge of the cups. 'There's something a bit seedy about this side of the canteen, I'm afraid,' she began, lighting a cigarette. 'I would have preferred to have invited you to a waitress service lunch over there of course.' She coughed and nodded towards a section that was cordoned off, where the tables were laid with cloths and Dexter was reminded of a holiday hotel on the Costa Brava. 'But you seemed keen to meet me this morning, so this seemed like the best place.'

Her make-up had been applied thickly that morning but with great dexterity. She looked as if she was about to walk on stage rather than be interviewed by detectives from New Scotland Yard. But Dexter preferred it. By larding on the make-up, Jane Pargeter seemed to have regained the charm and sharpness she displayed on television but lacked on the afternoon following the murder. 'I love sitting here sometimes, watching the world go by. All of human life is here, you know. It's a bit like a pavement café in Paris.' Her eyes, set amongst crow's-feet when she smiled, flickered over the other people in the canteen. She rattled on breathlessly, perhaps encouraged, Dexter thought, by a desire to delay Blanche coming to the point of the meeting. 'It's particularly fun when all the actors come in dressed up in costume – it's like being in some surreal painting.'

The superintendent smiled, watching Jane carefully. Blanche looked a little ragged at the edges, her sergeant noted indulgently, but was otherwise unmarked by just four hours' sleep the night before. Her eyes were sparkling and her legs bustling when he had staggered into the incident room an hour late at nine o'clock: he had been so

160

tired he had slept through the high-pitched beep of his alarm clock. Dexter had expected her to say that the day was to be spent seeking more evidence against David Parkin. Blanche explained however that since her sergeant had rifled through all the available files and drawers at TV London there was nothing more to be done. Better, she believed, to while away the leaden hours until evening by talking again to three people. Two – Parkin's wife and Jim Lancaster – had both opportunity and motive to murder Nicola while the third, Jane Pargeter, had at least a conceivable motive. All three on the other hand, and here Blanche was imagining what Parkin might say in his defence once in the interview room, had a good reason to want to see the blame for the murder transferred to Parkin should they have killed Nicola themselves. All three might have planted the pair of scissors in the reporter's desk.

The superintendent sipped her coffee. 'You told me the other day that you couldn't remember the farewell party very clearly,' she began. 'Have you remembered anything important since? Anything that's come back to mind?'

The TV presenter sucked extravagantly on her cigarette and blew out the smoke over her left shoulder. Her eyelashes, clogged with thick make-up, flickered together. 'No. I can't say I have. Why?'

'I'm interested in checking the times when various people were seen to leave the party.'

Jane Pargeter said nothing for a moment, tugging back her cheeks in a wince that looked to Dexter as if she was attempting to suppress a smile. 'I told you everything I saw when you interviewed me before.'

Blanche nodded. 'That's right. You said you saw Jim Lancaster, Maggie Parkin and David Parkin all go out of the boardroom.' She counted them off on her fingers.

When pressed by Blanche she added nothing to what she had said before. Dexter admired the way in which his boss disguised who she was really interested in. But when the superintendent mentioned David Parkin's name, Jane Pargeter flicked her cigarette nervously

161

and a curl of grey tobacco fluttered into the porcelain pot. Although it was faint, Dexter was sure he smelt the sour staleness of alcohol on her breath. 'David was out of the room for – I don't know, ten or fifteen minutes I suppose.'

'Did you see him come back?'

'No. I didn't. I just happened to look up and he was back. That's all.' She fingered the brooch at her neck – Victorian gold plate with an amethyst in the centre, held in place by a fierce pin.

Blanche sighed. 'From what you know of David Parkin's character, Jane, would you say he was a violent man?'

The TV presenter stared at the female detective for a second and then her face twisted into a sly smile. 'If you're asking whether I think David could be the murderer, then I'm afraid the answer is yes. He's got a cold, violent side.' She paused and touched her cheek. Dexter noticed her hand was shaking faintly and she struck him as keeping her self-control with great difficulty. 'He hit me once, you know. I suppose it's possible he had a row with Nicola and killed her.'

Blanche squinted with concentration. 'You're still quite bitter about him ending your affair, aren't you?'

A look of watchfulness stole across Jane Pargeter's eyes. She inhaled deeply, like a participant in a yoga class. 'Superintendent, I don't know why you keep harping on about this. As I told you that was all a long time ago. Time's a great healer.' Pargeter looked away and stubbed out her half-finished cigarette. She shuffled in her seat, smoothing out the wrinkles from her skirt. The last thing you are, thought Dexter, is healed.

The sergeant watched his boss scrutinise Jane Pargeter, her lips pulled into a look of scepticism to match his own. Suddenly her face relaxed and a new twinkle animated her brown eyes. Dexter had seen the look many times before: Blanche had had an idea. She leant forward, saying she wanted to go back for a moment to what the TV presenter had said about Jim Lancaster.

The flinty look in Pargeter's face told Dexter that

Blanche had struck home in some way. The woman's shaking hand plucked another cigarette from the packet. Her shoulders slumped a little as she sucked the smoke into her lungs. She smiled – a mouthful of perfect if yellowing teeth, Dexter noted coldly – and spoke in an excellent, though female, imitation of Jim Lancaster's accent. 'Hello, my name is Jim Lancaster. I'm a teacher and I'm really boring.' She chuckled and her voice returned to normal. 'What else is there to say about him?'

Blanche stared into the woman's eyes without blinking. Dexter wondered what the superintendent's idea was, except that it must relate in some way to Jim Lancaster. He decided to sit back and wait. 'You remember that farewell party better than you pretend, don't you?' prodded Blanche.

'I remember it all right – I enjoyed it.'

The female detective glanced around the canteen and spoke in a confidential whisper, her eyes drilling into Pargeter's so as to miss none of her reactions. 'Did you enjoy telling Jim Lancaster that his wife was having an affair with David Parkin?'

Dexter watched the flintiness harden back into Jane Pargeter's face, as she pondered how much the superintendent knew. So that was it, Dexter reflected. Of course. Despite her protestations, it was evident Jane Pargeter still resented David Parkin for dumping her for another woman. He and Blanche also knew that Jim Lancaster had lied to them about when he stumbled across his wife's adultery. He had learnt about it much closer to the time of the murder. Why not at the party, from a woman who suddenly saw a way to wreak her spite not only on Parkin but on his ambitious young lover?

Pargeter's tongue crawled over her yellow teeth. She drained off the last of her tepid coffee. 'He's told you, has he?'

Blanche lied with a nod. The black detective watched anxiously, wondering whether Pargeter would take the bait and confirm the superintendent's theory.

'To answer your question with brutal honesty – I *did*

rather enjoy it. I didn't when I discovered what happened afterwards of course.' Hardly surprising, considered Dexter. Jane Pargeter probably just thought she would fulfil her petty revenge and leave Jim Lancaster to have a row with his pushy wife. Instead the wife was a corpse within the hour. Dexter studied the TV presenter's face for a clue as to her sincerity about regretting Nicola's death but all he saw was brittle nervousness. He suddenly felt some sympathy for her: her intentions had been evil but Jane could hardly have foreseen the appalling results of her maliciousness – if indeed Jim Lancaster had stormed off and murdered his wife.

'You'd better tell me exactly what happened.' Blanche's voice was calm and authoritative.

Jane scratched the side of her nose with a manicured fingernail. 'Well, I bumped into Nicola's husband at the party. And whenever I meet the spouse of someone who's having an affair with someone else, I always ask myself whether they know. And, if they do, how they feel about it.'

'So you decided to ask him, did you?' Dexter saw that Blanche could not hide a faint sneer of distaste at how the TV reporter had behaved.

Jane detected it. She slid a hand through her newly washed hair and her eyes rolled desperately from Dexter to his boss. 'I assumed the poor man already knew, you see. I had no idea he'd been kept in the dark for so long. As it turned out, I was doing him a service.'

'Doing him a service?' asked Blanche, her voice pitched high with incredulity.

Jane realised her desperation had led her to saying something foolish. 'OK, maybe I wasn't doing him a service. But he had to find out at some stage, didn't he?' Jane Pargeter inhaled and blew the smoke out with a pout of self-righteousness, reminding Dexter of a spoilt and naughty child. She shrugged. 'I had no idea he was going to storm off and try to find her there and then, did I?'

Blanche's eyes were cold with dislike. Dexter decided that although he understood her predicament, he no longer warmed to her either.

'He just collapsed. It was quite dramatic really. He obviously didn't have the faintest idea it was going on.' Jane pulled on a dry smile, making the skin crinkle round the margins of her eyes. 'It was stupid of me. I shouldn't have done it, of course. It was an act of petty revenge. But I have to say, when I saw his eyes start to dart round the room looking for Nicola, I felt better for it. That little bitch had it coming to her.' God, you did hate her, reflected Dexter, and the thought fired through his brain that perhaps Jane Pargeter had foreseen Nicola's murder after all. Willed it at least, even though she had not carried it out.

'And where was Nicola when you were telling her husband all this?' asked Dexter.

Pargeter turned her alert eyes to the sergeant. 'She wasn't in the boardroom because I'd seen her leave. Her husband muttered something to me about going to find her and then stormed off.'

'Did you actually see Jim Lancaster leave the room?'

Jane Pargeter shook her head. 'Once he'd disappeared I didn't take any more notice. I carried on drinking and talking until Ken O'Mara rushed into the room and screamed that he'd found the body.'

The superintendent pushed her chair back on its aluminium legs. Her head drooped to one side, and her heavy-lidded eyes stared at the ashtray, even though they did not focus on it. She looked slightly strange when she was deep in thought, as though in a trance. Dexter was used to the superintendent's mannerisms but after a second or two, Blanche caught Jane Pargeter's look of puzzlement, and the detective smiled apologetically. She glanced round the canteen with a twinkle in her eye. 'You television journalists have a job a bit like mine, don't you?'

'What do you mean?'

'We're both meant to be seekers after truth. And no one wants to let us near it.'

Pargeter laughed cynically. 'I think people take television far too seriously.' She was more relaxed now, her shoulders less hunched, as if she realised the interview

165

was coming to an end.

'So why do you do it?' commented Blanche, as she stood to say farewell.

'Because it gives me a buzz. I get recognised in the street. Above all, it's better than working all your life in a fish-finger factory like my mum did.' The TV presenter twitched her cheeks into a smile of farewell.

The sergeant understood for the first time just how tough a woman Jane Pargeter was underneath, steely and unforgiving, hardened by life. He watched her all the way to the swing doors, her head of brown hair held high and bobbing slightly as her heels clipped the floor. 'I bet she's heading for the bar – if it's open yet.'

While they were talking in a corner, the room had drained of people. Three women in nylon overalls sat at a table eating the food they had prepared for the canteen lunch. Through the window Dexter saw the silver arrow of a jet flare in the sun as it turned to make its descent to Heathrow. 'It was clever of you to work out the connection with Jim Lancaster, ma'am.'

Blanche smiled appreciatively. She began to trace circles on the table top with the drops of spilt coffee. Her eyes only focused on the sergeant a couple of seconds after he posed the question. 'It was a guess really. When someone discovers they've been betrayed by their partner they get angry. I should know, Dexter.' The sergeant saw her eyes were dim with sadness and he guessed she had been thinking about her former husband. 'The art of interviewing is to put together various theories on the basis of the *available* evidence, not the evidence you'd like to be there. Then you try it out. And sometimes you're lucky, and sometimes you're not.'

'Well, we're doing all right. If only we can get some proper evidence against Jim Lancaster, we'll have two kosher suspects rather than one.'

Blanche smiled and strode towards the swing doors. Dexter loped along behind, knowing things were not as simple as the woman detective liked to make out.

CHAPTER
FIFTEEN

'Oh, it's you again.'

'Yes, it's us.'

Jim Lancaster fingered the open door of his house, unable to hide a look of worry. He had good reason to look apprehensive, Dexter thought. After all, it was the third time the police had visited him in as many days.

'I'm fed up with this. Can't you just leave me alone for God's sake?'

'I'm sorry. I know how you must be feeling – '

'Do you? Do you really?' His voice was staccato with anger. 'It's bad enough – with Nicola being killed – but you keep coming round here – harassing me.'

The sergeant considered Jim Lancaster was going to slam the door and he prepared to thrust his right foot up against the jamb.

'I'm sorry . . . ' pleaded Blanche with an expressive shrug. 'But it could be important.'

Nicola's husband hesitated for a moment, rubbing his nose. Dexter watched the man's annoyance drain away: he was the sort who could not stay angry for long. Walking with his gauche, bouncy tread, his shoulders hunched, Nicola's husband led Blanche and Dexter down the steps into the kitchen and gestured for them to sit down round the kitchen table.

The sergeant gazed out at the suburban garden with a gardener's informed eye. It was not just the flower-beds marked by dying crocuses and the general air of neglect, with last autumn's leaves left to rot in sunless corners, that made him depressed. It was also the cold: a chill wind had risen during the morning and ruffled the feathers of a sparrow which stood shivering on the window-ledge.

Blanche looked at Lancaster with a quizzical smile and did not say anything for a full ten seconds. Dexter counted them off by the hand of his watch. He wondered where she was going to begin: with the stains or Jane Pargeter. 'I'd be grateful if you could start to tell me the truth,' she said finally.

'About what?'

'Everything. But I'd like to start with just one thing for the moment – when you learnt your wife was having an affair with David Parkin.'

Jim Lancaster blinked behind his spectacles. 'But I told you – '

'You told me you learnt about it a couple of weeks before Nicola was murdered.'

'That's right.'

'But the truth is the first you knew about it was at the party.'

His lips parted as if about to shape some words. But none was said. He stared back blankly. His mouth closed to moisten suddenly dry lips. The kitchen window was flecked by a new fall of drizzle whisked against the glass.

Blanche leant forward on her chair, her eyes watchful. 'We've been talking to Jane Pargeter.' Dexter saw Lancaster's eyes flicker as he registered the implications of what Blanche had just told him. 'It must have been terrible when she told you about Nicola's affair with Parkin. I want to give you a chance to put the record straight. Tell me what really happened.'

Jim Lancaster looked confused for a moment, blinking furiously behind his spectacles. 'If you've already spoken to her there's not much point . . . It's like what she said.' He crossed his arms. 'She told me Nicola was having this affair . . . At first I didn't believe her but there was something in her eyes that told me it was true. And I'd also had some suspicions.' His voice was so gentle the police officers had to strain to hear. He gulped. 'I was so shocked and

168

angry. Hurt. Like some wounded animal. I had to speak to her, to Nicola. So I ran off. And I found her.'

Dexter had seen it happen many times before: the moment when a human being slips from conversation into confession, the moment when what seemed like a universal desire to atone for wickedness overwhelmed the conflicting wish for self-preservation. That moment of clarity could be all too brief, later twisted and defined out of existence by clever lawyers when the criminal came to court. If only the police and the criminal could reach an agreement on punishment or rehabilitation there and then, the sergeant sometimes thought, justice would more often be done.

Lancaster breathed out slowly and looked down at the table when he realised what he had said.

'Where did you find her?' Blanche had difficulty controlling the excitement in her voice.

'In her office.'

'Alone?'

A faint smile crossed Lancaster's face, as though he was laughing at a cruel joke in dubious taste. 'Parkin wasn't with her if that's what you mean. She was alone all right.'

The fridge suddenly switched itself on, the buzzing hum sharpening the tension. Dexter sensed every nerve in his body vibrant and alert. 'What happened? Did you have a row?'

He shook his head in a daze. 'Nothing happened. We didn't row. I didn't hit her. I couldn't say anything to her.' His voice was drained of emotion, his eyes lustreless, as Dexter imagined the memory of her body floating back into his mind. The sergeant became aware of the tick of his watch against his ear. 'She was dead.'

Blanche's chair creaked as she leant forward, hands on her knees. 'What time was that?'

'God knows – half past nine or so, I suppose. I had more important things to worry about than the time.'

'Did you see anyone? See anything suspicious?'

Nicola's husband did not hear the question. Instead he murmured to himself, his eyes glazed. 'I can still see her.

169

Lying there, covered in blood. It was the sort of thing I'd have done I suppose if I'd had the chance. Only someone else got there first.'

Blanche and Dexter exchanged glances. The superintendent asked if he really meant what he had just said.

'Oh, yeah. I was angry enough, ashamed enough.' He took off his spectacles and began to clean them with his handkerchief. 'I can still remember standing there at the party when that woman Pargeter told me. I felt sick. Covered in a kind of prickly heat. I just wanted to get out, escape, find her. Tell her what I thought of her.'

Dexter found Lancaster's performance quite convincing, but not convincing enough to win him over. 'So if you didn't kill Nicola, why didn't you call the police when you found her body?'

Nicola's husband looked up wearily, his voice no more than the rustle of dead leaves. 'I wasn't thinking straight. It was the shock I suppose and the wine – I must have drunk almost a bottle. I just wanted to get out. And I did.' He glanced out at a gang of starlings fighting over some breadcrumbs that had been tossed on the lawn.

The superintendent enquired calmly what happened next.

'Does it matter?'

Blanche apologised with a smile. 'You never know.'

'I went down in the lift. I asked the security guard to order me a taxi.'

'Which one?' Dexter realised that Blanche wanted to check out his story. At the moment they only had the word of Nicola's husband for what had happened.

Lancaster thought for a moment. 'There was only one there. An Asian I think. Anyway, I sat there for a couple of minutes and then the cab came.' He looked up, a glint of desperation in his eye. 'You've no idea what I felt like when I found Nicola. She might have been having it off with Parkin. But I loved her.'

Blanche squinted thoughtfully, fixing the man in front of her with an inquisitive stare. Dexter wondered whether the superintendent believed Lancaster's story: she was so difficult to read. The sergeant was not sure himself. How do you judge whether a human being is telling the truth? The signs were so varied, so liable to misinterpretation, all Dexter could rely on was instinct. And his instincts havered between guilt and innocence.

Blanche asked whether Nicola's husband had seen anything suspicious at the party.

'Not really. You see when Jane Pargeter told me, I suddenly looked round for Nicola at the party. And she wasn't there.'

'Was David Parkin?'

'No, he wasn't either. And I remembered what Nicola told me about her having to meet someone. I thought it had to be him. And she hadn't come back. I know it sounds mad but I suddenly had an image of them doing it on the carpet in the office like a couple of dogs.' His voice was flat with sadness. 'Sounds silly, doesn't it?'

Blanche shrugged sympathetically, or so it seemed to the sergeant, as if to say, 'I understand. It wasn't silly.'

'But the room was empty, you see. I looked in the editor's office but no one was there.'

'What about the viewing booth?'

'Well, that was one strange thing. I remember trying it and finding it locked. I was so paranoid I even listened at the door. But I couldn't hear anything.'

Blanche's eyes widened and she sat forward on the kitchen chair. 'You're saying you went to the office *twice* then?'

'Yeah, that's what I said, isn't it?' whined Lancaster with irritation.

He had not, as Dexter well knew. The detective wondered whether Nicola's husband was deliberately misleading them or had had a genuine slip of memory.

'And the first time the door to the viewing room was locked in some way?'

'Yeah, of course. Otherwise I'd have got in.'

'And do you think someone was inside?' interrupted Dexter, suspicious of this latest revelation.

'I don't know. I couldn't hear anyone. So I stormed off

171

down to reception. Couldn't see her there. So I went up to the bar, back to the party, and still couldn't find her.'

'And was Parkin there then?' asked Blanche.

'Oh, yeah. I ran across to him and asked him where the hell Nicola was. He looked embarrassed and said he didn't have the faintest idea. I felt like punching him but knew it was stupid to start a fight. So I stormed off again down to the office and that's when I found her. The door was unlocked then.'

Blanche sighed, stood up and wandered over to the window. 'You weren't too upset finding her dead, were you? In fact, you'd have quite liked to have done it yourself.'

'She had something coming to her all right, Superintendent. But she didn't deserve that.'

Lancaster's voice had suddenly become animated and loud as he recalled the sting of his betrayal. Dexter even wondered for a moment whether he was drunk. But the sergeant knew he was not, it was simply the effect of a quiet man suddenly giving vent to his anger.

Dexter moved his chair over the kitchen tiles causing a squeak that exploded round the kitchen. He felt it was time to ask about the stains on the clothes that Jim Lancaster had taken to the dry cleaner's.

Nicola's husband gave a nervous smile. 'Yeah, the owner said you'd been in.'

'What exactly were the stains by the way?'

Dexter saw Lancaster moisten his lips before he spoke. 'Coffee, Sergeant. Just coffee. I spilt some on the jacket.' The sergeant was sure Nicola's husband was lying and that the stains were blood but knew he had no evidence to prove it. If only that bloody dry cleaner had been as inefficient as most of them usually were.

Dexter did not see Blanche for another few hours. While she was driven over to Greenwich to interview Maggie Parkin, the superintendent sent him back to Scotland Yard to harry the forensic science laboratories over the blood-stains on the pair of scissors. They told him, however, that

172

they were short of staff and the earliest they could give a result was nine o'clock that night.

Blanche reappeared just after four, throwing off her coat and beckoning Dexter into her office in the same gesture. Her skin had become paler during the afternoon, Dexter noticed, and her energy almost feverish. She looked worried and preoccupied, her eyelids lined with red. Fatigue was creeping up on her. Blanche plugged in the electric kettle and spooned coffee into the percolator while she listened to the sergeant's account of his afternoon, swearing softly when he told her the news from the forensic labs.

'And how was Mrs Parkin?' asked Dexter, while Blanche took a packet of chocolate digestives from her filing cabinet and arrayed them on a plate. It was a typical gesture of hers, thought the sergeant, a sign of gentility, of her desire to guard her feminine standards in a male world of sloppiness.

'I think she's still hiding something,' murmured Blanche, biting into a biscuit.

'What?'

'If I'd been trained in mind-reading rather than riot control, Dexter, I'd tell you.'

The sergeant rubbed the palms of his hands up and down on the side of his chair and waited for his boss to continue.

'She was on edge, talking not so much the hind leg off a donkey as off an African elephant. And she was puffing away at those wretched cigarettes like there was no tomorrow. The smoke made me feel quite sick.' Blanche extracted two cups and saucers from her filing cabinet and Dexter made the coffee. 'I got out of her that she *did* know about Parkin's goings-on with Nicola Sharpe.'

'So it was just a front?'

'Yes. She said she did it because she knew her husband was innocent and she didn't want him implicated. Of course, it ends up making things look worse for him – as if she was trying to cover his tracks.'

Dexter leant forward and slipped two more lumps of

sugar into his coffee: Blanche was always trying to reduce his sugar intake and make his diet healthier. The sergeant wondered aloud whether Maggie Parkin did secretly believe in her husband's guilt.

'It's certainly possible. She protested his innocence a bit too loudly: she was the one who actually brought the subject up.' The superintendent narrowed her eyes, crinkling the dark flesh of the lids. 'The alternative, of course, is that she did it. Don't forget that phone-call, remember – the one to Nicola at the party. It was from a woman and we've only got two female suspects, Parkin's wife and Jane Pargeter.'

'What did she say when you asked her about it?'

'She said she didn't know anything about it.' Blanche sipped her coffee and licked a dab of chocolate from the end of her forefinger. It struck Dexter as a very sensual act, at odds with what he thought of as the female detective's self-control and cautious approach to the world. She smiled. 'Who are you betting on then?'

The sergeant sat back and rubbed his fingernails thoughtfully. He was uncertain, and could not see the point of hazarding a guess before the forensic labs had reported on the pair of scissors. But he always liked being asked for his opinion: it made him feel important and he had never understood why people needed to go on assertiveness courses. Dexter decided to make a joke of it. 'I think it could be Nicola's hubby. He's the sort of creep who'd do that kind of thing.' Blanche nodded. 'On the other hand, there's a lot of evidence against Parkin. I'm not sure about his wife either. And then I've got my – '

Blanche smiled good-naturedly. 'Thanks, Dexter. That's very useful.'

Dexter smiled back. 'I do my best to please.'

A constable appeared at the door to say that DI Eddy Russell was on the phone for the superintendent. Dexter had forgotten about the Drugs Squad and detected excitement crackle in Blanche's voice, the excitement of being a sexual quarry. He listened to Blanche's nervous laugh as she agreed a rendezvous but then saw her brow

174

wrinkle as she replaced the receiver.

'He says he's got to bring someone else along tonight, someone he's got to entertain.'

Dexter chuckled to himself. He was amused that Blanche still felt the need to maintain the pretence that her interest in the handsome detective inspector was solely professional. 'How's that going to fit in with David Parkin by the way – if the lab results are positive?'

Blanche studied her watch. 'Easy. You say the earliest we're going to get the results is nine, so let's just phone in around then. There's no point in sitting here twiddling our thumbs.'

The sergeant nodded with approval, knowing that he needed some way to dissipate his nervous energy in the coming hours. He suddenly remembered that Stephen Blufton's information about drug smuggling was due to be put to the test that day. He asked Blanche what was happening but discovered her gaze was locked on the other side of the room. He followed her eyes but found she was only staring at a door. Blanche caught his look. 'I've just had an idea, Dexter.' She stood up, her eyes shining. 'Let's pop in at TVL again. I want to walk through what Jim Lancaster told us. And also I think it's high time you and I watched a bit more television.' She hovered for a second, selecting the right words. 'By the way, I'd appreciate it if you came along tonight. I need you to act as my chaperone,' she added with a mischievous laugh.

CHAPTER
SIXTEEN

'People are coming back to work in the office downstairs from Monday, you know. Some of them even think it's haunted.' The security man swung open the door to the boardroom where the party had taken place and switched on the lights, revealing the room as Blanche and Dexter had last seen it the day after the killing. 'I was glad I was part of a different shift. It was a real shock to the boys who were on that night.' The security guard – a tall, friendly man with dishevelled, greasy hair and a distant Irish brogue – stood by expectantly. Dexter found him too talkative.

'I'm sure,' said Blanche, launching into a genteel chat with the security man about his work and colleagues. Dexter sometimes thought the superintendent took the need to be polite to the public too far. He wandered off to find Simon Franks and arrange a viewing of Nicola Sharpe's last few reports. These were the 'bit more television' Blanche wanted to watch, since she believed they would help freshen her image of the murdered woman.

When Dexter met the superintendent twenty minutes later, Blanche stood outside the *Inside Out* office still chatting to the security guard. Blanche thanked the man for his help and he loped off down the corridor, jangling his keys.

'So, did you find what you were looking for, guv'?' asked Dexter as the lift jerked into motion and hummed downwards.

Blanche yawned and leant back against the aluminium

bar that ran round the inside of the lift. 'Possibly. I'm sure Jim Lancaster isn't telling the truth about that door to the viewing room being locked.'

'Why's that?'

'Well, you need a special key and no one on the programme's officially got one. I've just checked.'

Simon Franks stood in the basement corridor and shook Blanche's hand gingerly, as if it might crumble. He made some remark about being surprised to receive Blanche's request so long after the murder and not being sure what she hoped to gain from viewing the tapes.

'We'll see,' the female detective merely shrugged in reply. To Dexter the producer seemed much more self-confident than on the morning after the murder, talkative and charming. The prickly distrust had faded to be replaced by an almost oily helpfulness.

Franks led them through some swing doors with a flourish and into another corridor, explaining that normally he would not waste money by taking them to a full editing suite. But one happened to be free for a couple of hours along with the picture editor who cut Nicola's last report. Franks said he thought the superintendent might find it interesting.

Their footsteps suddenly cracked like pistol shots as the carpet was replaced by plastic tiles. On either side were a series of editing suites, visible through small windows in the doors. In the dimness of the rooms Dexter made out blurred figures and machinery bedecked with lights, knobs and dials. It reminded the sergeant of mission control for some dark and mysterious space flight. They had to pick their way past trolleys loaded high with videotapes – some in large plastic containers, others in small plastic boxes plastered with labels. The TV producer led them to one of the last suites on the left and a young man in pullover and jeans swung round on his chair. Franks introduced him as Terry, the picture editor. On the desk in front of him were a pile of grey videotape boxes.

The superintendent picked one up. 'This is all of Nicola's work in the last few weeks of her life, is it?'

'Yeah. Everything,' replied Franks. He picked up the tapes and sifted through. 'A few reports for the local news. The *Inside Out*s we did together on homelessness and cancer cures. Even the farewell tape.'

'The farewell tape?'

Franks snorted dismissively. 'It's the thing I put together for Ken O'Mara's party — a sort of piss-take.'

'And Nicola's in it?' asked Dexter.

The producer turned to him with an apologetic smile, his voice injected with what the sergeant considered a theatrical dose of concern. 'Yeah. In a rather bad taste way, I'm afraid. We were due to show it at the end of the party and of course . . . well, you know what happened. No one ever got to see it complete, except me and Terry of course.' Terry nodded and looked away to one of the machines, twiddling the knobs to hide his nervousness.

Blanche did not linger long over the local news reports. One was about a new initiative to help people dying of AIDS; another about the closure of a London theatre; a third about a motorway pile-up on the M25. Dexter noticed that each report ended with Nicola addressing the camera, even in the third one, where it was unnecessary and intrusive. Terry smiled. 'She did a piece to camera on every single thing she did. She was quite a girl, Nicola. But my God, she could be a pain in the arse sometimes as well, you know.'

Franks flashed him a look of irritation, as if it was disloyal of the picture editor to criticise Nicola now that she was dead, indeed criticise her at all. That, the producer seemed to be signalling, is my job. You are a mere picture editor, a workman, whose views on editorial staff are of no account. Dexter wondered what Terry would say about Simon Franks behind his back.

Terry ignored the glance and pressed the homelessness film into the slot of one of the machines. The tape laced up and showed a figure five on a TV screen.

'This didn't get shown either,' commented Franks. 'It got pulled because of the murder. The management want me to put another voice on it so the rushes don't go to waste. But I've refused. As a mark of respect.' In the half-light of the editing suite his face appeared more than ever like a mask, the nose attenuated, the skin smooth and polished.

Terry leant forward and languidly pressed the 'play' button. He then disappeared to buy a round of teas from the canteen. Dexter liked the picture editor and felt at ease with him. With his gruff, Cockney drawl and lack of pretentiousness, he was the first person he had met on the production side of TV London who was not part of the middle-class mafia, and who seemed relaxed and at ease with himself. Mind you, Dexter thought, Terry was probably playing a role as much as anybody else.

He found the film boring: tramps sleeping rough on pavements, women with grimy children in bed and breakfast hotels, men in suits pontificating. Lots of talk about the Problem. Just the sort of thing he avoided on his television at home. The only interesting thing about the film was the revelation that in one London borough some local councillors owned several of the bed and breakfast hotels where conditions were particularly dreadful. Blanche watched without expression, sipping at her cup of tea, except when Nicola appeared in one of her numerous pieces to camera. Then she leant back and narrowed her eyes with concentration. When the report was finished, Blanche made an appreciative comment.

Franks smiled – obviously pleased by Blanche's approval, Dexter believed, although trying not to show it. 'It's so hard to capture poverty on video, you know, Superintendent. Some of the places we went to were absolute tips – paper peeling off the walls, damp patches on the ceilings – and video just glosses over it all.'

'I'm sure,' said Blanche. 'And was this film important to her in any particular way?'

'She was proud of that piece to camera at the end,' murmured Terry, in his flat London accent.

Simon Franks' smile was tight with irritation. 'I wanted to cut it out at one stage in the editing but Nicola went

179

mad. She said it was the best one she'd ever done. She said she'd put it on her show-reel.'

Dexter recalled that halfway through the homelessness report Nicola had delivered a short lecture about the appalling conditions in which one family lived while managing to look stunning at the same time. It *was* quite a performance, Dexter had to admit, and Nicola was a beautiful woman.

Simon Franks picked up another grey box containing the film for Ken O'Mara's farewell party. He handed it to Terry with a show of false reluctance, preceding it with a string of apologies. For Christ's sake, just cut the crap and show it, thought the sergeant with a sigh.

The film only lasted for about ten minutes and began with a satire of Ken O'Mara's eating habits. Dexter registered the narrator's voice immediately. It was David Parkin, whose gravelly tones gave the report an air of spurious authenticity. O'Mara's wife was shown meekly pushing a trolley along the aisles of the local Sainsbury supermarket, stuffing it with packets of biscuits. At home she unloaded and stacked them in the basement. The film then cut to plates of biscuits on every conceivable ledge in every room of the house. Parkin interviewed a giggly Mrs O'Mara who said her husband ate tons of biscuits every week but added that, now Ken was to leave TV London, she would have her revenge. The camera panned away from her to rest on a gleaming exercise bicycle.

David Parkin was next shown outside a pub in Pimlico, where he delivered a piece to camera with mock gravity about Ken O'Mara's commitment to investigative journalism and to recruiting more female reporters. 'This is Nicola's bit,' hissed Franks.

Nicola was shown on a bar stool in a black skirt that barely hid her crutch. The word 'RECONSTRUCTION' flashed up on the screen. 'And now at last we can reveal Ken O'Mara's recruitment techniques,' intoned Parkin's commentary.

'Hello, my dear,' said a male Irish voice off camera, imitating O'Mara. 'How would you like to be in TV?'

Nicola turned from the bar, eyelashes fluttering, lips pouting. 'Oh, I'd be thrilled,' she said, standing up. 'Is there an interview?'

'Don't worry,' continued the Irish voice, 'it's easy. It's just to get the *feel* of your personality. It's the *shape* of your body – sorry, mind – that matters.' The film cut to a close-up of what was supposed to be O'Mara's hand pinching Nicola's bottom.

The next shot was of Nicola hunched over a table in a darkened room. Her right hand was scribbling in a note-book whose page was headed 'Drugs Investigation'. Dexter saw Blanche lean forward in the dimness, her eyes alert. Parkin's commentary talked of Ken O'Mara's insistence that all new reporters had direct experience of the stories they were investigating. At that moment the camera tracked to the left and zoomed in to reveal that Nicola had a tube of paper up her left nostril and was pretending to sniff cocaine from the table top. Just like Nicola's note to Parkin, Dexter remembered, with the threat to expose him. He turned to meet Blanche's steady gaze, wondering whether the murdered woman wished to transmit a message through the scene.

The humour was heavy-handed and, in response to Simon Franks' nervous laugh, Blanche smiled politely.

Nicola appeared next knocking on Ken O'Mara's door. An Irish voice told her to come in and the rest of the scene was filmed from the point of view of O'Mara's chair. Parkin's commentary said that another notable feature of Ken O'Mara's time as editor was his commitment to running controversial films – whoever they might embarrass. Nicola approached the desk. 'That drugs story you asked me to investigate, Ken, has turned out amazingly.'

'Really? Come a bit closer, my dear,' crooned the mock O'Mara voice.

Nicola tottered round the table on her high heels and slid her buttocks on to the table. 'You've got to run it, Ken. I've got all the interviews in the can and some fantastic sequences.'

'What's the story?'

Nicola leant forward. 'Ken, I've discovered the whole bloody Cabinet – the people who run Britain – are drug smugglers. They're in a secret conspiracy with the Colombian cocaine barons and the Mafia to flood this country with cocaine.'

Melodramatic music flared on the soundtrack to accompany close-ups of a mouth – supposed to be O'Mara's – sagging open, and of Nicola's look of tough determination.

'Great story,' gasped the O'Mara voice finally. 'But I'll think I'll just need to talk it over with a few people before we run it though.'

'But, Ken, it's cut. It's ready to run. You've got to go with it tonight,' Nicola pleaded.

'Don't worry, I'll have a look at it straight away. Have you got the tape?' Nicola handed it across. 'That's wonderful.'

'Great, I'll just go and tell everybody,' gasped Nicola, full of breathy enthusiasm, running towards the door. Suddenly she halted. 'You *will* be showing the drugs film, won't you?'

'Of course.'

After the door closed, a pudgy hand picked up the videotape gingerly as if it were a dead bird and, pausing for a moment so that the viewer could read 'GOVERNMENT DRUGS SCANDAL', dropped it into a wastepaper bin. His hand reached into a drawer and took out another videotape box marked 'HAVE THE ROYALS GOT A FUTURE?'

Everyone in the editing suite sat in silence, their faces softened by the gentle light. Terry tapped his fingernails on the table.

'I'm glad to see the art of satire isn't dead,' commented Blanche.

Franks leant forward, resting his hands on his thighs. 'Ken's got a good sense of humour. He'd have known no offence was meant.'

Dexter saw Blanche was not listening to him. 'Who suggested the drugs idea by the way? Was it Nicola?'

'Yeah. She'd been looking into it for Ken anyway – as I

told you. And it seemed a good laugh. She came up with the wonderfully whacky idea of the Cabinet all being drug smugglers.'

'It's probably true,' said Blanche with a chuckle. The superintendent gazed at the blank TV screen before suddenly turning to Franks, her eyes drained of laughter. 'Do you think there was any link at all between her research and the video?'

'What – the Cabinet being drug smugglers?' The producer paused for a moment to make sure he had heard correctly and then burst out laughing, flicking a nervous glance at Terry.

Blanche smiled and said she did not mean that, but the reference to Colombian cocaine barons and the mafia.

The producer shrugged, adding that he knew no more than what he had told Blanche before. 'I think you've been reading too many thrillers, Superintendent.'

Blanche's strong features softened into a grin in the dim light.

Dexter was still mulling over the scene in which Nicola pretended she was taking drugs. 'Did Nicola actually sniff coke?' He deliberately posed the question in an open way.

The producer groaned dismissively. 'No, of course not. It was just a joke. I think you've got the wrong idea about the people who work in TV, Sergeant. There's the odd junkie or alcoholic but they're the exception rather than the rule.' Terry nodded agreement.

Dexter glanced at his watch and was surprised to see it was almost seven o'clock. Time no longer had the same meaning down in the basement of the TV company, windowless and illuminated only by artificial light. For a moment, the sergeant had that same sense of disorientation when the lights went up at the end of an afternoon programme in the cinema and he felt he had just flown back from another world.

The superintendent eased herself up with a sigh. 'It's strange to think that pile of tapes is all that's left of Nicola's life, isn't it?'

'It's more than most people have,' bridled the producer.

'I suppose you're right,' Blanche shrugged. 'I'm afraid I think of TV as a bit like a McDonald's hamburger – easily digested and soon forgotten.'

'I love them myself – hamburgers. Can't get enough of them,' interrupted Dexter with a broad smile, anxious to push the superintendent off her soapbox before she started to sound off about the worthlessness of most television. If only, he thought sometimes, Blanche would not worry so much about wasting time and let the minutes trickle like sand through her fingers.

Even the glasses on top of the cigarette vending machine quivered in time to the music. The raucous beat of Rod Stewart thumped through the whole pub – jogging the fag ends on the worn-out carpet, stomping over the heavy brown paintwork, beating the dust from the velvet curtains draped across the windows and setting Dexter's toes tapping. Three large bronzed fans whirred above in the smoky air. A few lonely men nursing a half-empty glass patted the floor in time to the music. Most of the young, rather shabbily dressed people in the pub shouted over it or craned their heads closer to hear. For them the din increased rather than destroyed the intimacy of conversation.

With a smile Dexter noticed Blanche wince as soon as the swing door closed behind her. He knew the youthfulness of the clientèle – hardly any could have been above thirty – and the loud music would make her uncomfortable. 'I suddenly feel old, Dexter,' she shouted, paddling through the crowd towards Eddy Russell, who sat by himself on a huge mahogany settle on the right of the door.

The warmth of the detective inspector's greeting cooled when he caught sight of Dexter behind Blanche's shoulder. It was what Dexter had feared: two was company and three very much a crowd. He stiffened and wondered how he might escape. Blanche caught his look and explained smoothly to the inspector that since Eddy said he was going to bring along a guest so would she. DI Russell was too amicable to take offence and, after ten minutes' conversation and a drink, the three slipped into the easy amity of fellow professionals, exchanging grumbles and gossip.

'I'm afraid I've got a confession to make,' said Eddy Russell finally, taking a swig from his pint of bitter and wiping the foam from his upper lip. He turned to Blanche, who sat beside him on the settle, his face grave. Dexter leant forward across the table to hear better what was about to be said. Eddy smiled submissively, the smile of the good companion, the smile of one who wishes to be liked. His face was flat and wide, clean, the skin marked only by a few freckles on the right cheek, the eyes set far apart and shallow in their sockets. A handsome face, Dexter thought once again, admiring the aggressive, stubby nose. 'I told Nicola Sharpe more than I should have done.'

'What in particular?' asked Blanche.

'About the Mafia.'

The superintendent's forehead crinkled. 'The Sicilian Mafia?'

Russell nodded and sipped some more beer. 'I told her we'd had a tip-off. They're meant to be operating in Britain again, smuggling drugs.'

Dexter whistled under his breath. Nicola had told Stephen Blufton the truth after all. No wonder she thought Jane Pargeter's job was in the bag. He asked how much the Drugs Squad knew about them.

Russell swung his grey eyes across to Dexter. He looked puzzled. 'Well, that's the point. We and customs didn't know much at all till you phoned last night with the stories about the lorries and the baggage handlers at Gatwick.'

'So that information didn't come from you?' Blanche interrupted.

Eddy shook his head. 'Not from me.' He stared out at the people in the pub, plunged in thought.

'So are customs taking our tip-off seriously then?' Dexter shouted above the din.

'Oh, yeah. Don't worry. They've been going through all the lorries that've come into Dover today with some sort of connection with the Balkans. It must be like looking for a needle in a haystack – assuming there's a bloody needle there.'

Dexter tapped his feet in time to the music and eyed a handsome youth leaning by himself against the bar. The sergeant admired the man's chiselled chin and ebony black hair glistening with gel. He was pondering how to chat him up without attracting too much attention from Blanche and Eddy, when he heard the superintendent ask the man from the Drugs Squad who exactly had given them the tip-off in the first place.

'It was the Italian police. They told us a few months ago. But they were vague. They just said the Mafia were back in Britain again – running drugs, money-laundering. You name it. That's free trade in Europe for you.'

Blanche's eyes had focused on a group of American youths at the bar sporting baseball caps. Suddenly she turned to the inspector, sipping her whisky. 'So why did you tell all this to Nicola?'

The detective sipped his beer. 'Because I was bloody stupid.'

'You were threatening the whole of your investigation, weren't you?'

A flush of colour shot through the inspector's pale face. 'I thought this was meant to be a friendly chat not a bloody interrogation.'

Blanche ran her tongue over her lips. She spoke in a hoarse whisper. 'I'm sorry, Eddy. But don't forget, Nicola was murdered. I have to know *all* the facts that might be relevant, not just some of them.'

The inspector heaved a great sigh. He glanced from Blanche to Dexter and back again. He had the hopeless look of a cornered animal to the sergeant. 'My marriage is on the fucking rocks, if you really want to know. I was lonely. Nicola seemed to fancy me and I fancied her. So, I told her more than I should have done.' He wrenched the words out painfully, like rotten teeth. 'I was infatuated with her. She kept tagging me along, and bit by bit she wheedled the story out of me.'

The superintendent tightened her lips. 'In bed?'

186

'No. It never got that far. Believe me, Blanche, it never got that far.' He pleaded with his eyes and sighed again, running a hand through his hair.

The female detective sat back and glanced round the bar to see if anyone was taking any notice of them. No one was. There was too much noise, too much animation. 'What about Blufton?'

'What do you mean?'

'Blufton gave us some important details you didn't know,' Blanche continued. 'The dates of the lorries and this name Della Torre for a start. Now, assuming they're true, Blufton is hardly going to shop a drug smuggling ring he's in on, so it's safe to assume Nicola had another source of information. One we haven't found yet,' she said, smiling at Eddy.

Dexter nodded. What she said made sense. Trust Blanche to be thinking so far ahead. And an idea flipped up in his mind. 'Perhaps it was this bloke Kennedy she was supposed to be meeting. Perhaps he existed after all.'

Before Blanche could respond, Eddy Russell glanced at his watch and jumped up. 'Talking of Blufton,' interrupted Eddy, with a sly smile, 'we better be on our way. This guy we're meeting tonight has some interesting things to say about him.'

187

CHAPTER
SEVENTEEN

The hotel was a drab, modern affair just off Gloucester Road: six storeys of brick and concrete, its façade studded with double-glazed windows. At the reception Eddy Russell asked for Mr Casamento. A girl with an air of exaggerated efficiency phoned up to one of the rooms.

'Casamento is Scaglione's side-kick, a sergeant. But it's Scaglione I really want you to meet,' the inspector said.

'And who's Scaglione?' asked Dexter, faintly irritated by Eddy's conspiratorial air.

Eddy Russell sucked in his breath and raised his eyebrows. 'Commissioner Scaglione is number two in Palermo's Flying Squad. He's the man who's got the nasty job of watching the Mafia.'

The lift doors slid open and two men appeared. One was short and neat, with beautifully groomed black hair, a moustache and great, drooping eyes. Dexter noted approvingly the mixture of quality and style in his wardrobe: a cashmere jacket, bold tie of blue and yellow silk and a Burberry neatly folded over his arm. There was no doubt in the sergeant's mind that this had to be Scaglione. His companion was taller and fatter with an air of unkemptness: tie crooked, raincoat crumpled and a dusting of dandruff over his shoulders. Scaglione hardly smiled when he greeted them, extending a quick, dry handshake that was over before it had begun. A cautious and intelligent man, thought Dexter, on first impression. Casamento, on the other hand, pumped each of their hands for several seconds in his warm, damp grasp.

When Eddy asked them where they wished to eat, Scaglione shrugged his shoulders. The reply, translated by Sergeant Casamento into American-accented English, was terse: 'It don't matter to the chief. Provided it's Italian.'

It was a chill night despite the puffs of cloud smeared on the sky. As they walked back towards Gloucester Road the streetlights cast their shadows long on the pavement. Scaglione looked about watchfully, his eyes flickering ahead like searchlights, eyeing a group of American students, a whooping drunkard and a telephone booth plastered with stickers advertising 'Sadie Queen of Correction' with the same impassive air. They were in the heart of London's tourist land, the young foreign visitors – whether Japanese, Spanish or American – all dressed in the international uniform of jeans, anorak and mocassin shoes. Although the scene around them appeared innocent, in the presence of Scaglione Dexter sensed a brooding menace. He knew how easily fear transmits itself from human being to human being and told himself to stop imagining things. Even in the restaurant, Scaglione's melancholy eyes roved about for a few seconds as if expecting an ambush. He only relaxed when he slipped off his raincoat and took a first luxurious pull on his cigarette.

He sat self-contained and apart, like an aristocrat obliged to share his table with commoners. By the light from the rustic metal chandeliers above, Dexter noticed the sallow brown bags beneath Scaglione's eyes and the delicately chiselled face. An aura of expensive *eau de toilette* hung about him. The commissioner in turn examined Dexter critically, with just a glint of disdain in those magnificent eyes.

The commissioner murmured something in Italian and looked at Blanche. His assistant translated it as how pleasant a surprise it was to discover that the superintendent they were to dine with that evening was a woman.

Blanche smiled and said she imagined it was indeed a surprise, because there were probably even fewer women of high rank in the Italian police force than in Britain.

189

Good on you, Blanche, reflected Dexter. Give as good as you get.

'Naturally,' replied Scaglione smoothly. 'And especially in Sicily. Most of the women officers there are used for handing out parking tickets.' He spoke calmly, without passing judgment. Dexter saw that Blanche was staring at the commissioner with a look of frustration: she was finding it impossible to penetrate the commissioner's inscrutability.

Food was ordered and they talked inconsequentially until the commissioner had finished picking at his pasta. Dexter discovered that Casamento was obsessed by soccer so the two sergeants exchanged anecdotes about the last World Cup.

Blanche wiped her mouth with her napkin and asked Scaglione why he was in London. Dexter noticed that she pronounced his name with an accent that sounded genuine. He experienced that twinge of irritation that many of the English feel when one of their number makes the effort to speak a foreign language properly. He knew Blanche was not intending to show off but it sounded like it.

'Business,' replied the commissioner through his assistant. 'I was invited to London to pass on some new information about the Mafia to your drugs intelligence and organised crime people.'

Dexter frowned. He did not know much about the Mafia apart from what he had gleaned from watching *The Godfather* twice on video. He knew the Mafia made its money from protection rackets and drugs, and had an image of sweaty men in New York restaurants fingering suggestive bulges in their jackets. He was also aware of another branch of the Mafia operating down in Sicily.

Rather than ask Scaglione to repeat everything he had already told Eddy, the inspector explained what had been learnt from Palermo's Squadra Mobile or Flying Squad. A few months before, a high-level *mafioso* from just outside Palermo had fallen foul of other Mafia leaders. His wife and three children had been murdered and the man, under police protection in Rome, had given a full confession to investigating magistrates. One of his most devastating revelations was confirmation that the Sicilian Mafia was prospering, like some phoenix that had risen from the pyre of the so-called Maxi-trial when hundreds of Mafia gangsters were jailed in Palermo in the late 1980s. In particular, the Mafia was profiting from the international drugs trade as much as ever. Informal pacts had been struck with Colombian cocaine barons and the shady men who controlled organised crime in Turkey.

The reason Scaglione was in London was that the *mafioso* told the investigating magistrate in Rome that some of the heroin was ending up in Britain, where the Mafia had re-established itself. The previous boss in Britain, Francesco Di Carlo, had been jailed in 1987 and the Metropolitan Police had assumed that the Mafia network had been broken. But a new man had been sent to London from Sicily to control the Mafia's financial interests in the United Kingdom. Until Blanche had passed on the name of Della Torre he had not been identified.

Casamento interjected frequently during Eddy's narrative. Scaglione puffed at a series of cigarettes and gazed round the restaurant, seemingly intrigued by the bizarre interior: a mansard roof of red plastic tiles set high up on the walls, while above the diners' heads artificial vines curled their way around plastic beams.

'And you told all this to Nicola?' Dexter overheard Blanche whisper to Eddy Russell.

The inspector nodded sheepishly.

The sergeant suddenly experienced a feeling of unreality. Perhaps it was the wine – a slightly vinegary Valpolicella. Or fatigue. After all he was short of sleep. Or perhaps it was the gnawing fear that he and Blanche had got it all wrong and the Sicilian Mafia was behind Nicola's murder. He just did not know any more.

Scaglione murmured something to his sergeant, who translated. 'The commissioner says the food is terrible at this restaurant. He says Superintendent Hampton should visit him in Palermo and he will be delighted to show her

191

what real Sicilian food is.' The commissioner smiled for the first time that evening.

'Tell Signore Scaglione that I thought he was a married man,' replied Blanche.

Casamento translated. And back came the reply, thick with the sergeant's American accent. 'He says he thinks you're probably married too. But that just gives you an even better reason to come out alone to Palermo to try the food.' Blanche laughed politely, rather enjoying the flirtation despite herself, Dexter believed. Scaglione spoke again, this time looking at Blanche intently. 'Superintendent, the commissioner wants to know why you are here tonight – why are you so interested in what he has to say?'

'Tell him I'm investigating a murder. A woman TV reporter learnt more about this Mafia drugs-running operation than she should have done. It may have something to do with the fact she got killed.'

Scaglione shrugged. 'The chief says he don't think it's very likely.'

'Why?'

'It's not the way their criminal – how do you say?' Casamento broke off to grasp the air for the right word. 'Their mentality works. They threaten journalists rather than kill them.'

'*Sfortunatamente*,' grunted Scaglione, chuckling and lighting another cigarette.

'Unfortunately, he says.'

Blanche leant forward and asked Casamento to find out from the commissioner if he knew anything about a man called Leonardo Della Torre.

Scaglione leant his elbows on the table and gestured outwards with his hands. '*Naturalmente*.' He sucked on his cigarette and then twisted the gold ring on his left hand round and round.

'Yeah, the chief says he's heard of the guy. Della Torre comes from a little town between Palermo and Corleone. We never managed to pin much on the guy but we do know he's an expert mover of junk.'

'Heroin to us,' clarified Eddy Russell. 'Is that all you

192

know about him?'

Scaglione's eyes flashed as the waitress arrived with the main courses. He said nothing more until she had finished serving and moved away. 'We know he spent some time in England in the early eighties. Apparently he knew Liborio Cuntrera and the Caruana brothers.'

'Who the hell are they?' asked Blanche, eyeing her veal hungrily.

'These were the big guys who worked with Francesco Di Carlo. And the chief says when Di Carlo got picked up, Della Torre must have thought it was getting too hot, so he came back to Sicily.'

Blanche rubbed her chin thoughtfully, her eyes moving from Eddy Russell to Scaglione. 'And what does the commissioner know about a man called Stephen Blufton?'

Casamento turned with a look of puzzlement to the inspector. 'We told you what we knew about him a couple of months ago, Eddy.'

The inspector explained it would be better if the commissioner gave what information he had directly to Blanche.

Scaglione shrugged in a gesture of conciliation and sipped at his glass of wine. '*Va bene.*' He explained that Blufton's name had cropped up during the confession of the *mafioso* in Rome. It seemed that back in the seventies, Blufton was implicated in Mafia money-laundering operations. One used Blufton's antiques businesses, another his pizza restaurants. In others Blufton had helped set up import-export companies which acted as fronts to launder the profits of drug smuggling. One also defrauded the Italian government of subsidies for Sicily's citrus fruit farmers. Worldwide, said Casamento, with an expansive gesture of his hands, this scam alone netted the Mafia three hundred and fifty million dollars.

Dexter whistled. 'I never thought oranges and lemons would make you rich.'

'You can if you get paid for ones that don't exist,' chuckled Eddy Russell. 'That was the whole point of the fraud. Blufton's front companies ordered the fruit from

Sicily, the bills arrived from Palermo but the fruit didn't. Clever, eh?' commented Eddy Russell.

With each revelation, Dexter sat further back in his seat, thinking through the implications of what Casamento and the inspector were saying. Blufton was a criminal. It was as simple as that, a fraudster and a money-launderer, if not a smuggler of drugs himself. He was such a smooth bastard and he had taken them in. Dexter had fallen for it hook, line and sinker. What was equally annoying was that DI Russell had not told Blanche and Dexter what he had known earlier. After all, they could have worked out that Nicola had another source of information apart from the inspector and that the dead woman had stumbled on information that might have put her at risk. He glared resentfully across at the inspector, hoping to God that Blanche was never silly enough to go to bed with him and, if she was, that Russell suffered from brewer's droop.

'What was even cleverer was that Blufton seems to have got away with it,' commented Dexter snidely.

The inspector smiled at the implied criticism. 'Don't worry, we checked him out. He's as clean as a whistle now. And there's nowhere near enough evidence to nick him for something he did years ago.'

Dexter was lolling back on his chair so that it balanced on its rear legs. Suddenly, he had a flash of inspiration and all was clear. He threw his weight forward and his chair landed square on the carpet tiles with a dull plop. His words poured out in a torrent. 'Don't you see, ma'am. It must have been Blufton that did it. It's suddenly come to me.' Blanche stared back at him impassively. 'Blufton must have a handle on this new Mafia heroin thing. He finds out Nicola's getting too close for comfort so he has her bumped off. It's obvious.' He sat on the front of his seat, palms spread in a gesture inviting Blanche's support.

Blanche shrugged her shoulders, tugged at her skirt and sat back. 'Contract killers don't murder people in offices using pairs of scissors. And, if Blufton *were* involved, he wouldn't bust one of his own operations, would he?'

194

Dexter held his mouth open for a moment to reply but changed his mind. Blanche was right. It did not make sense. He sighed. Back to the drawing board and their cast of suspects.

'That reminds me,' said the inspector. 'I've got an arrangement with customs to call them in Dover tonight to see if they've had any luck. I'll just give them a ring.' He wandered over to the public phone screwed to the wall at the back of the restaurant. He returned a few minutes later to say they had found nothing so far.

Scaglione asked what was going on and Eddy Russell explained without going into details. The commissioner tautened his cheek muscles as if he suddenly detected bitterness on his tongue and growled something to his sergeant. 'The chief says be careful. The Sicilian Mafia don't have the same worries about killing cops as their American cousins do.' Scaglione murmured something else, his eyes glittering. 'The commissioner's friend got blown up by the Mafia in his car only a year ago. His intestines got found a hundred yards away and one of his feet ended up in the front yard of a villa nearby.'

All four grew quiet, contemplating the horror of such a death. The commissioner skimmed the froth on the top of his *cappuccino* with a spoon and mumbled something under his breath. 'He says they're just a bunch of murdering mother-fuckers,' translated Casamento. 'The chief's seen men strangled, shot, mutilated – you know, with their, how do you say? balls? – stuffed in their mouths. He says there's nothing glamorous about the Mafia.'

Dexter glanced at his watch, feeling faintly queasy, a flutter of fear in his stomach. He thought there was probably a side of Scaglione that dined off the very violence he was meant to be controlling. It was two minutes to nine. His turn for a phone-call. He nodded to Blanche and wandered over to the pay phone in the corner.

'We think we've got him, Sarge,' burst out the voice of the young DC who answered first, unable to contain his excitement. 'We've just got a positive result back on the scissors. And Fingerprints say they *can* match the partials

195

against David Parkin.'

Dexter flexed his fists with joy and relief. About bloody time, he thought.

David Parkin looked up through narrowed eyes when Blanche and Dexter walked into the interview room. He had taken off his raincoat and jacket and hung them over the back of a chair in the corner. Then he had rolled up the sleeves of his shirt to just below the elbows. It gave him the air of someone who was about to grapple with some serious intellectual work. He stood up and rested his hands on his hips, confident and defiant, his skin glowing leathery brown under the fluorescent lights. 'Could you tell me what this is all about, please, Superintendent?' His bass voice quavered with irritation. 'I was sitting at home having a quiet supper with some friends when a couple of police officers knock on the front door and ask me to go with them to the station. I refuse and so they arrest me for Nicola's murder. This is bloody ridiculous.' Dexter noticed for the first time how bristly Parkin's eyebrows were: it was strange how you could never take everything in about a person at the first meeting.

Parkin's 'brief' stood up at the same time as his client, looking embarrassed by the outburst. Dexter guessed the solicitor was about forty, with a thin, whittled-down face and expensive brown spectacles.

Blanche introduced herself to the solicitor in her emollient way and said she wished to ask his client some questions.

'OK then,' snapped Parkin. 'I can't imagine why it can't wait until tomorrow. But since I'm here, for God's sake get on with it.' He sat down and crossed his legs. He was dressed casually, in grey trousers and a cream Viyella shirt crossed with lines of green.

Dexter settled himself in a chair and switched on the tape-recorder at the side of the desk, intoning the names of the people in the room and the date and time. It was almost eleven o'clock and the sergeant made a quick calculation about how long they had before Parkin had to be charged: twenty-four hours in the first instance, with a twelve-hour extension if needed. If Blanche wanted to hold Parkin longer they would have to go before a magistrate for a three-day lay-down. The sergeant hoped Parkin would crack well before then.

He glanced across at Blanche and wondered whether she would begin the interview in a roundabout way or confront him with the pair of scissors immediately. The sergeant always preferred the direct approach, and a twinge of disappointment plucked at his throat when he heard Blanche pose the first question with all the restrained politeness of a guest at a Buckingham Palace garden party.

'Mr Parkin, you work in two offices at TV London, don't you?'

His lips tightened with suspicion. 'Yes, that's right.'

'One is the *Inside Out* office and the other one is for a documentary you're working on, is that right?'

Parkin sighed. 'Yes. One is on the fourth floor and the other on the second.'

'And how do you divide your time between the two offices?'

'It varies. I probably split my time between the two about fifty-fifty.' The television reporter sat back on his chair and stretched out his legs. The way David Parkin stared unflinchingly at Blanche underlined his self-confidence, Dexter considered. The sergeant reviewed his memories of Parkin on the television screen. Over the years he remembered watching him interview dictators and presidents, stand by bloated corpses rotting under the African sun, explain the terror of young soldiers in the deserts of Iraq, and be beaten up and left for dead in some dreary South American country whose name he had forgotten. The sergeant was sure that one thing Parkin had learnt over the years was how to recognise danger. And he was certain he had scented it then, in the seemingly sleepy eyes of the superintendent. 'I hope you're going to ask more interesting questions than these, Superintendent. The answers I've given you so far hardly seem worth arresting me for.'

'If you'd just bear with me, Mr Parkin.' Blanche smiled. 'Is your office on the second floor locked most of the time?'

'No, it's open during the day from Monday to Friday. Anyone can wander in and out. But it's locked most evenings though and at weekends – unless someone is working. I haven't been in there at all this week.' He gave a lopsided smile. 'Why are you so interested in my office arrangements all of a sudden?'

Blanche reached down and slid the plastic bag containing the pair of scissors across the table. 'Do you recognise these scissors?'

The solicitor pulled his chair forward. A nerve twitched on Parkin's forehead as his eyes slid from the superintendent's face down to the scissors. Dexter registered no other sign of recognition. One of his small, elegant hands reached out instinctively towards the packet. The sergeant's concentration was so intense he took in every single grey hair on the top of his knuckles. But the hand froze a foot away from the bag. Parkin glanced up, his eyebrows cocked in an unspoken question.

'Go ahead,' said Blanche.

To Dexter's eye, Parkin made it appear that his curiosity had triumphed over his irritation. He turned the package over on the tips of his fingers as if it were a rare miniature. 'They look like a normal pair of scissors to me – just like the ones we have at . . . ' He looked up at Blanche and flicked his tongue across his lips. His eyebrows bristled with distrust.

'Have at where, Mr Parkin?'

He seemed to regain his composure. 'I was going to say have at work.'

'So do you recognise this pair of scissors or not, Mr Parkin?'

'Not this pair in particular, no.'

'But you said they reminded you of ones at work.'

Parkin studied Blanche, his eyes sliding from side to side. Dexter saw his right hand shaking on the side of the table. He was nervous, preparing for an ambush. 'Yes . . . They do. They look like . . . the ones that everyone uses at the office. So what?'

The superintendent took a handkerchief from her handbag and blew her nose. Throughout, though, Dexter noticed that Blanche's brown eyes hovered on Parkin's leathery face, smooth like a lizard's. 'This pair of scissors was found yesterday in your desk on the second floor.'

'Have you been searching in my desk?' he snapped.

Blanche shrugged. 'The management gave us permission to search wherever we liked, Mr Parkin. We are investigating a murder.'

Yes, he looked like a lizard, Dexter decided – his tongue flickering over his lips, his head flickering from side to side – a lizard discovering it has been trapped. If the police had searched his desk then they would have discovered the letter from Nicola. The sergeant was sure Parkin's mind was whirring ahead in a panic.

All Parkin could murmur was, 'So what?'

'Well, do you recognise the scissors as yours?' Blanche's voice was calm and cool. There was no trace of hostility in her voice.

Parkin glanced down at the scissors and then at his solicitor. 'No. They could be anyone's as far as I'm concerned. I keep a pair of scissors in my desk but I've no idea if these are the same ones.' His voice sounded more confident, as if he were making an effort to regain his composure.

'So, you're not denying that these scissors could have been used by you?'

'No.'

Blanche breathed out with relief, as though she had surmounted an important hurdle. 'These scissors *were* found in your desk yesterday, Mr Parkin. Have you any explanation as to how they got there?'

'Well, presumably I put them there when I last used them.'

'And when was that?'

He pinched his lips – whether through concentration or

worry Dexter found it impossible to say. 'God knows. Could have been a week ago, two months ago. I've no idea.'

'And what would you have used them for?'

'Look, what the hell are you driving at?' flared the TV reporter suddenly. Dexter wondered if the outburst was not a trifle too theatrical: the cry of a guilty man pretending innocence. 'If these scissors have something to do with Nicola's murder, why don't you just tell me?'

Blanche's face was expressionless. If Parkin was a lizard, the sergeant thought, then his boss reminded him of an owl, wide-eyed, waiting and watching. She continued, as though deaf to what Parkin had just said. 'These scissors have traces of Nicola Sharpe's blood on them. Have you any idea of how it got there?'

Parkin snorted indignantly. But behind the anger Dexter smelt fear. "Course not. I've got no idea at all.'

Blanche paused. 'The pair of scissors also has your fingerprints on. Do you have any explanation?'

The reporter turned to his solicitor, grasping for words. 'I've got no idea . . . It's got nothing . . . Look, for all I know, these scissors could have come from my desk but I've no idea how the blood got there. It's got nothing to do with me.'

Blanche reached into her case and drew out the note from Nicola. Dexter watched the television reporter's eyes flicker as he confirmed his worst fears. Parkin had always looked youthful and energetic to Dexter but now, suddenly, he seemed to age. His shoulders sagged, the wrinkles on his face deepened and his vitality drained away. The old defiance and arrogance had disappeared. He did not seem to care any more. He took the letter and read it through, hollow-eyed. He confirmed that he recognised the note in a low grumble.

Blanche pulled herself up in her chair and squared her shoulders. 'Nicola Sharpe was threatening to ruin your career unless you agreed to continue the affair with her. It's all there in the letter. I put it to you that you panicked – pulled between your wife and child on the one hand and

200

Nicola on the other. And that it was you who murdered Nicola Sharpe.'

Dexter tried to conceal a smile. It was the same smile he wore at the end of a Hollywood film when star-crossed lovers are finally reunited or evil is overcome. He always felt tense when someone he thought guilty was confronted. He knew the murder squad would be tense as well, waiting, sipping coffee, exchanging speculation, eager for any news from the interview room. A confession would be so much easier. There would be a whoop of victory from the murder squad. Parkin would be sent down to the cells and he and Blanche could retire to bed for the first proper night's sleep in three days. If only Parkin would crack.

All the reporter did was shake his head, looking desperately from Blanche to his lawyer and back again. The spool of the tape recorder continued to turn remorselessly. 'It wasn't me. I didn't kill her. I didn't even know Nicola had left the party.'

'I put it to you, Mr Parkin, that you'd agreed with Nicola to pretend she was meeting a man called Kennedy at nine o'clock. It was just an excuse for Nicola to leave. You met her down in the *Inside Out* office and you had a row.' Parkin's mouth flopped wide open with amazement. 'In the heat of the moment you grabbed the first weapon that came to hand – a pair of scissors in the viewing room. And you stabbed her to death. Isn't that what really happened?'

The silence was so profound that Dexter noticed for the first time the faint hum from the tape-recorder. He could not tell the reason, whether it was being confronted by the truth or the necessity to combat it, but a defiant glint sparked again in Parkin's eyes. 'No. That's complete rubbish. Nicola was certainly trying to . . .' He halted when he caught the warning look in his solicitor's eye. 'She was certainly putting pressure on me to keep the affair going but I wouldn't have dreamed of . . . killing her.' He slumped back in his chair. 'I'll say one last thing before I shut up. Those scissors were planted on me. I don't know by who, but they were planted on me.'

201

*   *   *

David Parkin refused to answer any more questions that night. He sat in the interview room, protesting his innocence while his solicitor struggled to remain awake. In the end, Blanche gave up with a sigh and ordered that Parkin be sent to the cells. It was almost two o'clock in the morning.

CHAPTER
EIGHTEEN

The smell was overpowering: stale sweat. Mr O'Sullivan
knelt next to Dexter, red, peasant hands clasped together
on the pew in front, clad in a grubby anorak and brown
trousers, a wisp of grey hair folded over his left ear. The
man's eyes rested immobile on the priest, unaware of the
discomfort he was causing to Dexter's nostrils. The
sergeant tucked down his chin and breathed deeply to try
to stifle the smell of Mr O'Sullivan with a blast of his own
eau de toilette. But it was no use. The stench of the middle-
aged Irishman would not go away. Dexter wondered how
Jesus Christ coped with body odour – not so much a policy
of turning the other cheek, he thought, but turning the
other nostril.

Then, blissfully, the moment of eucharist arrived. Mr
O'Sullivan shuffled along the parquet floor to join the
knot of other celebrants: the ragged handful devoted or
lonely enough to attend early mass on a weekday. Dexter
somehow felt he had been uncharitable to Mr O'Sullivan,
but comforted himself with the thought that he had resisted the temptation to move away when the man had
come and sat down beside him.

The sergeant at last felt able to lift up his head and
breathe in the details of the small church. He had been in
grander ones and more beautiful. But he always found a
special comfort in his own church in Shepherd's Bush –
the one he had first walked into almost ten years before.
The lobby was unchanged since then, panelled in oak with
leaded windows looking on to the aisle, when Dexter had

picked up a postcard which he sent to the Catholic Enquiry Centre. He had been received into the Catholic Church six months later to the consternation of his family, who were strict Seventh Day Adventists.

Although most of the congregation were Irish and there was only a sprinkling of blacks, Dexter had immediately had a sense of belonging. The Irish in London, he discovered, were more welcoming than the English, being themselves exiles in a foreign land. In fact sometimes London seemed to him no more than a bundle of outsiders, tossed together by accidents of history.

A line of Gothic arches led up to the altar and a brass cross that was the focus of worship. Placed strategically round the walls were carved Stations of the Cross. High above, the first rays of April sunshine streamed in through the stained-glass windows on to the panelled roof. Dexter's eyes came to rest on a sculpture of Christ on the Cross above the pulpit – a listless plaster figure who did not seem to have anything to do with the messy reality of death. The sergeant was reminded of how Scaglione's friend had been murdered by the Mafia. As morning hardened on the walls of the church, the stories the commissioner had told with so much credibility the night before now seemed improbable. How could swarthy *mafiosi* be operating in the same city as the friendly, pasty-faced Irish people he saw all around him? He pinched himself and repeated again and again that what Scaglione had said was true. The commissioner had even warned Eddy Russell not to let Scotland Yard repeat the same mistake it made before and imagine Britain was clear of the Mafia. Then Dexter remembered how he had first seen Nicola Sharpe, her body soaked in blood, lying slumped on the floor of the viewing room. *That* was also death. But in the cold light of morning he realised how stupid he was to think Nicola could have been murdered by the Mafia. Her corpse was messy: the killing did not have the cold and clinical air of a contract killing. Dexter was convinced David Parkin was guilty and he uttered a prayer for a quick confession.

Dexter genuflected and joined the other communicants.

Other images from the murder enquiry span through his mind like Nicola's last reports they had viewed in the editing suite. As usual he and Blanche had been plunged into another world by the investigation. Not the world he saw around him in the church, of Irish exiles living in the council estates and rented rooms of Shepherd's Bush, but the glamorous, middle-class world of television. It was rather like going to the zoo, looking at a number of exotic animals that he would not normally see in the flesh. Most of them, he felt, were on the make: smooth, clever with words, obsessed with their careers, and incapable of recognising a moral even if it savaged them in the calf.

A draught suddenly cut across Dexter's legs. He shivered as he imagined what it must have been like for Nicola in her last moments, trying to ward off the blows with her soft, manicured hands. People might philosophise about it, kid themselves that they would welcome it when it came, but death was terrifying. Dexter smiled to himself. That was why he had become a Christian: he was scared by death and he could never understand those who were not. Blanche for instance. He had asked her once what she thought happened to people after they had died. 'Nothing,' she had replied. 'Death's the end. And a jolly good thing too, if you ask me. I've enough trouble as it is avoiding people I don't like in this life without bumping into them in the next.' She was being light-hearted of course. But Dexter felt sorry for her, for her loss of faith, her belief in the power of reason to solve life's problems.

The sergeant wondered what might happen next between Blanche and Eddy Russell. At the end of the meal in the Italian restaurant Dexter had overheard the inspector saying he would phone Blanche. Dexter felt protective towards his boss. She deserved a break and, before he knew what he was doing, Dexter closed his eyes and recited a short prayer for her, asking God to find her a kind-hearted man rather than the shits she always seemed to be attracted to. And then he asked God to do the same for him. It was soppy of him, Dexter knew, but no one would know.

As he turned from the priest, the dry taste of wafer on his tongue, Dexter caught the smile of a youth he had never seen at the church before. He had long, blond hair parted down the middle and the sort of full, red lips that the sergeant found irresistible. Dexter hesitated. He saw with alarm that it was already half past eight and glimpsed the confessional box in the dimness. The sergeant gulped and strode out of the church. He wore a smile of self-satisfaction, the smile of someone who has temporarily forsworn pleasures of the flesh for those of the spirit.

Something had happened. Blanche's cheeks were glowing and eyes sparkling. She strode around the incident room with an air of easy relaxation, like an exhausted but victorious marathon runner. Dexter noticed that she had even applied her make-up with more than usual uninterest that morning. But she also looked preoccupied, rolling a biro round and round in her hand, her left eye puckered up with concentration. Dexter cradled a coffee – stiffened by three spoonfuls of sugar – in his hand and waited for her to speak. 'The customs at Dover found sixty kilos of heroin hidden in a container lorry early this morning. DI Russell phoned half an hour ago.'

'So Nicola got it right then?'

'Looks like it.' Blanche was about to speak again when her eyes swung away from Dexter and focused on the room behind.

DS Wootton waddled in and smiled obsequiously at the superintendent. The sergeant nodded at Dexter, trying to stifle a glance of dislike. Dexter now knew why Blanche's eyes had regained their old sparkle overnight: she had a plan. She explained that although they probably had enough evidence to charge Parkin, they needed more. She ordered Dexter to check out the Parkins' bank and telephone accounts to discover if there were any irregularities. Wootton was 'actioned' to do the same for Nicola Sharpe and her husband. Blanche wanted to find out if any blackmail money had been paid or received. Wootton suggested they reallocate the work, because he had a mate who had been 'in the old Bill' but who was now in BT's Investigation Unit. The superintendent agreed. Wootton would look into the phone-calls while Dexter would examine the bank accounts.

Blanche sprang up from the desk and reached for her coat. All her movements spoke of urgency, the need to trap Parkin before their time had slipped away. 'Dexter, I also want you to try and dig up anything new you can on Blufton when he was involved with the Mafia. Who worked with him, where, when – you know what I'm after. There might be a link there somewhere. I'll phone in at lunchtime.'

Dexter shrugged his shoulders. 'Dead easy,' he drawled, his London accent laced with irony.

Blanche chuckled. 'Start with Eddy Russell. He probably doesn't know much himself but he can ask Scaglione.'

'And what about you, ma'am?' asked Dexter.

'I'm off to see one of the security guards. He phoned in this morning to say he'd remembered something that might be important.'

'What?'

'He didn't say. It was actually his wife who called – an Asian woman.'

'So if anyone calls where shall I say you are?'

Blanche tugged on her raincoat. It was rumpled and shadowed with grime. Dexter made a mental note to remind her to take it to the dry cleaner's. '"Come friendly bombs and fall on Slough,"' recited the superintendent with a smile. 'That's where I'll be. Slough. Investigating the curries.'

Dexter watched the superintendent stride out towards the door, waving a cheery good morning to one of the computer operators who had just arrived and the constable who was to drive her to Slough.

'Dexter?'

'Yeah. Hi, guv'.'

'Any news?'

'Yeah. Both the Parkins are probably worth a look. The

Investigations Department of their bank have tipped me the wink. They say there are some big unexplained receipts and payments.'

'That's great. Any details?'

'Come off it, guv'. I ain't got the search order yet. What I don't know is how much of it is part of the tax fiddle Nicola talked about and how much might be something else.'

'What about Nicola and Jim Lancaster?'

'Well, I'm getting a search order on Nicola's account as well. She paid a lot of dosh into her account a few weeks ago. Lancaster looks clean though.'

'What about Wootton – has he had any luck on the phones?'

'Not so far.'

'Did you find anything out about Blufton?'

'No. I drew a blank on that.'

'Didn't Scaglione have any ideas?'

'You must be joking. It took ages to find the bugger as well. We finally tracked him down to Madame Tussauds. How did you get on – how was the curry?'

'Hotter than I expected. I'm at TV London at the moment.'

'What are you doing there?'

'Getting a job in Personnel. In fact, the file I wanted to look at has just arrived. I'll ring you later.'

'Dexter?'

'Hi, ma'am.'

'I've been trying to get hold of you for the past half-hour.'

'Yeah, sorry. I've just got back to the office. I was getting the search orders sorted out.'

'That doesn't matter now. I've already spoken to Wootton and he's getting things organised. I want you and him down here with a couple of DCs like greased lightning.'

'Where's here?'

'For Christ's sake, Sergeant, haven't you spoken to

208

Wootton yet?'

'No. I've been out of the office for a couple of hours. I've just got back in and happened to pick up the phone.'

'Well, find Wootton and get down to TVL in the next five minutes. I want to make an arrest.'

CHAPTER
NINETEEN

The superintendent's car was parked in the lee of some drab council flats, opposite a block of Victorian houses, their ground floors rusticated with stucco. Dexter slid into the front seat and just had time to register an old man stumbling across the road in front of them before he heard the click of a rear door and the grunt of DS Wootton as he sank his bulk into the back. Blanche glanced at Wootton's reflection in the rear mirror. 'There are only two ways in and out of the TVL building – one at the front and one at the back. Wootton, I want you to cover the rear with your DC. Dexter, I want you and the other DC to come with me and make the arrest.'

'Who are we nicking then, ma'am?' asked Dexter. In the panic no one had told him.

Blanche edged her car door open. The cold air rushed in even though there was little wind. 'A man called Jason Savage. You know him as Bill Southgate. He's one of the security guards and he's the man who murdered Nicola Sharpe.'

Before he could ask any more questions, Blanche had slammed her door and was striding towards the river.

Blanche stood with Dexter and a detective constable on the river embankment fifty yards from the TV London head-quarters. The familiar stump of smoky glass rose up, reminding Dexter of a great, black crystal. Its facets reflected the leaden sky – somehow making the clouds darker and more oppressive. Down below, seagulls picked their way on stiff legs over the bricks, mud and mangled metal that made up the river bank. The Thames was ruffled only by a faint breeze and eddies churned up by the pillars of the railway bridge. Behind rose two rusty and derelict cranes, back to back like sentries, and beyond them the four cream chimneys of Battersea Power station. Blanche ordered the constable to guard the main door while she and Dexter approached the main desk to make the arrest. 'And don't forget,' she said. 'He's violent.'

Blanche and her sergeant strode over the pedestrian crossing, slightly ahead of the constable. The sergeant's heart thumped in his ears and he clasped and unclasped his hands to relieve the tension. He had experienced this excitement before when making an arrest: the cocktail of elation, fear and hope. And he knew the exhilaration could easily lead to mistakes: he had to appear calm and relaxed so as not to arouse suspicion.

Bill Southgate sat slumped on a chair at the security desk when they walked in. His ginger hair and air of suppressed violence were unmistakable. He was looking down, perhaps reading a newspaper, Dexter thought. In reception there were more people than the sergeant would have liked: two squeaky-voiced girls and three men scattered over the sofas, and a despatch rider in black leathers. Blanche glanced instinctively over her shoulder to check the constable was in position by the swing doors. He was, pretending to watch one of the television screens on the wall.

'Hello, again,' said Blanche with a polite smile. Southgate flicked up his head, suddenly watchful, his narrowed eyes shifting from Blanche to Dexter and then back again. 'I wonder if you might be able to help. I don't know if you remember me – '

'Don't worry, superintendent, I remember all right.' He showed no sign of being suspicious yet. His voice sounded calm enough to the sergeant. Southgate slid from his seat like an awakening snake. 'What can I do for yer?'

'Well, I wondered if we could have a quick word out the back. There were a couple of things I wanted to ask you.'

211

Dexter saw Southgate's green eyes flicker over his shoulders. Had he guessed? Why did not Blanche just say you are under arrest and get it over with? The sergeant flexed his fists. "Fraid it's a bit tricky just at the moment. I'm the only one 'ere. Do you think you could pop back in an hour or so?' Don't worry, Dexter, the sergeant told himself. False alarm. Something just caught his eye. Stay cool, man. Dexter had not noticed before just how thin Southgate was, even though he gave an impression of muscular force. His skin, despite the freckles, was also paler and blotchier than Dexter remembered.

'Not really,' Blanche replied. 'It's pretty urgent. I'm sure you could just step out the back for a second.'

'OK.' He eased himself through the gate that separated the security desk from the body of the reception.

Later Dexter wondered what it was that alerted him. Perhaps it was the determined edge to Blanche's voice; perhaps the inch or two that Dexter moved closer to the desk; or even the detective constable turning from his television screen to check what was happening. In a whir of movement, the security guard's fist thumped into Dexter's stomach. The sergeant staggered backwards, an agonising breathlessness clutching at his lungs. Dexter saw Blanche lunge at Southgate but miss. A second later and the security guard was through the swing doors.

His lungs rasping and burning for breath, Dexter gathered himself and followed. By the time he had staggered through two sets of swing doors, Blanche was no more than a clattering shadow at the end of the corridor, pursued by the detective constable. He saw Blanche yank open a door and disappear.

The sergeant ran so fast that by the time he arrived the door was just about to close, sucked back by an invisible pneumatic device. Dexter plunged into an airless booth. No one was there. He sprinted through the padded door at the far end, stumbling over skeins of cabling.

Towering up in front of him was a tiered structure supported on metal struts. He heard shouts from the other side, and sprinted towards the right to find an opening. He swung left and stood in a pool of blazing light. Three scene-shifters were manhandling a desk on to the set of a games show. Behind them was a painted flat studded with coloured lights. 'What the fuck's goin' on?' shouted one man as the sergeant skidded to a halt on the rubberised floor.

'Police!' screamed Dexter. 'Did you see where they went?'

'Yeah,' said one, pointing towards the other side of the studio. 'Right through 'ere and out the other side.'

The sergeant sprinted across, his stomach churning, jumping over more cables. An exit sign glowed red in the gloom. He dived towards it and down a set of concrete steps. Suddenly he was out in the open – chill air brushing his cheeks. Then he saw her, Blanche, glimpsed in the space between a parked lorry and a trolley crammed full of scenery. Dexter ran forward, causing a forklift truck to swerve and skid. 'Fuckin' bastard,' screamed the driver.

Dexter staggered up and found Blanche in an enormous hangar, her eyes wide with adrenalin, her forehead glittering with sweat. Her chest heaved as she fought for breath. She stabbed out her right hand. 'There's one exit – over there. I've sent James – round the back to cover – the other.'

Behind them Dexter registered a blank wall; in front, lines of stalls containing scenery for different programmes, each separated by an aisle. A dismembered suburban sitting-room, the mantelpiece on its side, jostled against an enormous polystyrene globe which in turn lay next to a dismantled courtroom. Pillars supporting the roof stretched away into the distance, their bases protected against accidents by cylinders of steel. The hangar echoed with a confused knocking and the murmur of distant conversation.

'James!' shouted Blanche through cupped hands. 'Where are you?' Her voice reverberated among the pulleys that looped down from the ceiling.

'Here, ma'am!' floated back a reply from the far side of the hangar. 'Over here!'

213

Dexter swung round to the superintendent. 'Do you know where he went?' he groaned, clutching his stomach.

He watched Blanche's eyes scan round the hangar. They flickered over the vaulted ceiling, the piping that snaked over the walls, the line of offices high up on the right, the spiral staircase that rose to meet them.

Nothing moved.

Dexter twitched as the bell attached to a telephone began to ring high up above. Ring. Pause. Ring. He was starting to catch his breath back now, although every few seconds a spasm of vomit shot up from his stomach. Some scene-shifters in pullovers and running shoes slouched into the entrance. Blanche ran across and asked them to guard the entrance. She then called Wootton on her walkie-talkie.

Dexter sensed, rather than saw, her arrival back by his side. He stood, crouched, with his hands on his knees. He sensed Blanche put her arm across his shoulder. 'Are you all right?'

'Yeah,' he lied.

Nothing moved.

'OK,' said Blanche in a harsh whisper. 'Let's try to flush him out. You take the left aisle. I'll take the right. He must be in there somewhere.'

The sergeant edged forward on the balls of his feet, his legs shaking. Each stall was delineated by lengths of scaffolding. The first on his left was crammed with scenery flats covered in a wallpaper of cornflowers, no more than hardboard on a deal frame. The next contained a classical column about five feet high, a dresser and a desk – all painted to look like stained oak. To his right, Dexter glimpsed Blanche between some corrugated aluminium and a mock wooden staircase. She stalked forward, gingerly placing one foot in front of the other. She caught Dexter's eye and frowned.

Nothing moved.

Water trickled through a pipe above Dexter's head. Suddenly a pair of feet rattled down a metal staircase to his left whistling 'A Hard Day's Night'. The sergeant span

214

round to confront a young man in a patterned jumper. He stood still, wide-eyed, the last note of his whistle dying on the cold air when he saw Dexter raise his finger to his lips and whisper 'Police'.

Nothing moved.

Dexter saw everything with a sharpened focus. He looked down at his right hand. It had an unhealthy, yellowish cast because of the halogen lights above, but the sergeant thought he could distinguish every throbbing vein, every line on his knuckles. He swallowed a fleck of puke in his throat and steadied his legs. In the next bay two enormous cylinders of cardboard slid into view. Both were painted to look like steel held together by rivets. Blanche appeared, eyes wide, in a gap in the scenery. Her deep concentration made her look worried.

The telephone bell sounded again, insistent, irritating. Dexter had tiptoed about thirty yards down the aisle.

Suddenly he heard Blanche's voice. 'James! You still there?'

'Over here, ma'am.' The constable's voice was detectably closer.

'Stay where you are.'

Nothing moved.

A train clattered by outside.

Dexter saw something at the end of the aisle that made him feel queasy again: a painted flat of terraced houses that had been turned on its side. A moment of disorientation swept over the sergeant. He imagined he had stumbled into some surreal world, full of distorted fragments of reality: the solid wall on his right proved to be no more than another sheet of board, the bricks just moulded plastic. A notice was pinned to it with the name of the programme and the word 'DEAD' scrawled across the top.

Nothing moved.

Dexter froze when Blanche shouted again. 'Come on out, Jason,' she shouted. The use of Southgate's Christian name sounded strange and insincere to Dexter. 'Jason! We know who you are. It's better to come quietly. We just want to ask you a few questions.'

215

The only movement was a pigeon which had strayed into the hangar by mistake. It took wing and flapped out through the main entrance.

Dexter tiptoed forward again past a huge fan, eight feet in diameter, encased by a grille.

The hangar echoed with the clatter of feet running up a metal staircase. 'Dexter!' screamed Blanche. The sergeant did not see Southgate at first but only heard him: the lower level of the spiral staircase was hidden behind stalls of scenery. Dexter scrambled over some boxes and squeezed past a photo blow-up of the Prime Minister. Southgate was almost at the top of the spiral staircase with Blanche scrambling up twenty feet below. The walkway above only led to another door: there was no way down except the staircase. Dexter threw himself on to the bottom rung and rattled upwards. He bumped past a fat woman who had come out of her office and dived through another door. He found himself in a service stairwell, the walls no more than rough concrete. Footsteps scraped above and he jumped on to the first step. His foot slipped and he cracked his shin on a sharp edge of concrete. 'Shit,' he hissed, anaesthetised to the pain, emerging one storey up in a corridor to find Blanche scrambling through an open window.

Once on the flat roof the security guard jumped over some piping and disappeared behind a wall. Dexter was only a couple of yards behind Blanche when they reached the corner. The security guard, his head a ginger blur, climbed over the parapet and began clambering down a fire ladder. By the time the sergeant reached the ladder he was level with the superintendent, his hands clasping the cold steel of the ladder just before hers.

Dexter sprang on to the ladder. He saw Southgate between his feet, almost close enough to touch. Thirty feet below was another flat roof built next to a boundary wall. If Southgate got there first he could escape. The security guard quickened the speed of his descent, sensing the approach of the wall. Dexter felt the smoothness of the painted metal on his pink palms, one hand below the

216

other, one foot below the other. 'Faster,' he ordered himself, 'faster.' His hands and feet became a blur.

He looked down and Southgate suddenly seemed closer, as though he had stopped on the ladder. The man's mouth hung open. His arms flailed the air as he fought to regain his balance, a fingertip scraping one of the metal rungs. In slow motion Southgate toppled backwards. It was then that Dexter heard the wailing scream that quivered on the air and died only when the man crumpled on to the roof below.

Dexter glanced up at Blanche and down again at the security guard. The smoke drifting from a distant chimney seemed to pause. There was a terrifying stillness.

The sergeant scurried down the ladder, Blanche descending above him. Southgate lay on his back, his right leg at an unnatural angle, blood trickling from his mouth.

He sneered when Dexter crouched over him. 'Black bast . . . ' he started to murmur.

Blanche knelt beside them, bringing her face close to Southgate's. 'Did you kill her, Jason – Nicola Sharpe?' she whispered.

The man smiled, drawing his lips back to reveal a line of small, bloodied teeth. He made an attempt at a nod. 'Yeah. It was me.'

Blanche turned and shouted up to the detective constable, who had appeared at the top of the ladder, to call an ambulance. She paused. 'Did someone pay you to do it?'

Dexter knelt down beside her to listen. He was trying desperately to piece together what he had learnt. Obviously Blanche had discovered that Bill Southgate had carried out the murder but believed he had done it on someone else's behalf. The sergeant strained to hear.

Southgate smiled again. "S funny. Can't feel a thing,' he moaned.

'Who paid you, Jason?' She paused again. Dexter still found it strange hearing the alien Christian name. What did she say his real name was? Jason . . . Jason Savage. That was it. He must remember. Not Bill Southgate but Jason Savage. 'We've found out about the fifteen grand in

217

your account. We know all about it.'

Savage gulped and then winced with the pain. 'Parkin.'

'David Parkin?'

Another spasm of pain passed across Savage's face. He opened his eyes and sneered at the superintendent. 'Think you're so fuckin' clever, don't you?' His breathing rattled in his chest. 'The wife.'

'Maggie Parkin?'

The security guard coughed more blood. 'Yeah.'

'Was it you who planted the scissors?' Blanche asked. The security guard did not seem to hear so Blanche leant forward and repeated the question into his ear.

Savage attempted to nod. 'Her idea.' He suddenly caught sight of Dexter and his eyes burnt with contempt and hatred. 'Black bastard,' he murmured. He closed his eyes and his head slumped to one side, unconscious.

Dexter stood up, restraining the urge to spit on the man's face. Blanche took off her coat and laid it over the security guard, tucking it up to his neck. 'Come on, Dexter,' she said, with a wry smile. 'Let's have yours.'

The sergeant slipped the leather jacket from his shoulders, shivering. He turned from the black stump of the TV London headquarters towards the misty roofs of Chelsea, the peppermint-green spire of a church pricking through the gathering twilight. That sneer in Savage's eyes had released a memory, something he had tried to smother, a memory that explained his unease whenever he saw the TVL building.

He had been only six. He had just finished his first year at primary school and it was the summer holidays. The days had seemed longer then, sunnier. The rye grass pushing through the cracks of the pavement on the council housing estate had been scorched brown. And he was kicking a ball against a garage wall. Suddenly, even though it was the middle of the day, the air seemed to grow chill. He looked round. A group of white boys had surrounded him. Looking back none had been younger than ten and none older than twelve. But to young Dexter they all towered up like the trees in the local park.

The ringleader had looked at him in exactly the same way as Savage before he closed his eyes, the same look of hatred and contempt. 'We've got some food for you, nigger boy. Found it over there in the bushes,' he drawled, pointing towards the scrub that hemmed in the council blocks. 'C'mon, John. Better show 'im 'is dinner.' Another boy held up a jam jar containing a huge black beetle, its antennae twitching. 'You're gonna like this, nigger. Very tasty.'

Dexter screamed and ran towards them, fists flailing. He was punched and then pinned down on the concrete: two of the boys holding his arms, another sitting on his legs. A fourth forced his mouth open, and held the struggling beetle above his face. The TVL building reminded him of that beetle in its sleek, black shell. Laughing, the boy forced the insect into Dexter's mouth and smacked his jaw shut. Dexter would never forget the terror of that bitter taste, the crackling sensation of the beetle's crushed shell on his tongue. When he refused to swallow it, the ringleader punched Dexter in the stomach. Then the boys wandered off laughing into the summer's day, leaving Dexter to be sick on the dry earth.

The sergeant blinked back the tears. It was on that day he discovered he was black. The colour of his skin did matter. And those who later pretended they were blind to it were either fools or hypocrites.

Blanche eased herself up and straightened her skirt. The detective constable appeared at the top of the ladder. He scrambled down and ran across. 'The ambulance is on its way, ma'am.'

The superintendent looked across to the pale face peeping from out of the coats. Blanche thought for a moment and walked over to the security guard. She flicked back the coats that were covering him, and rolled up the sleeve of Savage's shirt. His forearm was peppered with red scars from a hypodermic needle.

CHAPTER
TWENTY

'I was blind, Dexter. Blind as a bat.'

'What do you mean, ma'am?'

'Not to have seen earlier that one of the security guards could have done it.'

Blanche gazed out of the car window at the ponderous block of Dolphin Square. The sergeant gripped the wheel of the unmarked police car with one hand as they sped east along the Embankment. They were on their way to pick up Maggie Parkin from her publishing house. It was the next obvious move in the enquiry. Dexter was still in a daze, nervous, impatient to catch up on the missing episodes of the day and plot their next move. They had now tracked down the man who had stabbed Nicola Sharpe to death, the one who had wielded the murder weapon. But that was not enough. They had to find the person who had paid him to do it. The sergeant was resentful. It was like completing a ten-mile run and then being told at the finishing line that the race had been doubled in length without informing the competitors. And this petty annoyance of Dexter's was supplemented by a new anger. He had a certain bizarre respect for contract killers. They were cold and heartless, inhuman, but at least they had a dark, animal courage. They had the guts to trespass into the unthinkable and actually take another's life. The person who hires the killer on the other hand has the murder on his conscience but not the vivid memory – the blood, the terror in the victim's eyes. A person who bought murder, Dexter reflected, was nothing but a coward.

The superintendent lifted a hand to conceal a yawn, blinking her tired eyes. She was sifting through Maggie Parkin's recent bank statements, trying to collate unexplained payments that might match the one to Jason Savage. Dexter had to keep reminding himself of the murderer's real name. Not Bill Southgate but Jason Savage. He would ask Blanche how she found out in a minute. It would be better to hear the story from the beginning.

Dexter had already found two cash withdrawals of five thousand pounds in the past month from Maggie Parkin's account, but there were others over the preceding year. Dexter waited patiently for Blanche to speak. 'It was that Asian guy, the security guard, who finally put us on the right track, you know. The one I saw in Slough this morning. He was on duty with Savage on the night of the murder. He's called Goel Prakash.'

They slid on to Millbank and up ahead Dexter saw the Houses of Parliament, shimmering in the misty distance like some medieval castle of legend.

'There was a really strange atmosphere when I arrived – you know when a couple have just had a row. The husband was washing his car in the road and his wife was clattering pots and pans in the kitchen. Anyway the security guard said his wife had made a mistake. She'd phoned up without asking him first and he had nothing to say.'

Dexter had been to Slough once and imagined the scene in a road of red brick council houses, the tarmac broken, the gardens grey and untidy.

'The wife must have realised what was happening. The next thing, she appeared at the front door – a fiery little thing in a sari – and started going hammer and tongs at him in Hindi. She was obviously afraid Prakash had got himself into trouble and told him to tell the truth or else. The effect on him was amazing. He stormed inside and started talking.'

Dexter braked as they hit a queue of cars drifting on to Parliament Square in the dusk. A group of Japanese were being shepherded along the pavement towards Westminster Abbey. The tourist season was just beginning, the spring flutter before the summer rush, the bridges clogged with open-top buses. And what were most of them after, Dexter thought? A London of the past, a London of picture-books, a London that only existed in their imagination.

'Prakash said Savage had lied to us. Apparently he wasn't ill at all – like he told you. He'd gone off just before nine o'clock to do a regular check round the building. But Savage got back much later than usual – about a quarter to ten.'

'And of course you didn't know Savage's real name at this point?'

'That's right. Anyway, Prakash asked what had kept Savage so long and he said he'd let himself out the back door to meet a woman friend. Savage said he wanted to keep it secret, and asked Prakash to return some favours by saying his mate had been ill at the time of the security check if anyone asked. When Prakash looked doubtful, Savage threatened his children.'

Dexter nodded. 'He's obviously a right bastard, this Savage.' He recalled the two security men when he interviewed them on the night of the murder. No wonder the Asian was so muted and kept throwing watchful glances at his colleague. 'And presumably the Asian bloke agreed to this before he knew about the murder?'

Blanche turned to Dexter with a dry smile. 'Oh, yeah. When we turned up Savage told Prakash he knew nothing about the murder, and he'd better stick by his mate or else his kids would be in real trouble. Savage said the woman he'd met couldn't come forward and back him up because she was married.'

It was a clever plan, Dexter considered. Perhaps too clever for a man like Savage. The sergeant sensed the plan must have been organised by someone else, someone cleverer, like Maggie Parkin, who wished Nicola dead but with the minimum threat to herself. But if it was Maggie Parkin, Dexter considered, why should she risk leaving the party around the time of the murder? He was still confused. He went back to listening to Blanche.

222

'Prakash said he had no reason to suspect Savage wasn't telling the truth. He assumed he'd had sex with the woman somewhere and that was why his mate had taken a shower and changed his uniform.'

Of course. Dexter nodded. He remembered Southgate's damp hair now. The security guard must have taken a shower after the murder. The sergeant had not realised its significance at the time but now he gripped the steering-wheel tighter with the realisation of his stupidity. If only . . . If only . . . Bollocks, he thought, I'm not going to start blaming myself for that. Anyone could have made the same mistake. 'Did he know Savage was on drugs?' he asked, to distract himself.

Blanche shook her head. 'No. Sometimes, though, he said Savage acted pretty strangely – big swings of mood, that kind of thing.'

'So what happened next?' It was obvious to the sergeant that the information from Goel Prakash was not enough in itself to persuade Blanche of Southgate's guilt.

'Well, I remembered what Jim Lancaster said about the door to the viewing room. He said it was locked the first time he went into the office looking for Nicola. It was such an unlikely story I felt it might just be true. But that door can only be locked by a key – there's no knob or anything to do it from the inside.'

'So the murderer must have had a key, right?'

'That's the theory I worked on. He must have been inside at the moment Jim Lancaster first came looking for his wife. Perhaps Savage heard Lancaster calling for Nicola when he came into the office or perhaps he had locked the door as soon as Nicola was dead – we'll ask Savage about it later. It was then a question of saying who had a key. None of the members of staff had one, including Nicola. But of course the security guards did – which all helped point the finger at Savage.' Blanche patted the photocopied bank statements on her lap into a neat pile and slipped them into her briefcase.

'A security guard could have wandered anywhere around the building with complete freedom. Up and down the lifts, along corridors, into offices. He'd have had no problem getting into Parkin's office to plant the scissors. And what's more to the point, people would have taken no notice of him: he was just another man in a uniform. Provided you're wearing the right uniform in the right place you become invisible.'

True, the sergeant thought. The best disguise does not need to be a false moustache or beard but only something that stops people paying attention.

The superintendent leant back and stretched her long legs under the dashboard. She yawned again. 'The idea of Savage being the murderer also fitted in with what I'd come to thinking about the mysterious Mr Kennedy – that he didn't really exist. He was just an invention to persuade Nicola to meet a stranger down in the office.'

The gearbox whined as Dexter changed down to third as they approached Trafalgar Square, jostling among the cars for the shortest queue.

Blanche explained that she still had no real evidence against the man whom she thought of at the time as Bill Southgate. So she had phoned in to the incident room when Dexter was out of the office, and 'actioned' Wootton to do an urgent check on Southgate's elimination fingerprints. She, meanwhile, had driven to TV London and read Southgate's personnel file. Dexter listened to Blanche intently as she told the story with zest and succinctness: she hated pointless verbosity. The file, it turned out, was remarkably thin, containing only a few personal details and a covering note marked highly confidential. It said William Southgate had a criminal record but his appointment had been personally approved by Stephen Blufton as part of his charity work with ex-prisoners. Blanche phoned Malbis Castle but Blufton's personal assistant said the chairman was out all day and was only expected back in the evening. The charity itself however was more helpful, although its initial hostility only weakened when the superintendent explained the urgency of her request to the director. He feared the police wanted to harass an ex-prisoner who was trying to integrate himself back into society. It was the director who reluctantly revealed Southgate's real name, Jason Savage, and that he had only been released from prison on the Isle of Wight six months before. Savage had been serving a long sentence for murdering a man who had seduced his girlfriend. Savage was also known to have been addicted to heroin but had undergone treatment. The charity director said Blufton had generously agreed to give Savage a job on probation, and it was decided to change the man's name to William Southgate as part of starting a new life.

From the personnel file Blanche had also discovered details of Savage's bank account. As luck would have it, she had an old friend from university days in the Investigations Department of Barclays Bank, who informally told her about the payment of fifteen thousand pounds. The superintendent had finally amassed enough evidence to arrest Jason Savage.

Dexter swung the police car across the front of the National Gallery, its porticoes measured and cool. The sergeant tapped his fingers on the steering-wheel while he waited for the traffic lights to change. He was slightly resentful that Blanche had not phoned him more during the day and told him what she had found out. But he knew it was not intentional. Blanche had simply been too busy.

A few minutes later the sergeant could see Oxford Circus, and beyond it the church of All Souls in Langham Place. He ran his tongue – a raw pink against black skin – over his lips. He understood the story now. A convicted murderer, a man who had returned to his heroin addiction, had been hired to kill. Money would have been enough, he was sure, to buy a man like Savage. Maggie Parkin must have found out about his background somehow and approached him discreetly. 'Do you believe what Savage said about Maggie Parkin?' he murmured.

The superintendent gazed out at the pedestrians scurrying across Regent Street. 'I don't know. We've got the evidence of what Savage said. And she's got a few questions to answer about her bank statements. Let's see what she's got to say.' Blanche sat back. She sometimes had a sudden desire for silence when she was thinking and the sergeant was happy to oblige. Dexter felt tired.

Blanche pushed a music cassette into the slot and closed her eyes. It was Bob Marley's 'I Shot the Sheriff'. The jovial bounce of the music cheered Dexter and he tapped his fingers on the steering-wheel. The words, 'If I am guilty I will pay!' made him smile. He was thinking that Maggie Parkin could have made the telephone-call that called Nicola down to her death.

Maggie Parkin sat in uncharacteristic silence at the table in the interview room while Blanche and Dexter pulled up two chairs. Blanche had said she wanted to speak to Mrs Parkin about her husband so Maggie had agreed to come voluntarily and was not under arrest. Deep inside Chester Row police station there was little noise except the occasional shout or clatter of feet from the corridor outside. The public relations lady extracted a cigarette from its packet with shaking fingers.

'I've got some good news for you, Mrs Parkin,' Blanche began.

She stared at the superintendent suspiciously, her eyes rimmed with red. Dexter guessed Mrs Parkin had passed a sleepless night after her husband's arrest, shocked by the possibility of his guilt or at the possibility of her own being uncovered. She sucked in the first draught of nicotine greedily, her rings glinting.

'Your husband's being released from custody about now.'

'You mean – you're letting David go?' Maggie Parkin could not stop herself smiling. She struck the sergeant as being at the mercy of conflicting emotions – joy, relief, suspicion, uncertainty.

Blanche nodded. 'We've arrested the person who actually murdered Nicola Sharpe. And that person's confessed.'

As she began to understand fully what the superintendent had said, a look of elation shot across Maggie Parkin's face. It appeared genuine enough to Dexter. Tears of relief welled up in her eyes. She wiped them away with the back of her hand, a silver bracelet jangling from her wrist. 'You mean – he didn't do it?'

'You mean . . . you thought he did?'

Maggie Parkin gulped and dabbed at her eyes with a handkerchief. 'No . . . of course not.' Dexter was not at all convinced by the lie. 'But things did look a bit suspicious. When someone's let you down once, you're willing to doubt them again.' She beamed through her tears and blew her nose. 'He shouldn't have been arrested in the first place, of course. But what's done is done – I'm just so glad. Tell me, is David at home yet? Can I phone him?' She stood up behind the table..

Blanche raised her hands, asking Maggie Parkin to sit down again for a few minutes. She said he was being released just at that moment but there were a few formalities to be gone through. Before then, she wanted to ask Mrs Parkin a few questions.

Dexter saw Maggie Parkin freeze when she heard the hardness in Blanche's voice. Her eyes, darkened by smeared mascara, drilled into the superintendent's. She sat down slowly, perching on the edge of her chair and drawing the aluminium ashtray across the table towards her. She was dressed in a long black skirt and black boots and had thrown a bright scarf over her shoulders to create an air of bohemian raffishness that Dexter considered rather dated. She sucked on her cigarette again, the arm holding it pressed nervously into her body. 'Well – fire ahead.' Her voice sounded thin and high-pitched as it bounced round the bare room.

'The man who murdered Nicola is called Jason Savage. He was working as a security guard at TV London. The murderer says he did it for money. It was a contract killing.'

Maggie Parkin laughed nervously and shrugged. 'What's that got to do with me?'

'He says it was *you* who paid him.'

She sat for a moment. Dexter registered the gleam on the top of her cheeks where the face cream made her skin shine. Her laughter began as a chuckle but built up over a second or two into an hysterical cackle, which left her rocking backwards and forwards, cradling her face in her hands. 'Me? – I'm supposed to have hired some hit-man? You must be joking.' It was a theatrical performance, the black detective felt, but an impressive one. Blanche sat calmly, her face expressionless. Maggie Parkin stopped laughing and flushed a deep red. 'Look, I had nothing to do with this whatsoever, Super–'

'He even said it was you who told him to plant the murder weapon in your husband's desk.'

'That's rubbish,' she flared. 'I had nothing to do with it.' Her voice was louder now and burned with irritation.

'You had a good enough reason to want Nicola dead, after all – she'd been having an affair with your husband.'

Maggie Parkin's eyes burned. She sucked greedily on her cigarette, her fingers quivering.

There was a knock on the door and DS Wootton gestured frantically to Blanche. Dexter followed her out. Wootton had a smile of triumph pinned across his face. 'My old mate at BT's come up with a result, ma'am,' he whispered. 'There've been around fifteen short phone-calls from the Parkins' house to Nicola Sharpe's in the past month. None of them longer than a minute. But they stopped five days ago.' The sergeant's eyes twinkled through his greasy spectacle frames.

'So the threatening phone-calls must have been made . . . ' Dexter's London drawl trailed away.

'Yeah,' grunted Wootton. 'By her in there.'

Blanche apologised to Mrs Parkin for the disturbance when they went back into the interview room. Dexter had noticed that the superintendent hardly ever lost her sense of courtesy. From her briefcase, Blanche pulled out photocopies of Maggie Parkin's bank statements with two transactions underlined. The superintendent asked to whom the two payments of five thousand pounds were made. Mrs Parkin's hands quivered as she examined the photocopy. At first she said she had forgotten.

'I put it to you, Mrs Parkin, that they were payments

228

to Jason Savage.'

The public relations lady gulped and stubbed out her cigarette.

'And apart from all those threatening phone-calls you made from home to Nicola –' Dexter saw Maggie Parkin's eyes flare with alarm – 'didn't you call her in the board-room at the start of the party? Wasn't it your job to lure her down to the office where she was going to meet Savage?'

Maggie Parkin ran a bejewelled hand through her hair. 'Look, apart from going out to change my dress and going to the loo, I didn't leave the party.'

'So what time *did* you go to the loo?'

'I can't remember, now. I think it was some time when we arrived.'

'You can't remember the time?'

'No, I can't remember the bloody time,' she shouted, throwing herself back in her chair. Maggie Parkin sud-denly wailed and crumpled like a paper bag. Dexter had seen people collapse before and when the moment came he knew it was sudden and complete. She covered her face with her white hands and wept. All Dexter could see was a mane of black hair and heaving shoulders. 'I hated her – I love David so much – I couldn't bear it any longer – I had to do something – but I didn't murder her – it wasn't me.'

Dexter swung round to Blanche, his mouth lolling open in puzzlement. The superintendent raised her hand to tell him to have patience. After a minute or so, the heavings became less dramatic. Only the occasional spasm shook Mrs Parkin's body and she dabbed at her eyes again with a handkerchief. She sat back in her chair, hunched and broken but also somehow less tense. 'It all started a few weeks ago – God, it seems a lot further away than that. I found a hotel receipt in David's suit – I've told you all this before – he told me he'd been with Nicola, but said it was just a fling and he'd break it off in due course – but I didn't believe him.' Her face stretched itself in strange involuntary motions as she wiped her eyes. Her face was flushed and blotchy. 'I sat at home watching the little bitch on television – wondering what she'd got that I hadn't – and decided to threaten her – make her break it off – so I found her home number and started making the phone-calls.'

'What sort of threats did you make?' asked Dexter, sceptical of her innocence.

'I didn't make any at the beginning – I just waited a few seconds and then put the phone down – the threats only came later.'

'What did you say?'

'I said she ought to get out of London quickly – that sort of thing.'

Blanche rubbed her chin. 'Do you think she guessed who you were?'

Maggie Parkin shook her head. 'I don't think so – I only said a few words – I just wanted her to feel threatened. I don't know what I was doing really.' She stared at her hands, listlessly turning a ring round and round.

Blanche sighed, squinting with concentration, as she asked Mrs Parkin what had happened on the night of the murder.

She nodded and smeared away the dampness from her cheeks. 'I'd never actually seen them together, you see, since I found out about the affair. David had refused to give Nicola up – I think at one stage he was even thinking of leaving me and the baby. I saw them chatting together in the pub first of all, then at the party I went off to the loo and when I came back the two of them were talking together as if I wasn't there. David was flirting with her. I was livid: you can't imagine what it's like having to pretend everything's fine and dandy when your husband's standing there with the little tart he's been sleeping with on his arm.'

Dexter turned to the superintendent. Blanche was nodding, her hazel eyes gentle with sympathy. Little do you know, Mrs Parkin, thought Dexter, Blanche knows what it feels like only too well.

Maggie Parkin offered a crooked smile. Her voice was faint and distant, as though talking to herself. 'As soon as he saw me David took his arm away and walked towards me. I just stood there stunned – I couldn't believe it – and David started chatting and moving me round from person to person. All I could think about was the two of them talking together – anyway David could tell something was wrong. I said I didn't believe him when he said he'd given Nicola up; he said I didn't know the pressures he was under. I suppose I got quite hysterical – I said I'd kill Nicola if David didn't end the affair – and the next thing I knew David threw a glass of wine over me.' She ran her tongue over her lips and sniffed. She wiped her eyes again and blew her nose. 'That's all there is to say. There's nothing else.' She sat back and blinked to clear the tears from her eyes. 'I didn't kill Nicola – and I didn't pay anyone to kill her either.' Her voice cracked over the last few words and she began to weep quietly.

Dexter wanted to believe in Maggie Parkin's innocence but his eye was caught by the bank statements on the table in front of her. 'But how do you explain those payments, Mrs Parkin? Who were they to?'

She sniffed back her tears. 'It's an antique jewellery business I run on the side.' She looked up. 'The tax people don't know anything about it.'

Blanche slipped her hands on to her knees and pushed herself upright. She looked puzzled and weary to Dexter, staring at the sobbing woman, her eyes heavy with judgment. The bleep the superintendent carried in the pocket of her jacket let out a shrill wail. She strode off to find a telephone while Dexter waited in the interview room.

A few minutes later Blanche snapped open the door and summoned Dexter with a wave. 'Trust our bloody luck,' she said, hammering the wall with her fist in frustration. 'Savage died on us on the way to hospital.' Two constables stopped talking and stared at the female detective. Silence stalked down the corridor. 'That's all we need. An inquest into a death in police custody.'

CHAPTER
TWENTY-ONE

Edgware Road shimmered and streamed with water, the rain no more than darts of silver in the headlights, bouncing off the queue of cars, swirling along the gutters, seeping into the drains. Above the Underground station was the flyover of the M40, a parabola of concrete that smashed across the roof line, hissing with cars seeking escape from the city. There was no tree, no grass, no softness. The coldness of damp concrete was everywhere, square and uncompromising. What few people there were huddled for protection in doorways or stood at the window of a fish and chip shop munching forlornly. Dexter loved it. Few people believed him when he said he found London on a wet night beautiful.

The sergeant swung left into a network of narrow streets, deserted now in the evening, and sluiced by the rain. Two police cars were drawn up outside the address Dexter had scribbled in his notebook: a late Victorian block of grimy brick, three storeys built on top of a line of shops which looked as if they never opened. Between two of the shops was an iron gate which creaked as Dexter pushed it open to follow the constable into a passageway. Water splashed down into an invisible courtyard while all that could be seen beyond were amorphous shapes – slabs of wall, window and railings – that made up another block of flats. Dexter and Blanche were led up a dank stairwell, the stone treads worn by generations of feet, past doors that were painted bright orange. The colour burned in the gloom and made the sergeant feel vaguely sick.

The door to Jason Savage's flat was ajar and from ahead in the main room came the noise of a television set and the smell of sweaty clothes. Under the naked light bulb in the centre of the ceiling sat DS Wootton at a cheap, veneered table. He was sorting through a pile of magazines and papers, a mug of coffee by his right hand. A detective constable was on his knees rolling up one corner of the carpet. Watching the television, slumped in an old armchair, was a young man in his early twenties dressed in a T-shirt and jeans. He rose gawkishly from the chair and, uncertain what to do with his hands, finally shoved them into his pockets. He was a good-looking boy, noted the sergeant appreciatively, letting his eyes run over the youth's sandy hair, firm neck, and thin but muscular arms. A gold ring sparkled on his left ear. The man said nothing but looked across to Wootton, who struggled up out of his chair.

'Have you found anything, Sergeant?' asked Blanche.

'Yeah, quite a bit, ma'am. Some stuff that might be heroin for a start. Some needles and syringes. And Savage seems to have come in to quite a bit of money over the past couple of weeks.'

He handed across three building society books. Two showed deposits of five thousand pounds and one of four and a half thousand. All three deposits had been made just two days before. The accounts, however, had already contained fifteen thousand pounds that had been paid in three weeks earlier.

Dexter found the room depressing. The wallpaper looked about twenty years old, a finicky pattern of faded brown flowers, selected more for the fact it was washable than its motif. The white paint on the ceiling was probably as old, shadowed with age. There was no fitted carpet, merely a rectangle of nondescript green studded by cigarette burns. A bed stood in one corner, the grey sheets ruffled, while a mattress slumped on the floor in the other. What little furniture there was looked as if it had come from the junk shops that Dexter knew so well in Shepherd's Bush, their windows and pavements crammed with fragile, Formica-topped tables and matchstick chairs.

Blanche turned to the stranger.

'He says his name's Chris, Chris Warrington,' intoned Wootton. 'He's Savage's flatmate.'

'Look, I've got nothing to do with all this,' began the youth, shuffling from one sports shoe to the other.

'Just shut up,' interrupted Wootton, although without any violence. 'We're doing the talking at the moment. You'll have your chance.'

The superintendent turned back to Chris Warrington and asked how long he'd been living there. 'I came to London about a month ago to find a job, right? I met Bill one night in the pub on the corner and when I said I needed a place to put my head down, he said I could doss down on the floor here.' His nasal accent was Liverpudlian. 'The next thing is you lot come round and say Bill's dead and that he murdered that tart on the telly who's been in all the papers.' The youth's eyes darted around the room as he spoke. He was scared, Dexter knew, but desperate not to show it.

Blanche suggested that Wootton and the detective constable waited outside. When they had left she switched off the television and sat down in one of the armchairs, inviting Chris Warrington to take the other. Her fingers tapped on the armrest. She asked him how well he knew Jason Savage.

'I thought I knew him pretty well, you know. But, what with the false name and this murder – I didn't know him at all, did I?'

'Was there any sort of relationship between you?'

'I'm not fucking gay if that's what you mean.'

Dexter winced at the aggression, the horror in the youth's eyes. He had seen it so many times before and often in the Met. It used to make him angry. Now it just made him sad.

Blanche paused to let the hostility seep away. The youth wiped his nose with the back of his wrist and explained that he paid Savage a small rent earned from various part-time jobs as a barman or porter. Blanche asked if he knew

234

Savage was a drug addict. Warrington tried to hide his nervousness by chewing his lip and looking across to the bamboo blinds let down over the windows. 'No idea.'

'C'mon,' remonstrated Dexter, pointing to the syringes and plastic bags that Wootton had found in an old biscuit tin and deposited on the table. 'You must have known. You can't live with a junkie and be blind to it. Jason's dead now. It doesn't do any harm to tell us. Unless *you're* chasing the dragon too.'

Warrington stared at the old gas fire, the orange glow of the clay bricks shining in his eyes. He ran a hand down the forearm of his shirt and, as if suddenly feeling chill, reached out for an old pullover which he pulled over his shoulders. 'He offered me some one night. Some of my mates back in Liverpool are junkies. But I'm not. It's a fucking mug's game.' He said Savage probably injected himself once or twice a week and that he had no idea who supplied him.

Sensing that Savage's flatmate was still very nervous, Dexter suggested they should have a drink. Warrington chose a can of lager from a pack by his armchair while Dexter was despatched to the kitchen to brew up two cups of tea. He boiled the water on top of an old gas stove which he was surprised to discover, underneath layers of grease, was finished in white enamel. The sink was crammed full of dirty plates and saucepans.

'It's a real fuckin' shock, you know. Only last night he was sitting where you are,' said Warrington. His face cracked into a wan smile. 'Tell you the truth I didn't get on with him all that well. He was a moody sod. I was thinking about getting out of here anyway.'

Blanche sipped tea from the cracked mug, fixing Warrington with her interrogatory stare. 'Did Jason talk about his job?'

Warrington pursed his lips and ran a hand over his hair. 'Not much. He knew he was lucky to get it. He said the TV company takes on a couple of ex-cons like him every year and he had to be on his best behaviour.'

Blanche dropped her head to one side and squinted.

235

She asked if Jason Savage ever mentioned any names at TV London. Dexter waited.

'Not really. There was this Indian guy he got on quite well with. He even went over to see him once. There was the boss security bloke Bill couldn't stand. Can't remember his name. And then there was the boss of the company himself, Stephen something.'

'Blufton?'

'Sounds right. He's the guy who's into all this prison reform. Bill — sorry, Jason, whatever his name is — even had to go up to his office and say hello when he started.'

Dexter remembered the theory he had first propounded in the Italian restaurant that Blufton could have been behind the murder. He decided to give it a try and wondered aloud if Jason had ever mentioned Blufton's name again.

Chris Warrington said he had not and yanked back the tab on another can of lager, the sharp hiss of air audible in the silence of the room.

Dexter turned to Blanche and was surprised to see her gazing at him as if he were a stranger. He had seen that look before. It meant either he had given her an idea or she was over-tired. The sergeant guessed it was the latter. Blanche smiled. She picked up Savage's three building society books and passed them across to the young man, asking if he had any idea how his flatmate had stumbled on to thirty thousand pounds in the previous few weeks.

The youth whistled. Dexter heard Warrington's chair squeak as he sat forward. He said he knew Savage had come in for some money but that he did not realise it was that much. 'It was a couple of nights ago. He'd been in a funny mood all evening — restless, you know. I was just sitting here watching the box. Anyway, I suppose it was about half eight or something and there was a knock on the door.'

'Who was it?'

Chris rubbed his right hand back and forth over the knee of his jeans. 'I dunno. I just heard Bill say "Oh, it's you," or something like that. And then I heard a woman's voice telling him to hurry up.'

'A woman's voice?' Blanche leant forward and rubbed her upper lip with her thumb.

The youth looked up at the stained ceiling for inspiration. 'Yeah. She said, "C'mon, hurry up," or something like that. She sounded quite upmarket. Then Bill came back for his coat. So I asked him who it was and he said just a friend. He said he'd be back in a couple of minutes.' As the lager seeped into Chris Warrington's blood, Dexter noticed that he had relaxed more and had begun to gesticulate with his hands. Warrington took another swig of beer. 'About five minutes later he came back. He had a zip-up holdall over his shoulder. He was laughing and so on, and said we should go off and get pissed together.'

'Did he give a reason?'

'He just said something about coming in to some money. One of his uncles had died or something and this friend had been round with some documents.'

'Did you believe him?'

'Why shouldn't I? He said he was goin' to wait a few weeks and then fly off to Australia.'

That bag probably contained fifteen thousand pounds in used notes, Dexter pondered. The second half of Savage's contract. He had probably slept with it under his bed until he woke in the morning with a throbbing hangover and vomited into the basin. He was lucky Chris Warrington was young and innocent. Another man might have smashed his skull and trotted off with the money. Fifteen thousand pounds was a lot of dosh.

Blanche plucked her bottom lip with her forefinger. The superintendent paused. 'And you've no idea who the woman was who came round?'

'No. Her voice didn't mean anything to me.'

Outside the rain had stopped and puddles shimmered on the tarmac below. The air wiped across Dexter's face like a cold flannel, chill and refreshing. In the darkness water still tinkled along the drain-pipes. Wootton and the sergeant were waiting on the stairwell outside the flat smoking. Blanche briefed them and ordered Wootton to take a full statement from Chris Warrington. Dexter watched her look out into the artificial dusk that was the closest London ever came to night.

Dexter lit a cigarette, cradling the precious flame between his hands. The woman who called round at the flat with the contract money could well have been Maggie Parkin, but Chris Warrington's evidence would be useless against her.

The superintendent nodded agreement. 'I think she's innocent, anyway. I believed her this afternoon when she said she had nothing to do with it.' Blanche leant on the parapet and breathed in the damp, night air. Away in the distance Dexter watched pinpricks of light join and separate, some static, some moving soundlessly in the mime of the living city. Although Blanche's hair was lustreless and ill-kempt, and her skin pale with fatigue, the sergeant saw her eyes glitter with a feverish determination. 'What happens if we forget about the woman for a minute?'

The sergeant edged forward and leant on the parapet beside her. 'What – assume she was working for someone else?'

'Yes. Who does that leave?' Blanche swung round to face the sergeant, her face cloaked in shadow. 'It's got to be someone who had thirty thousand to spare, desperately wanted Nicola dead, and did not want to do the job himself.'

'And someone who knew Savage would probably agree to do the job.'

'Yes,' nodded Blanche with a wry smile that quickly faded. 'Contract killers aren't like carpet cleaners. You can't just find them in the yellow pages.'

Dexter flicked through the suspects in his mind and eliminated them, one by one. Jim Lancaster could have murdered Nicola himself. Besides he probably did not have the money. David Parkin would hardly be likely to pay a contract killer and then get himself framed for the murder. His wife remained a credible suspect, though, apart from the fact that Dexter still found it difficult to believe she would pay thirty thousand pounds to have Nicola murdered and then ruin her alibi by stirring up a quarrel with her husband. And the sergeant dismissed Jane Pargeter because he did not believe she was mad enough to murder Nicola simply because she was trying to steal her job. He had already dismissed Hugh Parnham long ago. Besides, none of these people could have known about Jason Savage's background.

Dexter was drawn back to his original theory. 'It's got to be Blufton,' said the sergeant. 'I still don't know why he did it, but it's got to be Blufton.'

Blanche leant back from the parapet and straightened her shoulders. 'Yes, I've been coming to the same conclusion. What stopped me from accepting it was the lack of a motive. Why would Blufton want Nicola murdered?' She raised her eyebrows. 'But when you mentioned his name in there, I suddenly understood why. Nicola wasn't just blackmailing Parkin to keep their love affair going, I'm sure she was blackmailing Blufton with her knowledge of his old Mafia connections.'

A broad smile slowly trickled across Dexter's face. They had cracked it at last. He had come up with the theory, Blanche with the motive. All they needed now was the evidence. With a slippery man like Blufton it would be difficult to find but they would manage somehow. Dexter took a step towards the stairwell. 'How about a late night spin in the country, ma'am? I think we ought to have a word with our Mr Blufton.'

Blanche chuckled and began to follow him down the steps. 'What do you do, Dexter, when you realise you've been stupid?'

'What, in normal life, or on the job do you mean, guv'?'

'On a case.'

The sergeant clattered down a few steps. 'Pray, normally,' he shouted over his shoulder. 'It's a bit like an aspirin. Doesn't do much good. But it makes you feel a hell of a lot better.'

CHAPTER
TWENTY-TWO

All Dexter's concentration was centred on the car and the exhilaration of driving as fast as possible. He had always loved speed, the sound of the wind whistling over the paintwork, the squeal of tyres, the speedometer rising up the dial with the majesty of the tide. Not that there had been much speed in his first car – a battered Skoda he had bought for a couple of hundred pounds. He could probably have poured paraffin into the engine and it would still have run. That Skoda was like the dinosaurs now, rusting on some scrap heap, a monument to a Cold-War Europe that was gone for ever.

Image, the sergeant thought. It was all to do with image. Skodas had the wrong image. That was why he flogged it in the end, even though the car still got him from A to B. Every time he spluttered up to his police section house in the Skoda his mates came out to laugh. Television was all about images, pumping them out to an unknowing world. But you had to know what was behind them. It was like that with Blufton. He was the worst kind. All smiles and charm on the outside but underneath a ruthless sod. Nicola and Blufton were well matched, he thought with a cruel smile, which faded when he remembered her mangled corpse. They would have to check her bank account to see if she had extracted any money from Blufton as well as the promise of Jane Pargeter's job.

A shape suddenly scurried into the haze of Dexter's headlights. A pheasant. Dexter swerved and accelerated up to seventy again. Concentrate, man, the sergeant told himself. Don't let your mind wander. Don't cock it up now. The sergeant knew that if there were any delay their quarry might escape. The road stretched ahead, straight as a ruler, and the speedometer slid up to eighty. Now he had a good reason to drive as fast as possible even Blanche, who normally sat beside him in the car with a pained look as if she had bad toothache, abandoned herself to the sensation. Dexter had pride in his skill behind the wheel. He was fast and he was good, even if it was a struggle to deceive the heavy Ford Granada into thinking it was a Ferrari.

The sulphurous glare of the city faded into the suburbs – lines of dusty houses fronting on to the main road – the traffic thinning all the time, the noise dropping away behind them, the darkness thickening, and then they were free: in the black, enfolding night of the country. There was no sound except the revving of the engine, no lights except those of the odd car, which Dexter hounded mercilessly towards the ditch, or of the occasional house or shop which sank away into the darkness behind them. They were swallowed up by the no-man's-land that surrounds London, the countryside which is not countryside, the land that is not suburbs, the prosperous fields that are never truly silent, always within earshot of the railway track or the rumble of cars.

All they could see at first were the blue lights in the distance, throbbing through the trees like eerie beacons. Dexter wondered aloud, as he screeched along the country lane, if some kids had decided to have a fireworks party seven months too soon. Blanche murmured that it might be a couple of ambulances ferrying victims of a road accident to hospital. They were both wrong.

A police car stood parked across the gates of Malbis Castle, blocking the drive. Beyond it were two others, vague shapes in the darkness, figures drifting through their headlights.

'Who the hell are you?' growled a constable, his luminescent coat glowing. He strode towards them, an arm raised in a gesture of exclusion.

241

The constable studied Blanche's warrant card by the light of his torch. His look of hostility melted into one of puzzlement.

'What's happened?' asked Blanche, edging past the police car in the entrance.

'A couple of people have been shot dead, ma'am. The inspector says it looks as if some terrorists have done it.'

Dexter did not have time to think who it might be. Instead he followed the superintendent towards the Porsche which stood, unreal and frozen, in the headlights of the two police cars. It had skidded across the drive and smashed into a tree, its bonnet buckled by the impact. The windscreen was no more than a jagged black mouth, the side-windows, too, blank and empty. Dexter blinked as the police photographer switched on his halogen lamps and flooded the mangled metal of the car with an even more intense light. Pearls of water on the lower branches of the pine trees suddenly flashed where moments before there had only been shadow. Dexter started, as one drop brushed across his cheek like a cold fingertip.

On the driver's side of the Porsche, slumped back in the bucket seat, was the corpse of a man who the sergeant immediately recognised as Stephen Blufton. His skull had been so shattered by bullets that it was scarcely recognisable, a ball of blood and bone, the chin shot away. Dexter saw Blanche register Blufton's body with a tightening of the lips, an indication of physical distaste. He knew she always regretted a death, no matter whose it was. That was why she opposed capital punishment. 'It's easy to talk about,' she had once told him, 'but a terrible thing to do.'

Dexter on the other hand sensed no regret: Blufton was after all the murderer they had been seeking so frantically for the past few days, the man who had hired Jason Savage to kill Nicola Sharpe. It would have been difficult to make the murder charge stick against him. He would have left no trace of the thirty thousand pounds, no evidence of his conversations with Jason Savage, and now even Savage was dead. The businessman would probably have escaped the law. But he had not escaped justice. He had died too,

Dexter reflected, killed as brutally as the victim of the murder he had ordered. Vengeance is mine; I will repay saith the Lord.

When Blanche bent down to look across to the corpse beside Blufton's, she gasped and shook her head in disbelief. The body seemed at peace: the mouth lolling open, the lips newly rouged, the eyes staring with the vacancy of death. Miraculously the face had been untouched by bullets, although two had pierced the neck. It was as though the gunman had decided the woman's face should be sacred and unscarred by death. Instead the white pullover that covered Jane Pargeter's chest had been ripped apart by the bullets, the lambswool sodden with blood.

'So they were in it together,' murmured Blanche. 'I should have guessed earlier.'

So should I, thought the sergeant. But we did not. Jane Pargeter must have been the woman who brought the fifteen thousand pounds round to Savage's flat. Blufton would not have wanted to have been seen. And of course it all fitted in now. The way Pargeter had prepared her alibi so carefully by never leaving the farewell party. It must even have been her . . .

'The Met? What the hell are they doing here?' whined the inspector, addressing a uniformed constable, as he strode over. He was a nervous and jumpy man in his early forties, his hair cropped short to hide baldness. A faint lisp made his voice sound affronted and suspicious of interference – especially from a woman. 'Evening, ma'am. What *are* you doing here, if you don't mind me asking?'

Dexter saw Blanche pull on a charming smile to blunt the inspector's aggression. 'I came to interview the dead man, Stephen Blufton, about a murder. But I obviously came too late.' She nodded towards the crashed car.

The inspector's eyebrows lifted. Dexter guessed he was intrigued but keen not to show his interest. 'Which murder is that then, ma'am?'

'You've probably heard of her. A woman called Nicola Sharpe.'

'Not *the* Nicola Sharpe? The TV reporter?' Dexter

detected a faint country burr in the man's voice although he could not place it. All country accents sounded the same to him.

The superintendent nodded. 'That's the one. Blufton is chairman – or was chairman – of TV London.'

'And do you think Blufton had something to do with the murder?'

Blanche looked hard at the inspector. 'He's the person who hired the killer.'

The inspector's eyes narrowed for a moment, as if he thought Blanche was engaged on some practical joke. Dexter could tell she was getting impatient and wanted to speak to the officer in charge of the investigation. There was no point in repeating what she had to say.

Dexter interrupted the inspector's puzzled stare by asking him who had discovered the bodies. Blufton's personal assistant, the girl called Selina, had been working late in her office at the back of the castle about an hour before when she had heard a series of sharp cracks in the distance. She thought at first that one of the teenagers from the village was out riding a motorbike which was backfiring. But the bangs were too loud and too close, so she had thrown on her coat and gone out to investigate. She had found the Porsche quickly because even after the crash – by one of those bizarre slips of fate – the headlights were still on and the radio blaring.

'Did anyone see the killer?'

The inspector shook his head. 'We haven't found anyone so far, although there's a set of motorbike tracks under the trees. Whoever it was looks as if he was waiting there for the car to come and then opened fire.' The inspector said a rapid search of the car had revealed a couple of false passports and visas valid for Brazil as well as three packed suitcases.

The officer suggested Blanche and her sergeant should wait for his chief superintendent inside the castle. He was the man who was going to take charge of the case and was due to arrive from Reading at any moment. Dexter knew the inspector would want to show his boss that he had stood his ground, made it clear that the case was the responsibility of Thames Valley police and not the Met. The inspector paused and bit his lip, moving his weight from one foot to the other. 'I don't suppose you've got an idea who did it, have you, ma'am?'

Dexter had been pondering the same question since he had first seen the two corpses in the car. It was obviously an ambush, planned and executed with ruthless efficiency. It reminded him of terrorist murders in Northern Ireland he had seen on television – the endless litany of cars slewed across lonely, muddy roads, the windows splintered into sheets of white. But this killing could not have been carried out by terrorists. Malbis Castle, whatever else it was, did not house the cell of some shadowy paramilitary group.

'The Mafia.'

'*The Mafia?*' The inspector's gaze of incredulity swung from Blanche, to Dexter and then back to the superintendent. 'The closest we come to the Mafia round here is the Women's Institute.' The man narrowed his eyes at Blanche and laughed softly. 'You're pulling my leg, aren't you, ma'am?'

Blanche's gaze was drawn back to the corpses in the car. There was no trace of a smile on her lips. 'No. Not over something like that.'

The superintendent said she would wait for the local commanding officer inside the castle and strode off with Dexter. Two police cars were pulled up on the gravel of the car park, their blue lights silently strobing across the castle walls. The door to the kitchen was open and inside, sitting at the pine table with a woman constable, was Blufton's personal assistant, a blanket dragged over her shoulders. Dexter remembered her from their last visit and whispered the name Selina to Blanche in case she had forgotten. The woman's face was pale and drained and she cradled a cup of tea with shaking fingers. The WPC looked up, her eyes widening with surprise when Blanche slipped open her warrant card. The superintendent slid on to the bench beside Selina and signalled to Dexter and the WPC to wait in the shadows. Dexter understood: Blanche wanted to find out all she could from the personal assistant before the local chief superintendent arrived, and to do this she wanted to give Selina the illusion of intimacy.

When Selina finally spoke, Dexter had to strain to hear. Her voice was remarkably quiet, as though speaking a soliloquy. To seek comfort, she kept plucking at the brooch in the shape of a cat that was pinned on her elegant brown dress. Selina said she had been alone in the office catching up on some late work when at about half past eight Blufton rang her extension. He said he had suddenly had to leave on business and would be away for a few days. Any queries should be referred to his solicitor or stock-broker. Dexter saw Blanche nod at this, as if it confirmed a suspicion. Blufton had been planning his escape.

When the superintendent asked about Jane Pargeter, Selina's eyes focused on Blanche for the first time, scowl-ing through her tears. 'She was Stephen's mistress.' Dexter glanced at Blanche to share his surprise, finding her lips too parted in voiceless shock. It was the obvious conclusion of course, having found them in the car together with false passports. But none the less to hear the word 'mistress' uttered in so silent a room made Dexter start. It empha-sised the extent of their blindness, the size of their miscalculation.

The personal assistant swallowed from her mug of tea as if to wash away an unpleasant taste. 'I don't like to speak ill of the dead but . . . She was ghastly. A real bitch.' The harsh consonants of the last word echoed with even greater dislike in Dexter's ears because Selina's voice was so clipped and well articulated, the voice of money and private school privilege. He knew it was the sort of word the personal assistant would not have been brought up to use lightly. Selina said the affair had started several months before, after Blufton had met Jane Pargeter at a TV awards ceremony. The couple took elaborate pre-cautions to protect the secrecy of the liaison from the tabloid newspapers and TV London staff, with Jane Pargeter coming out to Malbis Castle once or twice a

246

week to pass the night.

Dexter exchanged smiles with the WPC. He watched the superintendent sit back, letting her eyes range over the clutter in the kitchen – a Victorian cut glass decanter of sherry, a French Empire clock and a chandelier hanging from a hook in the corner. 'Did you ever meet Nicola Sharpe?' Blanche enquired softly.

The woman looked down at the table and scratched her fingernail back and forth on the pine. 'Only once. Here at the castle.' Blanche's eyes narrowed. 'It was about a month ago, I suppose. It was all rather strange. You see, she'd phoned up out of the blue and asked to speak to Stephen.'

'Why was that strange?'

Selina nodded, tugging the blanket tighter over her shoulders. 'Well, Stephen didn't know her in particular. She was just a face on television as far as I knew.'

'And what happened?'

'Stephen asked for her to be put right through to his private office. A few minutes later he called up and asked me to cancel an appointment he had first thing the next morning.'

'Did he say why?'

'Yes. He said Nicola Sharpe was coming out to see him about some business idea.'

'And did she come?'

'Oh yes, she came all right. I met her when she arrived. It was a nice day so they went for a walk round the estate. I only remember her so clearly because of the murder. It gave me a real jolt when I heard about it.'

So that was it, thought Dexter, smiling triumphantly to himself: the moment when Nicola Sharpe put her proposition on the table. Blackmail. Give me Jane Pargeter's job or I will expose your past links with the Mafia and ruin you. Dexter recalled suddenly how the management had reversed its decision to sack David Parkin. Perhaps that had even been one of Nicola's demands. But the ambitious television reporter had overreached herself. She did not know she was asking Blufton to sack his own mistress. Nor could she have reckoned on Blufton's ruthless desire to protect the business he had built up over twenty years. Nicola had miscalculated with tragic results: the chairman of TV London chose to have her murdered rather than submit to her demands.

The superintendent asked the WPC if she would be kind enough to make a new pot of tea. Then she stood up and wandered over to the fireplace, stabbing the unlit logs with the toe of her shoe for a few seconds. 'I don't suppose you've come across a man called Leonardo Della Torre, have you?'

Selina puckered her brows and sipped some lukewarm tea. Dexter feared that Blanche's luck would not hold. But after a moment the woman's face relaxed. She explained he was an Italian businessman, a friend of a friend of Stephen's, and that he had visited the castle a few times to talk over some deals with Blufton.

'And did they do any deals?' enquired Blanche with a poker face.

'I don't think so. I certainly didn't have to write any letters about it.'

Before the sergeant had time to think through the implications of what Selina had said about Della Torre, and how it might be linked to the murder of Blufton and his mistress, a plump, self-important man blustered in. He eyed Blanche and Dexter warily and in a booming voice introduced himself as Detective Chief Superintendent Williams of the Thames Valley police. He transferred his cigar to his left hand and greeted the officers from the Met with a moist shake of his right. Although his face was florid and bold, its length emphasised by flowing mutton-chop whiskers, his eyes were small and full of cunning. Williams apologised for his delayed appearance – although without much sincerity, Dexter thought – and suggested they waited for him in another room while he was brought up to date by the inspector. He said he would be along in ten or fifteen minutes.

Blufton's study was not locked. Dexter instinctively moved over to the marble fireplace. The bottom of the grate was covered with black flakes, the remains of burnt papers. He stirred them with a poker but none of the paper had survived the fire. They could have been innocent notes or incriminating documents. But now no one would ever know. The sergeant pursed his lips and shook his head in reply to Blanche's enquiring look.

'Savage fell perfectly into Blufton's hands,' began the superintendent, sinking into an armchair. 'Just what Blufton was looking for. An evil man and a vulnerable one. It was a matter of sounding him out and seeing if he was desperate enough to carry out the murder. But carry it out to Blufton's plan.' Blanche folded her hands in her lap, one on the other, and scratched the topmost palm with her thumb. 'And it was a clever plan. He almost got away with it.'

Detective Chief Superintendent Williams puffed in a few minutes later. While Blanche told him about her investigation, Dexter's eyes kept wandering to the scene of rural bliss painted on the face of the grandfather clock. He found it restful and reassuring, an image of a world purged of evil and violence. No blood would ever be spilt there, he thought, no hatred engendered. The heat of the sun would never fade, and the hours would pass in an endless stupor of happiness.

The clunk of the pendulum still beat time peacefully in the sergeant's head as he and Blanche walked out through the castle, their footsteps echoing along the corridors of bare stone; past a suit of armour and a stuffed bear; through the Hall, crude candlesticks of forged iron on the table, the fireplace cold until the next, distant winter; and finally into the relative cosiness of the kitchen. Blufton's personal assistant had disappeared, driven off to a police station to give a formal statement.

The superintendent stood for a moment on the drawbridge outside, looking up at the newly cemented stones of the castle battlements. Away in the distance, the place where Blufton's car had come to rest was still marked by bright lights flickering through the trees. 'Blufton was always peddling dreams,' murmured the superintendent. 'If not some soap opera or chat show then this place.'

249

Dexter made a non-committal grunt. He did not know what Blanche was going on about. The castle was fun, a folly, romance, adventure. Much of the furniture and fittings might be fake but it gave people a chance to dream, an opportunity to lose themselves in another world, as he had sunk for a few minutes into the lost Arcadia of the grandfather clock. And where was the harm in that?

Blanche's voice had suddenly become flat with fatigue: the adrenalin that had sustained her for the past few days had trickled away. Dexter on the other hand wanted to talk. He felt his usual surge of elation at the end of a case, rather than Blanche's exhaustion. But all his attempts to spark a conversation were stifled by murmurs from Blanche to wait until tomorrow. As soon as the sergeant had completed a U-turn outside the castle and accelerated along the lane towards London, Blanche's head lolled against the window and her mouth fell open. She was sound asleep.

CHAPTER
TWENTY-THREE

The report came towards the end of the evening news bulletin and only lasted about a minute. It began with pictures filmed, in the early hours of the morning, of policemen milling round the entrance to Malbis Castle. A lorry swung out into the road with the bullet-ridden Porsche strapped on the back. These shots were followed by those of a line of policemen treading warily along the verges of the drive, their boots soaked with dew. The reporter appeared only at the end, a clipboard edging into view. The clear and husky voice filled out into a young woman, with shoulder-length red hair and a pale but attractive face. At that moment, she said, the police had no idea as to the motive for the 'murderous attack'. Friends of Stephen Blufton and Jane Pargeter said the murdered couple were universally popular.

'Oh, yeah,' said Dexter with a cynical smile, pressing the mute button on the television set. Watching the report seemed to crown their day's work and he slumped back with a groan, anticipating a few pints in the pub. Beside him Blanche sat with her arms folded and said nothing. 'A penny for your thoughts, ma'am?'

'They're worth a lot more than that,' she murmured, with a twinkle of self-mockery in her eyes. She and Dexter were alone in the incident room apart from a detective constable and a sullen woman who was emptying the rubbish bins. 'I was thinking how quickly the well-known faces on TV get forgotten. They're there for a few months, a few years. They're all over the newspapers. And then they disappear. And no one seems to notice. No one seems to care.'

Dexter was not in the mood for a discussion about the fleeting nature of fame – he would have been only too glad to become a television celebrity and quadruple his salary if he had the chance. He knew Blanche was clever but sometimes, like a lot of brainy people, he also thought she could be rather silly. He decided to change the subject. 'Well, it don't look as if Williams is giving much away, does it?'

Blanche sat back in her chair and smiled. 'He probably doesn't have much to give away. A few tyre marks, the type of gun. The killer probably took the first flight out of Heathrow this morning.'

The superintendent stretched out her arms like a cat, tensing the muscles. Dexter had hoped that after the deaths of Savage, Pargeter and Blufton the pace might have slackened. But that day had been as hectic as ever, skimming by in a whir of interviews and phone-calls. Blanche had refused to recognise any legitimate frontier between her enquiry into the murder of Nicola Sharpe and that into the killings of the people who had organised it, Stephen Blufton and Jane Pargeter. 'Now we've deduced who murdered Nicola Sharpe, we've got to try and prove it,' she had muttered.

The first surprise was sprung by Blufton's solicitor. His client, he revealed, had phoned him the night before and told him that he was resigning immediately as chairman of TV London. The solicitor was to tell the board the next day. The lawyer said Blufton sounded 'flustered' and when asked a reason for the resignation, had snapped back that it was none of the solicitor's business.

Once they had overcome their shock at the murder, Blufton's bankers and stockbrokers were reasonably co-operative. They confirmed that the businessman had various numbered bank accounts in Luxembourg and Switzerland and about four weeks before had instructed them to sell various blocks of shares. The proceeds were transferred abroad. Blanche asked sharply whether they had queried this. Why should we? came the reply. He was

252

a long-standing and valued customer of the bank. When the superintendent enquired whether they had had any inkling that Blufton had laundered drugs money in the past, the two pale and well-scrubbed faces behind the desk grew even paler. They said they certainly had had no suspicions of it during the past five years that Blufton had been their client. And as to what had happened before . . . well, that was the responsibility of Blufton's previous bankers. They of course had no record of the two cash withdrawals Blufton needed to pay Savage. Blanche showed no surprise. 'There was nothing he needed to be taught about money-laundering,' she murmured, packing her briefcase.

When Dexter searched Jane Pargeter's flat he found a few photographs of Jane and Stephen Blufton together – taken in Geneva and on some Caribbean island, the sergeant guessed from the background. The photos of David Parkin sniffing cocaine never surfaced, much to the relief, Dexter was certain, of the TV reporter.

Eddy Russell had appeared in the incident room earlier that afternoon. The superintendent had called in an Italian translator and together they prepared a set of queries about Blufton and Della Torre that were faxed by the Drugs Squad to Commissioner Scaglione in Sicily. 'We might get something back in six months if we're lucky, knowing the Italians,' Eddy had chuckled.

Blanche turned her heavy-lidded eyes from the mute television screen to Dexter's face. 'What do you think of DI Russell, Dexter? Do you think we can trust him?'

The sergeant knew that Blanche had agreed to go out with him later for a celebratory drink. He also knew what the superintendent's question was really driving at: should *she* trust him? He shrugged. 'Who knows, guv'? Only time'll tell.'

Blanche smiled to herself. 'I'm pleased the jigsaw's come together anyway.' Only an hour before, she had heard that another of her suspicions had proved correct. The heroin found at Savage's flat was found to be so strong that anyone who injected himself with it would have died from a fatal overdose. Although she had no proof, Blanche was sure Blufton had provided it as part of his deal with Jason Savage. The chairman of TVL knew Savage had been an addict when he agreed to take him on as an employee, and obviously hoped that the killer he had employed to murder Nicola Sharpe would in turn take his own life.

Dexter regarded the silent, flickering images on the TV screen and recalled Savage lying fatally wounded on the roof. 'Why do you think Savage said it was Maggie Parkin who paid him, by the way? He didn't have any reason to.'

Blanche pushed back her chair and stood up. 'Blufton probably told him to say it. It was the story he'd worked out to fit in with the planting of the scissors.'

Dexter nodded and stood up as well. 'But I'm still amazed Blufton decided to kill Nicola rather than tough out the blackmail.'

'Murder never seems worth while in retrospect. Especially if you get caught. But people still do it.' The superintendent's right eye narrowed to a squint while she meditated aloud. 'You've got to remember Blufton worked hard to create TV London. He'd got out of crime several years before and had been going straight. Now his past came back to haunt him. He wasn't going to have some jumped-up and over-ambitious TV reporter taking his business empire apart. Or his lover's job.'

Blanche slipped her hands into the pockets of her jacket. Her sigh of relief sounded abnormally loud to Dexter in the silence of the room. The desks were almost empty, the banks of telephones silent, the messages pinned to the walls like pleas uttered to an invisible God. 'Tomorrow we'll start packing all the exhibits up. They can go to that warehouse in Cricklewood.' She smiled goodnight: she was going for her drink with Eddy Russell.

Dexter knew a murder enquiry was never truly closed. The statements they had collected, the index cards filled in so attentively, the floppy disks of computerised information – all would moulder on the floor of that warehouse for years to come. But for all practical purposes the enquiry into the murder of Nicola Sharpe was over. He and

Blanche could relax for a few days while the administrative chores were settled. Then, with the rolling inevitability of the seasons, the routine would begin again. Probably not a murder – perhaps a rape, a serious sexual assault. An act that caused hurt and pain to a human being, but destined to become just another statistic in the mass of stupidity, fecklessness and evil that for the sake of convenience is known as crime.

The management of TV London at first planned to extend their thanksgiving service for the life of Nicola Sharpe to encompass Stephen Blufton and Jane Pargeter. The church of the Holy Innocents in Belgravia was booked and notices distributed around the office noticeboards. A few members of staff whose acquaintance with the dead was limited to a sighting in the corridor made a note in their diaries. Others who knew them better, and had been heard to express criticism varying from indifference to mordant hatred, prepared themselves to speak only good of the dead. The majority glanced at the notice with the apathy of forgetfulness.

One diligent newspaper, however, uncovered why Blanche's murder squad was so quickly disbanded. It splashed the story on the front page a few days later. Freed from any constraints of libel the journalist felt free to invent and embroider where the paucity of facts made him unable to report.

The plans for a thanksgiving service were suddenly dropped. There was no public explanation.